This book is t

All The Queen's Men

Also by Linda Howard

DREAM MAN

SHADES OF TWILIGHT

AFTER THE NIGHT

KILL AND TELL

NOW YOU SEE HER

LINDA HOWARD

All The Queen's Men

SIMON & SCHUSTER
A VIACOM COMPANY

First published in Great Britain by Simon & Schuster UK Ltd, 1999
A Viacom company

Copyright © Linda Howington, 1999

1 3 5 7 9 10 8 6 4 2

Simon & Schuster UK Ltd
Africa House
64–78 Kingsway
London WC2B 6AH

Simon & Schuster Australia
Sydney

A CIP catalogue record for this book is available from the British Library

ISBN 0-684-86065-1

Printed and bound in Great Britain by Caledonian International Book
Manufacturing Ltd, Glasgow

PART ONE

CHAPTER ONE

1994, Iran

It was cold in the rough little hut. Despite the blankets hung over the one window and the ill-fitting door, to block the escape of any telltale light, frigid air still seeped through. Niema Burdock blew on her fingers to warm them, her breath fogging slightly in the one dim battery-operated light that was all Tucker, the team leader, allowed.

Her husband, Dallas, seemed perfectly comfortable in his T-shirt as he calmly packed the Semtex blocks into secure sections of his web gear. Niema watched him, trying to hide her anxiety. It wasn't the explosive she worried about; plastique was so stable soldiers in Vietnam had burned it as fuel. But Dallas and Sayyed had to plant the explosives in the manufacturing facility, and that was the most dangerous part of a job that was already hair-raising enough. Though her husband was as matter-of-fact about it as he would be about crossing the street, Niema wasn't that blasé about the job. The radio detonator wasn't state-of-the art; far from it. This was deliberate, a precaution in case any of their equipment fell into the wrong hands. Nothing they were using could be traced to the United States, which was why Dallas was using Semtex instead of C-4. But because their equipment wasn't the best available, Niema had gone to great pains to make sure it was reliable. It was *her* husband's finger, after all, that would be on the switch.

Dallas caught her gaze on him and winked at her, his strong face relaxing from its normal impassiveness into a warm smile that he reserved only for her. "Hey," he said mildly, "I'm good at this. Don't worry."

So much for trying to hide her anxiety. The other three men turned to look at her. Not wanting them to think she couldn't handle the stress of the job, she shrugged. "So sue me. I'm new at this wife business. I thought I was *supposed* to worry."

Sayyed laughed as he packed his own gear. "Heck of a way to spend your honeymoon." He was a native Iranian who was now an American citizen, a tough, wiry man in his late forties. He spoke English with a Midwestern accent, the result of both hard work and almost thirty years in the United States. "Personally, I'd have picked Hawaii for my wedding trip. At least it would be warm there."

"Or Australia," Hadi said wistfully. "It's summer there now." Hadi Santana was of Arabic and Mexican heritage, but an American by birth. He had grown up in the heat of southern Arizona and didn't like the cold Iranian mountains in midwinter any better than did Niema. He would stand guard while Dallas and Sayyed planted the charges and was occupying himself by checking and rechecking his rifle and ammunition.

"We spent two weeks in Aruba after we got married," Dallas said. "Great place." He winked at Niema again, and she had to smile. Unless Dallas had been to Aruba another time, he hadn't seen much of it during their honeymoon, three months before. They had spent the entire two weeks lost in each other's company, making love, sleeping late. Bliss.

Tucker didn't join in the conversation, but his cool, dark eyes lingered on Niema as if assessing her; wondering if he had made a mistake including her on the team. She wasn't as experienced as the others, but neither was she a novice. Not only that, she could put a bug on a telephone line with her eyes closed. If Tucker had any doubts about her ability, she wished he would just come out and say so.

But if Tucker had doubts about her, then turnabout was fair play, she thought wryly, because she sure as hell wasn't certain about *him*. Not that he'd said or done anything wrong; the uneasiness that kept her on edge around him was instinctive, without any concrete reason. She wished he was one of the three men going into the plant, rather than remaining behind with her. The thought of spending the hours alone with him wasn't nearly as nerve-racking as knowing Dallas would be in danger, but she didn't need the added tension when her nerves already felt stretched and raw.

Tucker originally had planned to go in, but Dallas was the one who had argued against it. "Look, boss," he had said in that calm way of his. "It isn't that you can't do the job, because you're as good as I am, but it isn't necessary that you take the risk. If you had to, that would be different, but you don't." An indecipherable look had flashed between the two men, and Tucker had given a brief nod.

5

Dallas and Tucker had known each other before Tucker put this team together, had worked together before. The only thing that reassured Niema about the team leader was that her husband trusted and respected him, and Dallas Burdock was no one's pushover—to the contrary, in fact. Dallas was one of the toughest, most dangerous men she had ever met. She had thought he was *the* most dangerous, until she met Tucker.

That in itself was scary, because Dallas was something else. Until five months ago, she hadn't really believed men like him existed. Now, she knew differently. Her throat tightened as she watched her husband, his dark head bent as he once again focused all his attention on his supplies and equipment. Just like that, he could tune out everything but the job; his power of concentration was awesome. She had seen that level of concentration in only one other man: Tucker.

She felt a sudden little ping of disbelief, almost a suspension of reality, that she was actually *married,* especially to a man like Dallas. She had known him for just five months, loved him for almost as long, and in so many ways he was still a stranger to her. They were slowly learning each other, settling down into the routine of marriage—well, as routine as it could get, given their jobs as contract agents for various concerns, principally the CIA.

Dallas was calm and steady and capable. Once she would have described those characteristics as desirable, if you were the domestic suburban type, but basically unexciting. Not now. There was nothing staid about Dallas. Need a cat out of a tree? Dallas could climb that tree as if *he* were a cat. Need the plumbing fixed? Dallas could fix it. Need to be dragged out of the surf? He was a superior swimmer. Need someone to make a difficult shot? He was an expert marksman. Need to blow up a building in Iran? Dallas was your man.

So it took some doing to be tougher and more dangerous than Dallas, but Tucker . . . somehow was. She didn't know why she was so certain. It wasn't Tucker's physical appearance; he was tall and lean, but not as muscular as Dallas. He wasn't edgy; if anything, he was even more low-key than Dallas. But there was something in his eyes, in his characteristic stillness, that told her Tucker was lethal.

She kept her doubts about the team leader to herself. She wanted to trust Dallas's opinion of Tucker because she trusted her husband so much. Besides, she was the one who had really wanted to take this job, while Dallas had been leaning toward a diving trip to Australia. Maybe she was just letting the tension of the situation get to her. They were, after all, on a job that would get them all killed if they were discovered, but success was even more important than escaping detection.

The small facility buried deep in these cold mountains was manufacturing a biological agent scheduled to be shipped to a terrorist base in Sudan. An air strike would be the fastest, most efficient way to destroy it, but that would also trigger an international crisis and destroy the delicate balance of the Middle East along with the factory. A full-scale war wasn't what anyone wanted.

With an air strike ruled out, the plant had to be destroyed from the ground, and that meant the explosives had to be hand-placed, as well as powerful. Dallas wasn't relying just on Semtex to do the job; there were fuels and accelerants in the factory that he planned to use to make certain the plant didn't just go boom, but that it burned to the ground.

They had been in Iran five days, traveling openly, boldly. She had worn the traditional Muslim robes, with only her eyes revealed, and sometimes they had been veiled, too. She didn't speak Farsi—she had studied French, Spanish, and Russian, but not Farsi—but that didn't matter because, as a woman, she wasn't expected to speak. Sayyed was a native, but from what she could tell, Tucker was as fluent as Sayyed, Dallas nearly so, and Hadi less than Dallas. She was sometimes amused by the fact that all five of them were dark-eyed and dark-haired, and she wondered if her coloring hadn't played nearly as large a part in her having been chosen to be a team member as had her skill with electronics.

"Ready." Dallas hooked the radio transmitter to his web gear and shouldered the knapsack of plastique. He and Sayyed had identical gear. Niema had practically assembled the transmitters from spare parts, because the transmitters they had acquired had all been damaged in some way. She had cannibalized them and built two she had tested and retested, until she was certain they wouldn't fail. She had also tapped into the factory's phone lines, a dead-easy job because their equipment was of early-seventies vintage. They hadn't gotten much information from that, but enough to know their intel was accurate, and the small facility had developed a supply of anthrax for terrorists in Sudan. Anthrax wasn't exotic, but it was sure as hell effective.

Sayyed had slipped into the facility the night before and reconnoitered, returning to draw a rough floor plan showing where the testing and incubation was done, as well as the storage facility, where he and Dallas would concentrate most of their explosives. As soon as the factory blew, Tucker and Niema would destroy their equipment—not that much of it was worth anything—and be ready to move as soon as the three men returned. They would split up and each make their own way out of the country, rendezvousing in Paris to debrief. Niema, of course, would be traveling with Dallas.

Tucker extinguished the light, and the three men slipped

silently out the door and into the darkness. Niema immediately wished she had at least hugged Dallas, or kissed him good luck, no matter what the other three thought. She felt colder without his bracing presence.

After making certain the blankets were in place, Tucker switched on the light again, then began swiftly packing the things they would take with them. There wasn't much; a few provisions, a change of clothes, some money: nothing that would arouse suspicion if they were stopped. Niema moved to help him, and in silence they divided the provisions into five equal packs.

Then there was nothing to do but wait. She moved over to the radio and checked the settings, though she had checked them before; there was nothing coming over the single speaker because the men weren't talking. She sat down in front of the radio and hugged herself against the cold.

Nothing about this job had been a picnic, but the waiting was the worst. It always had been, but now that Dallas was in danger, the anxiety was magnified tenfold. It gnawed at her, that internal demon. She checked her cheap wristwatch; only fifteen minutes had lapsed. They hadn't had time to reach the facility yet.

A thin blanket settled over her shoulders. Startled, she looked up at Tucker, who stood beside her. "You were shivering," he said in explanation of his unusual act and moved away again.

"Thanks." She pulled the blanket around her, uncomfortable with the gesture, considerate though it was. She wished she could ignore her uneasiness about Tucker, or at least figure out *why* she was so wary of him. She had tried to hide her wariness and concentrate only on the job, but Tucker was no one's fool; he knew she was uncomfortable with him. Sometimes she felt as if they were in a silent battle no one else knew about, those rare times when their gazes would accidentally meet and distrust would be plain in hers, a slightly mocking awareness in his.

He never put a foot wrong, though, never did anything that would bring their discord into the open. His relationship with all three of the other men was both easy and professional. With her, he was unfailingly polite and impersonal, and even that was a measure of his professionalism. Tucker respected Dallas and certainly wasn't going to disrupt the team or endanger the job by openly antagonizing his wife. That should have reassured Niema on a couple of levels—but it didn't.

Until he put the blanket around her shoulders, there hadn't been a word spoken between them since the others left. She wished it had remained that way; keeping Tucker at a distance, she thought, was the safest place for him.

He sat down, as relaxed and graceful as a cat. He seemed impervious to the cold, comfortable in a black T-shirt and fatigue pants. Dallas had the same sort of internal furnace, because he seldom felt the cold either. What was it about men like them that made them burn so much hotter than the rest of the human race? Maybe it was their physical conditioning, but she herself was in very good shape and she had been cold the entire time they had been in Iran. She didn't wish they were cold, too, just that the damn anthrax facility had been built in the warm desert, instead of these chilly mountains.

"You're afraid of me."

The comment, coming out of the blue, startled her more than it had when he put the blanket around her, but not enough that she lost her composure. His voice had been calm, as if he were discussing the weather. She gave him a cool look. "Wary," she corrected. If he thought she would hasten to deny her uneasiness, the way most people would do when cornered, he was mistaken. As Dallas had learned, to his amusement more often than not, there wasn't much that could make Niema back down.

Tucker leaned his dark head back against the cold stone wall and drew one leg up, draping his arm loosely over his knee. Unreadable brown eyes studied her. "Wary, then," he conceded. "Why?"

She shrugged. "Feminine intuition?"

He began to laugh. Laughter wasn't something she had associated with Tucker, but he did it easily, his dark head tilted back against the wall. The sound was genuinely amused, as if he couldn't help himself.

Niema watched him, one eyebrow tilted as she waited for him to stop. She didn't feel the least impulse to join in his laughter, or even to smile. Nothing about this situation was funny. They were deep in Iran on a job that could get them all killed, and oh, by the way, she didn't trust the team leader one inch, ha ha ha. Yeah, right.

"Jesus," he groaned, wiping his eyes. "All this because of feminine intuition?" A shade of incredulousness colored his tone.

Niema gave him a stony look. "You make it sound as if I've been attacking you left and right."

"Not overtly, at least." He paused, a smile still curving his mouth. "Dallas and I have worked together before, you know. What does he say about your suspicions?"

He was utterly relaxed as he waited for her answer, as if he already knew what Dallas would have said—if she had mentioned her feelings to him, that is. She hadn't uttered a word of misgiving to him, though. For one thing, she had nothing concrete to offer, and she wasn't about to stir up trouble without proof other than her feminine intuition. She didn't discount her uneasiness, but Dallas was a man who dealt in hard realities, who had learned to disconnect his emotions so he could function in the dangerous field he had chosen. Moreover, he obviously liked, trusted, and respected Tucker.

"I haven't talked to him about it."

"No? Why not?"

She shrugged. Other than not having proof, her main reason for not talking to Dallas about Tucker was that her husband hadn't been wild about her coming on this job anyway, and she didn't want to give him an opportunity to say I told you so. She was good at what she did, but she didn't have the field experience the others had, so she was reluctant to cause trouble. And, she admitted, even had she known she wouldn't be comfortable with Tucker, she would have come anyway. Something primitive in her thrilled to the tension, the danger, the utter importance of what she did. She had never wanted a nine-to-five; she wanted adventure, she wanted to work on the front line. She wasn't going to do anything to jeopardize a job she had worked hard to attain.

"Why not?" Tucker said again, and a hint of steel underlay the easiness of his tone. He wanted an answer, and she suspected he usually got what he wanted.

Oddly, though, she wasn't intimidated. Part of her even relished this little showdown, getting their animosity out into the open and going one-on-one with Tucker.

"What difference does it make?" She returned his cool look with one of her own. "Regardless of my suspicions about you, I'm doing my job and keeping my mouth shut. My reasons aren't any of your business. But I'd bet the farm your real name isn't Darrell Tucker."

He grinned suddenly, surprising her. "Dallas said you were

stubborn. Not much of a reverse gear, was the way he put it," he said, settling his shoulders more comfortably against the wall.

Because Niema had heard Dallas mutter something very close to that, after one of the few times they had gone head to head about something, she found herself smiling, too.

In that more relaxed atmosphere he said, "What makes you think my name isn't Tucker?"

"I don't know. Darrell Tucker is a good-old-boy Texas name, and every so often I hear a little bit of Texas in your accent, so the accent and the name fit—but you don't, somehow."

"I've traveled a bit since I left home," he drawled.

She clapped her hands twice in mocking applause. "That was very well done. A homey piece of phrasing, the accent a little heavier."

"But you don't buy it."

"I bet you're very good with a lot of accents."

Amused, he said, "Okay, you aren't going to believe me. That's fine. I don't have any way of proving who I am. But believe me in this: My priorities are getting that building blown and all of us safely home."

"How can you get us home? We're splitting up, remember?"

"By doing all my preliminary work right, by anticipating as many problems as I can and taking steps to counteract them."

"You can't anticipate everything, though."

"I try. That's why my hair is going gray; I sit up nights worrying."

His hair was as dark as her own, without a silver thread showing. His sense of humor was wry, tending toward the ironic; she wished he hadn't shown it to her, wished he had maintained the silence between them. Why hadn't he? Why now, of all times, had he suddenly breached the armed truce?

"We're in."

She whirled to the radio set as the whispered words came plainly through the speaker. Incredulously she checked the time; thirty minutes had passed since she had last looked. She had been so focused on her confrontation with Tucker that she had forgotten to fret.

Like a flash, she knew: That was why he had done it. He had distracted her, using the one subject he knew she wouldn't be able to ignore.

Tucker was already at the radio, slipping on a Motorola headset. "Any problems?"

"Negative."

That was all, just three whispered words, but they were in her husband's voice and Niema knew that for now, at least, he was all right. She leaned back and focused on her breathing, in, out, keeping the rhythm regular.

There was nothing Tucker could do now to distract her, short of physical violence, so he left her alone. She checked the radio settings, though she knew they were right. She wished she had checked the radio detonator one more time, just to be certain. No—she knew it was working perfectly. And Dallas knew what he was doing.

"Has Dallas ever told you about his training?"

She flicked an impatient glance at Tucker. "I don't need distracting. Thanks for doing it before, but not now, please."

A faint quirk of his brows betrayed his surprise. "So you figured it out," he said easily, and she immediately wondered if distracting her had indeed been his intention. Tucker was so damn *elusive* that even when you thought you had him read, it was possible you were reading only what he intended you to read. "But this is more in the way of reassurance. Do you know about his training?"

"That he took BUD/S? Yes." BUD/S was Basic Underwater Demolition/SEAL training: extensive, and so grueling only a tiny percentage of men who tried actually completed the course.

"But has he told you what that training entailed?"

"No, not in detail."

"Then take my word for it, Dallas can do things no ordinary man would ever dream of doing."

"I know. And—thanks. But he's still human, and plans can go wrong—"

"He knows that. They all do. They're prepared."

"Why didn't he want you to go in?"

There was an infinitesimal pause, so brief she wasn't certain she had heard it. "Despite what he said, Dallas doesn't think I'm as good as he is," Tucker said with wry humor.

She didn't believe him. For one thing, Dallas respected him too much. For another, that tiny pause before he spoke told her he had been weighing his response, and his answer wasn't one that had required any weighing.

Whoever he was, whatever he was hiding, Niema accepted that she wasn't going to get any straight answers from him. He was probably one of those paranoid spooks everyone read about, who saw spies and enemies everywhere, and, if you asked him if it was supposed to rain the next day, would wonder what you were planning that required bad weather.

Sayyed's voice whispered over the radio. *"Trouble. Activity in the warehouse. Looks like they're getting ready to make a shipment."*

Tucker swore, his attention immediately focused on the situation. It was imperative the warehoused store of bacteria be completely destroyed before a shipment was made. The warehouse was usually deserted at night, with guards posted outside, but now there was activity that prevented Sayyed from planting his charges.

"How many?" Tucker asked.

"I make it . . . eight . . . no, nine. I took cover behind some barrels, but I can't move around any."

They couldn't let that shipment leave the warehouse.

"Dallas." Tucker spoke the name quietly into his headset.

"I'm on the way, Boss. My charges are set."

Niema's nails dug into her palms. Dallas was going to Sayyed's aid, but they would still be badly outnumbered, and by moving, Dallas was risking exposure. She reached for the second headset; she didn't know what she was going to say to her husband, but she didn't have the chance. Tucker's hand shot out; he jerked the plug out of the radio set and tossed the headset aside, his dark gaze cool and hard as he met her stunned look.

She found herself on her feet, her shoulders braced, hands knotted into fists. "He's my husband," she said fiercely.

Tucker put his hand over the tiny microphone. "And he doesn't need the distraction of hearing you now." He added deliberately, "If you try anything, I'll tie and gag you."

She wasn't without some training herself, and Dallas, once he realized he couldn't convince her to play it safe and sit home like a good little wife, had been teaching her how to fight in ways her self-defense class had never covered. Still, her level of expertise in no way matched his, or Tucker's. The only way she could take him, she thought, was to catch him totally by surprise, from behind.

But he was right. Damn it, he was right. She didn't dare say anything that could break Dallas's concentration.

She held up her hands in a brief gesture of surrender and

moved three steps away. The hut was so small she couldn't go much farther anyway. She sat down on a pack of provisions and tried to beat down the suffocating waves of anxiety.

The minutes crawled by. She knew Dallas was creeping toward the warehouse section, using every bit of cover available to him, trying not to take chances. She also knew that every passing second put the terrorists that much closer to leaving with the shipment of bacteria. Dallas would be balancing caution with expediency.

Tucker spoke into the headset. "Sayyed. Report."

"I can't budge an inch. The truck is almost loaded."

"Two minutes," Dallas said.

Two minutes. Niema closed her eyes. Cold sweat trickled down her back. Please, she found herself praying. Please. She couldn't form any words other than that.

Two minutes could be a lifetime. Time itself could be strangely elastic, stretching until every second was ponderous, until the second hand on her watch seemed almost motionless.

"I'm in position."

The words almost broke her control. She bit her lip until the taste of blood filled her mouth.

"How does it look?"

"Sayyed's got his ass in a crack, all right. Hey, buddy, how many charges did you get set?"

"One."

"Shit."

One wasn't enough. Niema had listened to them, knew how many charges Dallas estimated it would take to completely destroy the facility.

"Hadi?"

"In position. Can't help you much."

"*Start pulling back.*" Dallas's voice was even. "*Sayyed, arm all the charges.*"

There was another silence, then Sayyed's, "*Done.*"

"*Get ready. Throw the pack under the truck, then run like hell. I'll lay down covering fire. I'm gonna give us five seconds to get outta here before I hit the button.*"

"*Damn. Maybe you should make it six,*" Sayyed said.

"*Ready.*" Dallas was still utterly calm. "*Go!*"

CHAPTER
TWO

The staccato thunder of gunfire blasted from the radio speaker. Niema jerked as if some of the bullets had hit her, her hands pressed hard to her mouth to hold back the scream that clogged her throat. Tucker swung around to face her, as if he didn't trust her to keep silent. He needn't have worried; she was frozen in place.

There was an animal-like sound, cut short.

"Son of a bitch! Sayyed bought it."

"Pull out," Tucker said, but there was a renewed burst of gunfire that drowned out his words.

And from the tinny speaker came a sound that made the hair on Niema's neck stand on end, a kind of hollowed-out grunt, underlaid by gunfire and a thudding sound.

"Ah . . . shit." The words were strained, thin; she could barely recognize Dallas's voice.

"Hadi!" Tucker barked. "Dallas is down. Get him—"

"No." The word came on an exhalation, long and deep.

"Hang on, buddy, I can be there—" Urgency was plain in Hadi's voice.

"Save yourself . . . the trouble. I'm gut shot."

The world went gray around her. Niema fought back the shock, fought back the sensation of her entire body falling apart as the bottom dropped out of her stomach and her lungs seized, unable to pump. Gut shot. Even if he had been in the States, with a trauma unit nearby, the injury was critical. Here in these cold, isolated mountains, with safety and cutting-edge medical help days away, it was a death sentence. She knew this; her mind knew it. But she rejected it anyway, recoiling from the knowledge.

There were more shots, very close. Dallas was still shooting, still holding them off.

"Boss . . ." The whisper floated around the hut.

"I'm here." Tucker was still facing Niema, his gaze locked on her.

"Is . . . Can Niema hear?"

Dallas had to be going into shock, or he would never have asked, would have realized she could hear everything. She had wired the switch open.

Tucker's gaze never wavered from her. "No," he said.

More shots. The sound of Dallas's breathing, shallow and quick. *"Good. I . . . I've still got the detonator. Can't let them leave with . . . that shit."*

"No," Tucker said again. "You can't." His voice was almost gentle.

"Take . . . take care of her."

Tucker's face was a mask, his gaze locked on her face. "I will." He paused, and said, "Do it."

The explosion shook the hut, sending dirt cascading down from the cracks in the ceiling, rattling the door on its frame. The blast wave hadn't passed before Tucker was moving, ripping the headset from his ears and tossing it down. He picked up a hammer and began methodically destroying the radio; even though it was old and obsolete, it was functional, and their plan was to leave nothing that could be used. Reducing the radio to rubble took half a minute.

That done, he pulled Niema away from the packs of provisions and swiftly began repacking them, redistributing what they would carry. She stood numbly in the middle of the hut, unable to move, her brain frozen with shock. She was aware of pain; there was a great, clawing pain in her chest, as if her heart were exploding, and even that was somehow felt as if from a distance.

Tucker thrust a heavy coat at her. Niema stared at it, unable to comprehend what he wanted her to do with it. Silently he bundled her into it, putting her arms into the sleeves as if she were a toddler, zipping it up, tucking her hair under the collar as an extra buffer for her neck. He tugged gloves on her hands, and put a warm fur hat on her head.

He pulled a heavy sweater on over his head, then shrugged into his own coat. As he was pulling on his gloves, a low whistle sounded outside the hut, and he extinguished the light. Hadi slid in the door, and Tucker turned the light on again.

Even in the weakness of the single light, Hadi's face was drawn and white. He looked immediately at Niema. "God—" he began, only to be silenced by a quick motion from Tucker.

"Not now. We have to move." He shoved one of the consolidated packs into Hadi's arms, and slung the other two onto his own shoulders. He picked up a rifle, took Niema's arm, and led her into the night.

Their transportation, an old Renault, had died on them the first night, and all of Tucker's mechanical expertise could not repair a broken axle. Hadi glanced worriedly at Niema. She hadn't faltered during the two days they had been moving; she was like a robot, keeping pace with them no matter how hard Tucker pushed them. She spoke when they asked her a direct question; she ate when Tucker gave her food, drank when he gave her water. What she hadn't done was sleep. She would lie down when he told her to, but she hadn't slept, and her eyes were swollen with fatigue. Both men knew she couldn't go on much longer.

"What are you going to do?" Hadi asked Tucker, keeping his voice low. "Do we split up as originally planned, or stay together? You may need help getting her out."

"We split up," Tucker said. "It's safer that way. A woman traveling with two men would attract more attention than a man and his wife."

They were traveling northwest, through Iran's most populated area, but that was the only way to get to Turkey, and safety. Iraq was due west, Afghanistan and Pakistan were to the east, the splinter nations left by the breakup of the Soviet Union to the northeast, the Caspian Sea to the north and the Persian Gulf to the south, through very inhospitable desert. Turkey was their only feasible destination. From here on out, Niema would have to wear the traditional Muslim chador.

They had traveled at night at first, the better to avoid detection if there was any pursuit, though it was possible Sayyed and Dallas were thought to be the only saboteurs. It was even possible, Tucker thought, that no word of intruders had gotten out. The facility had been remote, with only one phone line going in. Dallas could well have pushed the button before anyone got to the phone, assuming any of the workers thought to make a call anyway.

The building was charred rubble. Tucker himself had reconnoitered, leaving Niema under Hadi's worried and watchful eye. As always, Dallas had been thorough; what the plastique hadn't destroyed, the fire had.

That was the one time Niema had spoken without first being asked something. When Tucker returned she stared at him, her dark eyes fathomless, haunted, somehow hopeful. "Did you find him?" she asked.

Startled, keeping it hidden, he said, "No."

"But—his body . . ."

She wasn't clinging to an irrational hope that Dallas was still alive. She wanted his body for burial.

"Niema . . . there's nothing left." He said it as gently as he could, knowing there was nothing he could do to cushion the blow but trying anyway. She had been a trooper all through the job, but now she looked so damn *fragile*.

Nothing left. He saw the words hit her, saw her reel with the shock. She hadn't asked anything since, not even for water. His own stamina was so great he could go for long periods before he was aware of thirst, so he couldn't rely on his own needs to remind him of hers. He set a time limit: Every two hours, he made her drink. Every four, he made her eat. Not that there was any *making* to it; she accepted whatever he gave her, without protest.

Now it was time for them to split up, as planned, but instead of Niema going with Dallas she would now be staying with him, while Hadi made his own way out of the country.

Tomorrow they would be in Tehran, where they would blend

in with the population. Tucker would then make secure contact and, if there was no trouble, acquire transportation. Another day after that, and they would be just across the border from Turkey. He would abandon the vehicle and they would walk across during the night, in a remote location he had already scouted. Hadi would cross over at another point.

Hadi scratched his beard. Neither of them had shaved for two weeks, so they were decidedly scruffy. "Maybe I could scrounge around tomorrow when we get to Tehran, find a pharmacy, buy some sleeping pills or something. She's got to sleep."

They had stopped for a brief rest, sheltered by the lone remaining wall of a small mud house that had long since been abandoned. Niema sat a little way off to the side, alone in a way that went far beyond the slight distance between her and them. She didn't fidget. She just sat. Maybe if she cried, Tucker thought. Maybe if she let some of it out, exhausted herself, she would be able to sleep. But she hadn't cried; the shock had gone too deep, and she hadn't yet recovered from that enough for tears. The time for crying would come later.

He considered Hadi's suggestion, but didn't like the idea of drugging her, in case they had to move fast. Still . . . "Maybe," he said, and left it at that.

They had rested long enough. Tucker stood, signaling that the break was over. Niema stood too, and Hadi moved forward to help her over some loose, unbaked mud bricks. She didn't need the help, but Hadi had become as protective of her as a mother hen.

He stepped on a loose board. It tilted up and dislodged some of the bricks just as Niema stepped on them, shifting them out from under her feet. She staggered off balance, slipped, and landed on her right shoulder in the rubble.

She didn't cry out, her training not to make any unnecessary noise still holding. Hadi swore softly, apologizing as he helped her to her feet. "Damn, I'm sorry! Are you all right?"

She nodded, brushing at her clothes, her shoulder. Tucker saw the slight frown knit her brows as she brushed her shoulder again, and even that much expression was so alien to her face these past two days that he knew immediately something was wrong.

"You're hurt." He was beside her before he stopped speaking, pulling her away from the rubble.

"Did you jam your shoulder?" Hadi asked, frowning with concern.

"No." She sounded puzzled, no more, but she twisted her neck to look at the back of her shoulder. Tucker turned her around. There was a small tear in her shirt, and blood was welling from it.

"You must have fallen on something sharp," he said, and thought maybe the damage had been done by a shard of brick, but then he saw the rusty nail protruding about an inch out of a rotten board.

"It was a nail. Good thing you had a tetanus booster." He efficiently unbuttoned her shirt as he spoke. She wasn't wearing a bra, so he only undid the first few buttons, then pulled the shirt off the injured shoulder.

The puncture wound was purplish and already swelling, sullenly oozing blood. The nail had gone in high and right of her shoulder blade, in the fleshy part just beside her arm. He pressed on it to make the blood run more freely. Hadi· had already opened their meager first-aid kit and extracted some gauze pads, which he used to mop up the blood as it ran down.

Niema stood motionless, letting them tend to the wound, which Tucker supposed was minor in relation to the concern both he and Hadi were showing. Any wound or injury that caused a delay was dangerous, because it would force them to stay in Iran even longer, so their concern was based in logic; but the biggest part of it, Tucker admitted, was the male instinct to protect the female. Not only was she the only woman with them, but she was already wounded, emotionally if not physically. Add in the fact that she was a lovely young woman who had quickly endeared herself to the team with her guts and wit, and of course they were jumping to protect her.

Mentally, he knew all the reasons, instinctive as well as personal. On a gut level, he knew he would move mountains to prevent anything from adding to the load of pain she already carried. He had promised Dallas he would take care of her, and no matter what it cost, he would keep that promise.

Sunlight gleamed on her bare shoulder, turning her skin to pearl. She had a pale complexion, despite the darkness of her hair and eyes. The elegant slant of her collarbone was exposed, and even as he applied an antibiotic ointment to the wound, Tucker couldn't help admiring the graceful structure of her body. She was remarkably feminine, despite her rough clothing and the fact that she wore no makeup, her hair wasn't combed, and all of them really, really needed a bath. She looked so female and elegant, he had constantly been surprised by her toughness.

"She looks like someone you want to put on a pedestal and keep from ever getting dirty or hurt," Dallas had said, before Tucker had ever met Niema, when he was putting the team together. "But she'd kick you in the teeth if you tried." He'd said it with intense male satisfaction, because she was his, and Tucker had shaken his head in wonder at seeing Dallas Burdock so obviously, unabashedly in love.

Tucker plastered a large adhesive bandage over the wound, then drew her shirt back up onto her shoulder. He would have buttoned the garment for her but she did it herself, her head bent over the task, her fingers slow.

Her reaction time was way off, dulled by shock and fatigue. If anything happened that necessitated quick action, he didn't think she could function. She *had* to get some sleep, he thought, one way or another.

He motioned for Hadi to step aside with him. "I'm not going to push her any further. According to the map, there's a small village about fifteen miles north of here. Think you can liberate some wheels for us?"

"Is the Pope Catholic?"

"Don't take any chances. We can't risk any pursuit. Wait until late at night, if necessary."

Hadi nodded his assent.

"If you aren't back by dawn, we'll move on."

Hadi nodded again. "Don't worry about me. If I don't make it back, just get her out."

"I plan to."

Hadi took some food and water with him and soon was out of sight. Niema didn't ask where he was going; she simply sat down and stared emptily at nothing. No, not emptily, Tucker thought. That would be easier to bear than the bottomless well of suffering reflected in her eyes.

The day wore on. He spent the time constructing a meager shelter for them, something to block the sun during the day and the wind at night. As they worked their way out of the mountains, the temperature had risen, but the nights were still damn cold. They ate, or at least he did; Niema refused more than a couple of bites. She drank a good bit of water, though, more than usual.

By nightfall, her cheeks were a little flushed. Tucker felt her face and wasn't surprised to find it hot. "You're feverish," he told her. "From the nail." The fever wasn't especially high, so he wasn't worried on that account, but her body didn't need this fresh assault.

He ate by flashlight. The fever robbed her of what little appetite she had, and she didn't eat anything that night; again, she drank a lot of water. "Try to get some sleep," he said, and obediently she lay down on the blanket he had spread out for her, but he watched her breathing for a while and knew she didn't sleep. She was lying there staring into the shadows, aching for the husband who wasn't there and never would be again.

Tucker stared at her back. She and Dallas had been circumspect in their behavior, refraining from public displays of affection, but at night they had slept next to each other, with Dallas spooned protectively around her and his big arm draped around her waist. She had slept like a baby then, utterly secure.

Perhaps she couldn't sleep now because she was alone and could feel the chill on her back. It was a simple thing, the kind of routine married couples seemed to develop so easily: the comfort of human warmth in the night, the sound of a loved one's breathing. Perhaps it was the trust, the intimacy, that meant so much. Intimacy didn't come easily to Tucker, trust even less so, but he knew it had existed between Niema and Dallas. Dallas's death had left her bereft, and she no longer found comfort in the night.

Tucker sighed inwardly. The sigh was for himself, because he knew what he had to do, and knew the cost.

He got a bottle of water and silently went to her, lying down behind her on the blanket and placing the water nearby. "Shhh," he murmured when she stiffened. "Just go to sleep." He curved his body around her, giving her his heat, his strength. Pulling a second blanket over them to keep out the cold, he anchored her to him with his arm around her waist.

He could feel the fever inside her; the heat emanating from her body wrapping around them both like a third blanket. Still, she shivered a little, and he pulled her closer. She lay on her uninjured left shoulder and held her right arm very still so as not to jar it.

"The fever's fighting the infection," he said, keeping his voice low and soothing. "There's aspirin in the first-aid kit, if you get too uncomfortable, but unless the fever gets a lot higher I suggest letting it do its job."

"Yes." Her voice was thin with fatigue, listless.

He stroked her hair, his touch gentle and tried to think of some way to occupy her mind. Maybe if she could just stop *thinking* she could sleep. "I saw a solar eclipse once. I was in South America." He didn't get any more specific than that. "The weather was so hot the air felt sticky. Cold showers didn't do any good; I was sweaty again as soon as I got toweled off. Everyone wore as little clothing as possible."

He didn't know if she was listening; he didn't much care. He kept that soothing, gently monotonous tone, his voice just barely above a whisper. If he could bore her to sleep, so much the better.

"It had been on the radio that there would be a solar eclipse that day, but the heat was so miserable no one much cared. It was just a little village, not the type to attract any eclipse chasers. I had forgotten about it myself. It was a sunny day, so bright the light hurt my eyes, and I was wearing sunglasses. The eclipse slipped up on me. The sun was still shining, the sky was blue, but all of a sudden it was as if a cloud had passed over the sun. The birds all stopped singing, and the village pets hid.

"One of the villagers looked up and said, 'Look at the sun,' and I remembered about the eclipse. I told them not to stare, that it would blind them if they looked too long. The light was eerie, if you can imagine dark sunshine. The sky turned a really deep shade of blue, and the temperature dropped at least twenty degrees. It kept getting darker and darker, but the sky was still blue. Finally the sun was completely covered, and the solar halo around the moon was . . . spectacular. On the ground we were in a strange, deep twilight, and everything was quiet, but overhead the sky glowed. The twilight lasted for a couple of minutes, and during that time the entire village stood still. Men, women, and children; none of them moved, or spoke.

"Then the light began to come back, and the birds started singing again. The chickens came off roost, and the dogs barked. The moon moved on, and it was as hot as it had been before, but no one bitched about the weather anymore." Two days later everyone in that little village was dead—massacred—but he kept that to himself.

He waited. Her breathing was too shallow for sleep, but at least she wasn't as stiff as she had been before. If she relaxed, her body might take over and let itself sleep.

Next he told her about a dog he'd had when he was a kid. There was no dog, but she didn't know that. The dog he made up was a Heinz 57, with a long, skinny body like a dachshund and a curly coat like a poodle. "Ugly little bastard," he said comfortably.

"What was his name?"

Her voice startled him. It was low, almost hesitant. Something painful grabbed his chest and squeezed. "She," he said. "I named her Fifi, because I thought that was what poodles were named."

He told her tale after tale of Fifi's exploits. She'd been an amazing dog. She could climb trees, open most doors by herself, and her favorite meal had been—God, what was some kid's cereal?—Fruit Loops. Fifi slept with the cat, hid shoes under the couch, and once really did eat his homework.

Tucker embroidered on the fictional Fifi for half an hour, keeping his voice to a melodic rhythm, pausing every so often to check Niema's breathing. It got slower, deeper, until finally she slept.

He let himself sleep, but lightly. A part of him remained alert, listening for Hadi's return, or for any suspicious sound. He woke completely several times, to check on Niema and make certain her fever wasn't getting higher. She was still too warm, but he was satisfied there was nothing critical about the fever, just her body healing itself. Still, to be on the safe side, he roused her enough each time that she could drink a little water. As he had suspected, once she let herself go to sleep nature got the upper hand, and though he woke her easily enough she went right back to sleep the moment she closed her eyes.

The hours passed and Hadi didn't return. Tucker was patient. People slept soundest in the hours before dawn, and Hadi would probably wait until then. Still, every time he woke from his doze, Tucker checked his watch and considered his options. The longer he let Niema sleep, the stronger she would be and the faster she would be able to travel. He couldn't, however, afford to wait too long.

At five o'clock he turned on the flashlight and drank some of the water himself, then gently roused Niema. She drank the water he held to her mouth, then snuggled against him and sighed drowsily. "Time to get up," he murmured.

She kept her eyes closed. "Not yet." She turned to face him, and slipped her arm around his neck. "Mmm." She nestled closer, pressing her face into his chest.

She thought he was Dallas. She was still drowsy, her mind

dulled by the hard sleep, and perhaps she had been dreaming about him. She was accustomed to waking in her husband's arms, to cuddling even if they didn't make love, and given the short time they had been married Tucker bet there hadn't been many mornings when Dallas hadn't made love to her.

He should shake her completely awake, get her fed, check her shoulder, and have her ready to move whether or not Hadi returned. He knew exactly what he should do, but for once in his life Tucker ignored the job. He tightened his arms around her and held her, just for a moment, something in him desperately hungry for the feel of her hugging him in return.

No, not *him*. It was Dallas she was holding, her husband she was dreaming about.

It cost him more than he wanted, but he took a deep breath and eased away from her. "Niema, wake up," he said softly. "You're dreaming."

Slumbrous dark eyes opened, as black as night in the dim glow of the flashlight. He saw the dawning of awareness, the flare of shock in her eyes, followed by horror. She pulled away from him, her lips trembling. "I—" she began, but no other words came.

The sob burst out of her as if it tore from her chest. She rolled away from him and lay on the blanket, her entire body heaving. She made a long, low, keening sound, chopped by the convulsive sobs that ripped out of her throat. The dam of her control, once breached, collapsed entirely. She cried until she gagged, until her throat closed and no more sound came out. She cried until he thought surely the spasm of grief had to ease, but it didn't. She was still weeping when he heard the sound of a vehicle approaching in the dark, cold dawn, and he stepped out to meet Hadi.

PART
TWO

CHAPTER
THREE

1999, Atlanta, Georgia

Delta Flight 183, Atlanta to London, was full. The first-class passengers had already boarded and made themselves comfortable, choice of reading material or drink, or both, in hand. The flight attendants had taken coats and hung them in the closet, chatted with those passengers inclined to be friendly, checked with the cockpit to see if the guys up there needed anything.

Congressman Donald Brookes and his wife, Elaine, were taking a vacation, the first in so long Elaine could scarcely believe Donald had agreed to the downtime. He had regularly put in eighteen to twenty hours a day on the job since first being elected fifteen years before. Even after all this time in government, there was a thread of idealism in him that insisted he give the taxpayers their money's worth, and more. She had gotten accustomed to going to bed alone, but she always woke when he came to bed, and they would hold hands and talk. In the early days they hadn't been on anyone's A list, so she had spent a lot of evenings alone with the kids.

Things had changed somewhat. Donald was chairman of the House Committee on Foreign Relations, and now they were A list; as often as not they were at some function somewhere, but at least they were together.

Oh, there had been times when they had gone back home to Illinois, when Congress was in recess, but though the pace slowed then, Donald had used that time to catch up with his constituency. They hadn't been on a real vacation since he was first elected.

Elaine looked forward to days of sleeping late, ordering room service, and leisurely exploring London. Five days in London, then a short hop to Paris for another five days, then Rome and Florence. It was her dream vacation.

Two rows behind them, Garvin Whittaker was already absorbed in the papers from his briefcase. He was CEO of a cutting-edge software firm that had exploded in value over the past seven years, edging toward fifty billion. Not in Microsoft's league, but then, what was? When his current projects hit the market, Garvin figured the firm would double in value within five years. At least, he hoped it would; he dreamed it would. He was biding his time, building his market and strength, taking care not to tread on any giant toes. But when he judged the time was right, he would unveil the operating system he had developed, a system so streamlined and simplified—and so bug free—it would leave everything else out there in the dust.

In the first row was a UN delegate from Germany, holding his icy drink against his head and hoping his headache would abate enough that he would be able to sleep on the long flight. In seat 2F was a World Bank official, her brow puckered as she studied the *Wall Street Journal.* Growing up, she had always dreamed of being something romantic, like a brain surgeon or a movie star, but she had learned that money was the most powerful kick available, far more potent than any drug. She traveled all over the world; she had dined in Paris, bought clothes in Hong Kong, skied in Switzerland. Life was good, and she intended to make it even better.

A career diplomat was in seat 4D. He had been ambassador to France in the Bush years, but since was relegated to more minor roles. He was newly married, to a Chicago socialite whose family's wealth provided considerable clout; he expected to be ambassador again soon, and not to any Podunk country no one could find on a map.

In the coach section, Charles Lansky wiped sweat from his brow and tried not to think of the impending takeoff. He didn't mind flying, once the plane was airborne, but he was sick with fear during takeoff and landing. After a brief stopover in London, he was flying on to Frankfurt, which meant two takeoffs and two landings. Only a vitally important meeting could have induced him to endure so much.

College students on a tour of England, Scotland, and Ireland crowded onto the plane, each of them carrying the ubiquitous backpack packed with essentials: a bottle of Evian, a portable CD player, a collection of fave CDs, makeup if the student was female, a handheld computer game if male; perhaps an item or two of clothing. They were tanned, healthy, as alike as Teddy Roosevelt's teeth but still young enough to be convinced they were unique.

The usual assortment of business people and holiday-goers filed in, milled around, eventually took their seats. One young lady anxiously clasped an overnight bag on her lap, until the flight attendant told her it needed to be stowed and offered to find a place in the overhead bins for the bag. The young lady shook her head and managed to stuff the bag under the seat in front of her, though it was a tight fit and she then had nowhere to put her feet. Her complexion was pasty, and she was sweating despite the air pouring out of the overhead vents.

Finally the giant L-1011 pushed away from the gate and taxied out to get in line for takeoff. Seventeen other aircraft were ahead of them, inching toward the runway. One of the pilots came on the intercom occasionally to give the passengers updates on their expected takeoff time. Most of the first-class passengers had already removed their shoes and put on the black travel socks provided in the gift bag Delta gave each first-class passenger on overseas flights. Magazines were thumbed through, books were hauled out, a few people already snored.

Finally it was Flight 183's turn. The big engines roared and the plane gathered speed and it rolled down the runway, faster and faster, until finally lift exceeded drag and they were airborne. There was some mechanical rumbling as the wheels lifted and folded and tucked into the belly of the aircraft. Flight 183 arrowed into the blue sky, steadily gaining altitude for the flight pattern that would take them up the east coast until, somewhere near New York, they would swing out over the Atlantic.

Thirty-three minutes into the flight, over the mountains of western North Carolina, Flight 183 disintegrated into a fiery ball that spewed flaming pieces of fuselage upward in a slow-motion arc, before the trajectory peaked and the pieces fell back to earth.

CHAPTER FOUR

Washington, D.C.

The two men sat companionably at a nine-teenth-century walnut desk; the wood shone with a velvety sheen, and the top was inlaid with rose Italian marble. A handsome chessboard, topped with hand-carved pieces, was between them. The library in which they sat was masculine, comfortable, slightly shabby; not because Franklin Vinay couldn't afford to spruce it up, but because he liked it the way it was. Mrs. Vinay had refurbished it the year before she died, and he found comfort among these things she had chosen for him.

She had also found the chess set at an estate sale in New Hampshire. Dodie had loved estate sales, Frank remembered fondly. She had kept the gift of enjoyment her entire life, finding pleasure in many small things. She had been gone ten years, and not a day passed that he didn't think of her, sometimes with lingering sorrow but more often with a smile, because they were good memories.

As always, he and John had flipped a coin to see who made the opening move. Frank drew white and had opened aggressively, if conventionally, by moving the pawn in front of his king two spaces forward. Sometimes he preferred the more popular moves, because sometimes doing the expected could be the most unexpected thing to do.

Frank knew he was a very good chess player. That said, it was difficult for him to best John at the game. The younger man was as analytical as a computer, as patient as Job, and, when the time was right, as aggressive as George Patton ever dreamed of being. In chess, as well as in his chosen field, that made John Medina a dangerous opponent.

Kaiser, an enormous German shepherd, snoozed contentedly at their feet, occasionally emitting puppylike yelps incongruous with his size as he chased rabbits in his dreams. Kaiser's peacefulness was reassuring.

The house had been swept for eavesdropping devices that morning and again that night when Frank arrived home. Electronic noise prevented their conversation from being picked up by a parabolic mike, should anyone try to eavesdrop using that method. The security system was state of the art, the door locks the strongest available, the windows protected by steel bars.

The house, which from the outside looked like the ordinary house of a moderately prosperous man, was a fortress. Even so, both men knew fortresses could be breached. Frank's 9mm was in his desk drawer. John's weapon was in his belt holster, tucked into the small of his back. Frank's position as deputy director of operations, CIA, made him a valuable commodity in the espionage community; for that reason, very few people knew where he lived. His name wasn't on any deed or any utility record. Any calls to or from his private number were routed through several switching stations that made them untraceable.

For all that, Frank thought wryly, if any hostile government was given the choice between snatching him or snatching John Medina, he would be the one left behind.

John studied the board, idly stroking the rook while he pondered his next move. Making his decision, he lifted his fingers off the rook and moved his queen's bishop. "How are my friends in New Orleans?"

Frank wasn't surprised by the question. Months, even a year or more, might go by without seeing John, but when he did, John always asked certain questions. "They're doing well. They have a baby now, a little boy born last month. And Detective Chastain is no longer with the NOPD, or a detective; he's a lieutenant with the state."

"And Karen?"

"Working in a trauma unit, or she was until the baby was born. She's taken a leave of absence, for at least a year, I think, maybe longer."

"I don't expect she'll have any trouble returning to her job when she's ready," John said, his tone mild, but Frank knew him well enough to read the request—or perhaps it was an order—underneath the tone. While he was formally John's superior, in truth John was pretty much autonomous.

"Not at all," Frank said, and it was a promise.

A couple of years before, both Karen's father and John's father had been murdered in a plot to cover up Senator Stephen Lake's hired killing of his own brother in Vietnam. In the process of uncovering the plot, John had become an admirer of both the plucky Karen and her tough-as-nails husband. Though they never knew his name, since then he had made a point of smoothing certain obstacles out of their way.

"And Mrs. Burdock?"

That question too was expected. "Niema's fine. She's developed a new surveillance device that's almost impossible to detect. The NSA has borrowed her for a couple of projects, too."

John looked interested. "An undetectable bug? When will it be available?"

"Soon. It piggybacks off existing wiring, but without causing a drop in power. Electronic sweeps can't find it."

"How did she manage that?" John nudged a pawn onto another square.

Frank scowled at the board. Such a small move, but it had moved the game in a different direction. "Something to do with frequency modulation. If I understood it, I could get a real job."

John laughed. He was a surprisingly open man, during those rare times when he could relax with people he could trust, and who knew who he was. If he liked you, then you were never in doubt of his friendship, perhaps because the majority of his life was spent in danger, in deep shadows, answering to different names and wearing different faces. He treasured what was real, and what was reliable.

"Has she remarried yet?"

"Niema? No." The pawn's position had him worried, and he continued frowning at the board, only half his attention on his answer. "She doesn't see anyone on a regular basis. She dates occasionally, but that's all."

"It's been five years."

Something in John's tone alerted Frank. He looked up to see the younger man frowning slightly, as if he were unhappy to learn that Niema Burdock was still single.

"Does she seem happy?"

"Happy?" Startled by the question, Frank leaned back, the chess game forgotten. "She's busy. She likes her work, she's very well paid, she has a nice home, drives a new car. I can take care of those things, but I can't direct or know her emotions." Of all the people for whom John was an anonymous guardian angel, Niema Burdock was the one he followed the closest. Since he brought her out of Iran after her husband was killed, he had taken an almost personal interest in her well-being.

In a flash of intuition, a leap of reasoning that had made Frank Vinay so good at his job, he said, "You want her yourself." He seldom blurted out his thoughts in such an unguarded way, but he was, abruptly, as certain of this as he had ever been of anything. He felt faintly embarrassed at making such an observation.

John glanced up, eyebrows lifted quizzically. "Of course," he said, as if it were a given. "For all the good wanting does."

"What do you mean?"

"I'm scarcely in a position to become involved with anyone. Not only am I gone for months at a time, there's always a good chance I won't come back." He said it coolly, unemotionally. He knew exactly what the risks were in his profession, accepted them, perhaps even sought them.

"That's true of other professions: the elite military teams, certain construction workers. They marry, have families. *I* did."

"Your circumstances were different."

Because Frank hadn't worked in black ops, he meant. John

was a specialist in those missions that never saw the light of day, financed by funds for which there was no accounting, no records. He took care of what needed to be handled without the government becoming involved, to preserve deniability.

Frank had been considering broaching a subject with John, and now seemed like a perfect time. "Your circumstances can be different, too."

"Can they."

"I don't plan to die in harness; retirement is looking more and more attractive. You could step into my place without ever losing a beat."

"DDO?" John shook his head. "I operate in the field; you know that."

"And you know that you can operate wherever you choose. You're a natural for the job. In fact, you're better suited for it than I was when I took over. Think about it for a while—" The phone rang, interrupting him, and he broke off. The call wasn't unexpected. He lifted the receiver, spoke briefly, then hung up. "An agent is bringing the report over."

The chess game was forgotten, the real reason for their meeting taking over. Since Flight 183 went down the week before, the FBI and NTSB had been combing the rugged Carolina mountains collecting fragments, trying to piece together what had happened. Two hundred sixty-three people had died, and they wanted to know the reason. There hadn't been any unusual radio traffic; the flight had been routine, until the plane fell from the sky. The flight recorder had been found and preliminary reports said that the pilots hadn't indicated anything was wrong. Whatever had happened had been instant, and catastrophic—and therefore suspicious.

From one of his untold shadowy sources, John had heard whispers there was a new type of explosive device that airport

X-ray machines couldn't detect, not even the CTX-5000 machines such as were used in Atlanta. He notified Frank, who quietly set about getting all the information available on Flight 183 as soon as NTSB and the FBI gathered it.

The crash site was difficult to work. The terrain was mountainous, heavily wooded, without easy access. The wreckage was strewn over an enormous area. Bits and pieces, both metal and human, had been found in treetops. Teams had been working nonstop for a week, first gathering the human remains and turning them over to forensic specialists for the almost impossible task of identification, then searching for even the smallest piece of the aircraft. The more pieces they found, the more complete the puzzle would be, and the more likely they were to discover what happened.

Fifteen minutes later an agent knocked on Vinay's door, rousing Kaiser. John remained in the library, out of sight, while Frank, with Kaiser beside him, collected the report.

Frank had requested two copies of the report, and on returning to the library he gave one to John. He sank back into his chair, his brow furrowed as he read. The report wasn't reassuring.

"Definitely an explosion. That wasn't really in doubt." People in the area had reported hearing an abrupt boom and seeing a bright flash. Whether or not anyone actually had seen anything was open to speculation, since the plane had gone down in the mountains where there wasn't a good line of sight in any direction. People generally didn't go around staring at the sky, though if the afternoon sun had glinted off the plane and caught someone's attention at just the right moment it was *possible* to have seen the actual explosion. More than likely, though, on hearing the noise, people had looked around, seen the smoke and arcing debris, and their imaginations took it from there and convinced them they had seen one hell of a fireball.

Rumors had immediately started that Flight 183 had been shot down by a missile. Congressman Donald Brookes, the House chairman of Foreign Relations, had been on Flight 183. Someone *had* to have wanted him dead for some reason, though all the reasons popping up on the Internet had been far-fetched, to say the least. Proof of the plot, the missile theorists said, was that Congressman Brookes, who lived in Illinois, was reportedly going on vacation but for some reason was on a flight originating in Atlanta, instead of Chicago. That was obviously suspicious. Even after it was revealed that the Brookes's oldest son lived in Atlanta and they had visited him for a couple of days before leaving for Europe, the bring-down-a-plane-to-get-one-man theory persisted.

There was, however, no evidence of a missile. The pattern of rupture in the metal, plus the burn patterns and residue on the pieces of fuselage, all gave evidence that Flight 183 had been brought down by an internal explosion that had literally ripped the plane apart, blowing out a huge section of the fuselage and all of the left wing.

Preliminary chemical analysis indicated plastique. They had not, however, found any evidence of a detonator. Even in such a catastrophic explosion, microscopic and chemical evidence would have remained; if something existed, then it left its print.

"To have done this much damage, the bomb had to have been sizeable; the machines in Atlanta should have detected it." Frank was deeply worried; all luggage for the flight had been inspected, either by machines or humans. If, as John thought, the device was undetectable by their current technology, then they had a big problem on their hands.

Every piece of luggage, both checked and carry-ons, would have to be hand searched, but airlines weren't the only ones vulnerable. The possible applications of such a device were staggering. It could be used in mail bombs, to destroy federal buildings—any public building, actually—disrupt transportation and communication. No one in America paid much attention to the security of bridges, either, but let a few of them come down and traffic would grind to a standstill.

The explosive could have been disguised as something else and slipped through the machines in Atlanta. The system failed occasionally; nothing was foolproof. There should still, however, have been evidence of the detonator. They should have found a radio, or a mercury switch, or a simple timer—anything by which the explosion could be triggered. The detonator was actually how most bombs were spotted, because they were more easily detected when scanned.

John rubbed his lower lip and tossed the report onto Frank's desk. He had been most interested in the chemical analysis. The explosive found had some components in common with plastique, but there were some anomalies. "I'm thinking R.D.X." R.D.X. was cyclonite, or composition C-1. By itself it was too sensitive to handle, so it was usually mixed with a plasticiser, which would give it some of the same chemical elements as plastique. R.D.X. could be molded into any shape including shoelaces.

Frank looked up. "How? You know how luggage and packages are thrown around; an unstable explosive would have detonated on the ground."

"But what if it wasn't originally unstable? What if the compound deteriorates, and sets off a chemical reaction that causes it to explode? If you know the rate of deterioration, the explosion could easily be timed."

"Something that starts out as stable as plastique, but deteriorates and becomes its own detonator? Son of a bitch." Frank closed his eyes.

"There's always the chance some lone sociopath in a lab somewhere cooked this up, but what I'm hearing is that it came out of a top-secret lab in Europe."

"IRA?"

"I'm sure they would be standing in line to buy, but I haven't picked up any hints that they bankrolled the development."

"Who, then?"

"Take your pick; we aren't short on candidates." Terrorist groups proliferated all over the world. There were at least twenty-five hundred known organizations; some came and went, others had thousands of members and had been around for decades.

"And they'll all have this new stuff."

"Only if they have the money to buy it." The terrorist organizations might cooperate with one another, but it wasn't one big happy brotherhood. A new explosive would be a big moneymaker, closely controlled for as long as possible so there would be only one producer of it. Eventually, as happened to all new technology, everyone would have it; by then the means of detecting it would also have been developed. It was like a chess game, with moves and countermoves.

"If it's in Europe, and big money is behind it, then Louis Ronsard is our man," John said.

That in itself was a large problem. Ronsard was a shadowy Frenchman who gave his allegiance to no one group; he was the conduit, however, for many, and he had made an enormous fortune providing what was needed. He probably wasn't behind the development of the explosive, but he would be the logical person to approach as a middle man, one to handle payments and shipments—for a fee, of course.

Ronsard could be picked up, or eliminated; he wasn't in hiding. But his security was extremely tight, making a capture far more difficult than an elimination. Even if he were captured, John doubted he would give up any useful information. Sophisticated interrogation techniques could be countered by intensive training and mind control. Added to the problem of Ronsard was that he had powerful friends in the French government. He had been left alone, for all of the above reasons, but also because he was neither the source nor the user of all the nasty things he provided. He was the conduit, the controller, the valve. Eliminate him and another conduit would take his place.

Finding the source was the key, but John also had to discover to whom other shipments had already been delivered. To do that, he had to get to Ronsard.

CHAPTER
FIVE

John Medina never stayed in the same place twice when he came to D.C. He had no home, literally. A home base gave anyone looking for him a starting point, and the thing about homes was that eventually, if you had one, you went there. So he lived in hotels and motels, condos, the occasional rented house—or a hut, a tent, a cave, a hole in the ground, whatever was available.

A condo was his preferred living quarters. They were more private than hotels, and, unlike a motel, had more than one exit. He didn't like sleeping in a place where he could be cornered.

The hotel he chose this time had wrought-iron balconies outside each room, which was what had made him decide in the hotel's favor. He had checked in earlier, checked for bugs, studied the security, then gone to meet Frank Vinay. Now, when he walked through the lobby to the elevators, no one who saw him would recognize him as the man who had checked in.

Disguise wasn't difficult. When he checked in he had been wearing glasses, had gray hair spray on his hair, cotton in his cheeks to fill out his face, and he had walked with a definite limp. He had also used a nasal Rochester, New York accent. His clothing had been the kind bought at a discount department store. There was no sign of that man now; he had removed the glasses and washed his hair, exchanged the gray polyester slacks for jeans, the plaid shirt for a white oxford, and the green windbreaker for a black jacket so exquisitely tailored it disguised the bulk of the weapon he wore and still looked fashionable.

He had hung the DO NOT DISTURB sign on his door to keep hotel employees out. Most people would be surprised to find out how often during the day, while they were gone, the hotel staff was in and out of their rooms. Housekeeping, maintenance, management—they all had a master key and could get into any room. Plus there were professional thieves who hung around hotels and noticed the businesspeople—when they left, how long they were gone, etc. A good thief could always get into a locked room, so getting into a room was nothing more than a matter of picking out the target, hanging near the desk to find out how long someone was staying, then discreetly following to see which room the person entered. Next morning, call the room to see if anyone answers. Then go on up, and, to be on the safe side, knock on the door. If there's still no response, go in.

A DO NOT DISTURB sign at least gives the impression someone was in the room. He had also dialed a certain untraceable number and left the phone off the hook, so if anyone called, he—or she; thieves were not gender specific—would get a busy signal.

Hanging on the inside door handle was a small battery-operated alarm. If anyone ignored the sign and opened the door anyway, an ear-piercing siren sounded, which was certain to attract attention. John turned off the alarm by pressing a button on the small remote he carried in his pocket. The alarm was just a gadget, but it amused him and would startle the hell out of anyone trying to get in. He wouldn't have bothered with it if he hadn't left his computer in the room.

The room was as he had left it. He scanned for bugs anyway, as a matter of routine, and thought of Niema's undetectable device. Technology was a leapfrog affair; something new was developed and for a while that side—whatever side it was—had the advantage. Then a countermeasure was developed and the other side had the advantage. Niema's bug would give them the advantage now, but technology couldn't be kept secret forever and eventually the bad guys—the terrorists and spies and hostile governments—would have the bug, too. It could be used against him, used to capture or kill him. Niema would probably be pleased if she knew her invention had led to his death. She wouldn't know, however; very few people would. He had no family, no network of friends or coworkers. Those people who worked with him didn't know who he was.

He didn't have to hide his identity with Frank Vinay, of course, or with Jess McPherson, an old friend of his father's. It was a relief to be able to drop his guard, those rare times when he was with one of them, and just be himself.

Sitting at the desk, he disconnected the call, then booted up the laptop and hooked it to the phone line. A few typed commands had him inside one of the CIA's data banks. He was one of the few people left in the world who still used the MS-DOS operating system, but when he was working he vastly preferred it over any system that required a mouse. A mouse was great for Net surfing or playing games, but he'd found that, when he was working, a mouse slowed him down. He could type in the DOS commands much faster than he could take his hand off the keyboard, guide the mouse, click, and go back to the keyboard. In his world, seconds shaved off operating time could mean the difference between whether he got the information he needed and got out safely, or if he was caught.

There was a wealth of personal information on Louis Ronsard—his parents, where he lived growing up, his school records, his friends, his extracurricular activities. Louis hadn't been a deprived child; his father had been a wealthy industrialist, his mother a well-born beauty who had doted on her children—Louis, the oldest, and Mariette, three years younger.

Louis was attending the Sorbonne when his mother died of ovarian cancer. His father was killed five years later in an accident on the Autobahn while on a business trip to Germany. Louis had taken over the reins of the family business, and, for reasons unknown, gone renegade. From that time to the present there was precious little personal information to be had about him, though he was far from a recluse.

Ronsard owned a heavily guarded estate in the south of France. He employed a small private army to ensure his security; to be hired, one had to meet stringent standards. The Company had planted one of their own, to no avail; the agent hadn't been able to discover anything useful, because his own activities were so regulated. He was still in place, though; John made a note of the agent's name and cover.

There was a recent photo; Ronsard was a striking man, with slightly exotic features and olive skin. He wore his dark hair long, usually secured at the nape, but for social occasions he left it loose. In this photograph he was emerging from some banquet, clad in a tuxedo, with a glowing blonde on his arm. She was smiling up at him with adoration in her eyes. She was Sophie Gerrard, briefly Ronsard's lover, but no longer in contact with him.

There was a long list of Ronsard's lovers. Women found him very attractive. His liaisons never lasted long, but he was evidently considerate and affectionate before his roving eye landed on some other lady.

There was a diagram of the mansions' grounds, but nothing of the house itself. Ronsard entertained occasionally, but the affairs were very exclusive, and the CIA hadn't yet been able to get anyone inside as either a guest or domestic help. True, Ronsard hadn't been at the top of their to-do list, so little effort had been expended on doing so.

That was going to change, however. Ronsard had just moved to the top of the list.

John maneuvered his way through a few more files, checking on Ronsard's known finances, who had designed and installed the mansion's security system, if there were any existing wiring plans. He found little information; Ronsard had either wiped his records, or they had never existed in the first place.

When he finished, it was two A.M. He stretched, suddenly aware of the kinks in his shoulders. He had another meeting with Frank the coming night, and maybe they would have more information on the crash. Until then, he could relax.

He showered and fell into bed. He had the warrior's knack of quickly and easily falling asleep, but tonight he found himself staring at the ceiling where the tiny red light on the smoke alarm blinked on and off. He didn't have to wonder about his sleeplessness; he knew the reason.

Niema.

Dallas had been dead five years. Why hadn't she remarried, or at least dated someone steadily? She was young—only twenty-five when Dallas died—and pretty. He hadn't let himself ask, these past five years, hadn't let himself personally check on her, but this time he had figured enough time had passed and it was safe to ask, to find out she had a hubby and a kid or two, and had gone on with her life.

She hadn't. She was still alone.

Had she changed? Put on weight, maybe gotten a few strands of gray in her hair? A lot of people began to go gray in their twenties. Did her big dark eyes still look so deep a man could drown in them, and not care?

He could see her. She would never know. He could satisfy his curiosity, smile a little at the physical pleasure seeing her gave him, and walk away. But he knew he wouldn't see her; some breaks were better made cleanly. He was still who he was and did what he did, so there was no point in daydreams, no matter how pleasurable.

Knowing that was one thing; turning off those desires was another. He would do what he had to do, but what he wanted to do was hold her, just once, and let her know it was him she was kissing, him making love to her. Just once he wanted to strip her naked and have her, and once would have to be enough because he couldn't dare risk more.

But he had a snowball's chance in hell of having that "once," so finally he turned off the daydream, rolled over, and went to sleep.

*   *   *

John arrived at Frank's house as he had the night before, in a car with blacked-out windows. He backed into the attached garage, the doors of which slid up as he approached and down as soon as his car was inside. He had spent the day digging out more details about Ronsard, trying to plot a course on getting inside Ronsard's mansion and getting the information he needed; nothing had immediately presented itself, but eventually it would.

Frank opened the door, an abstract expression on his face that was evidently due to the sheaf of papers he still clutched in one hand. Frank never quit working, it seemed, not even at home; he simply changed locations. While Dodie was alive he had made a real effort to put his job aside and just be with her, but more often than not he had become lost in his thoughts and she would laughingly shoo him into his office. Now, with Dodie gone, Frank often worked sixteen hours a day.

"I was just getting coffee," he said to John. "Go on into the library and I'll bring it in there."

John stopped in his tracks and quizzically regarded his old friend. Frank wasn't a domestic person; he tried, but he didn't have a coffee-making gene in his body. John had quickly learned, after Dodie's death, that if he wanted coffee in Frank's house he'd better make it himself if he wanted it to be drinkable.

Seeing the look, Frank said irritably, "I didn't make it, Bridget did." Bridget was his housekeeper, an Agency employee who had looked after Frank and Dodie since Frank became DDO. She went home after serving Frank his supper and cleaning up the kitchen, assuming he was eating at home that night; she must have made the coffee and put it in a thermos to keep it hot.

"In that case, yes, I'd like a cup." Grinning, John strolled out of the kitchen, with Frank's muttered "Smart ass," following him.

The door to the library was open. John walked in and stopped just past the threshold, his mind blank for a moment except for a silent, savage curse. Damn Frank and his meddling!

Niema Burdock rose slowly out of the chair where she had been sitting, her face pale in the mellow lamplight. Her eyes were as big and dark as he remembered; darker, narrowing as she stared at him and said one word, tight with disbelief: "Tucker."

John forced himself to move, to step inside the library as casually as if he had known she was going to be there. He closed the door; let Frank make of *that* what he pleased. "Actually," he said, as if five years hadn't passed, "you were right. Tucker *isn't* my name. It's John Medina."

He was never at a loss; he had been trained not to panic, not to lose focus. But this was a shock, the impact of her sudden presence as powerful as if he had been punched in the gut. He hadn't realized, he thought, how hungry he had been for the sight of her, otherwise why blurt out something he had kept from her five years ago?

Almost no one who met him knew his real name. It was safer that way, for both parties. So why had he told her, this woman who had every reason, if not to actually hate him, to at least avoid him? She had heard him tell her husband to, in effect, kill himself. She had been standing there staring at him with her eyes black as night, her face paper white with shock, when he told Dallas to press the button that would end his life as well as complete the mission. That wasn't something a woman forgot, or forgave.

She was almost as pale now. For a moment he hoped she

hadn't heard of him before. It was possible; he was in black ops, his name whispered among people in operations, but she worked on the technical side and would seldom, if ever, come into contact with field operatives.

Her throat worked. "John Medina is . . . just a legend," she said, her voice strained, and he knew she had indeed heard of him.

"Thank you," he replied casually, "though I don't know if I like the word 'just.' I'm real enough. Want to bite me to prove it?" He sat down on the edge of Frank's desk, one foot swinging, his posture totally relaxed despite the tension screaming through him.

"I thought pinching was the proven method."

"I prefer biting."

Color tinged her cheeks, but she didn't look away. "Your eyes were brown," she accused. "Now they're blue."

"Colored contacts. Blue is the real color of my eyes."

"Or you're wearing colored contacts now."

"Come look," he invited. As he had expected, though, she didn't want to get that close to him.

She gathered her composure and sank back into her chair. She crossed her legs, her posture as relaxed as his. Maybe more so; her movement riveted his attention on her legs, on the few inches of thigh she had revealed. He hadn't seen her legs before; she had worn pants, and often those had been modestly covered by the chador. They were very nice legs: slender, shapely, lightly tanned. She still looked to be in very good shape, as if she worked out regularly.

Abruptly aware of the response of his body, John snapped himself back under control. He glanced up and found her watching him, and automatically wondered if she had crossed her legs to distract him. If so, it had worked. He was irritated at himself, because sex was one of the oldest, most hackneyed distractions, and still he had let himself slip.

Frank opened the door, breaking the silence between them. He carried a tray on which there was a large thermos of coffee and three cups, but no sugar or cream. "Have you two introduced yourselves?" he asked smoothly, glancing at John so he could take the lead in giving Niema whatever name he chose.

"He says his name is really John Medina," Niema said. Her voice was cool and calm, and once again John had to admire her poise. "Five years ago I knew him as Darrell Tucker."

Frank flashed John another glance, this one full of surprise that he had so quickly revealed his true identity. "He goes by a lot of names; it's part of his job description."

"Then John Medina may be an alias, too."

"I can't give you any comfort there," Frank said with wry humor. "I've known him most of his life, and he's the real McCoy—or Medina, in this case."

John watched her absorb that, saw the quick suspicion in her eyes that Frank might be lying, as well. She wasn't a naive, trusting little soul, but neither was she experienced at completely hiding her thoughts and emotions.

"Why am I here?" she asked abruptly, switching her gaze to John.

Frank drew her attention back to him. "We have a . . . situation." He poured a cup of coffee and handed it to her.

"How does that involve me? Could I have some cream and sugar, please?"

The simple question rattled Frank, unused as he was to domestic duties. He gave the tray a panicked glance, as if he hoped the requested items would materialize.

"Ah . . . I—"

"Never mind," she said, and composedly sipped her black coffee. "I can drink it like this. What's this situation?"

John restrained a bark of laughter. As he remembered very well, she *always* drank her coffee black. This was just Niema needling Frank a little, getting back at him for setting her up for such a shock. She had always been able to hold her own with the team, and the realization was still as surprising now as it had been then, because she looked like such a lady.

Frank looked at him as if asking for his help. John shrugged. This was Frank's little show, let him run it. He had no idea why Niema was there, except as Frank's heavy-handed attempt at a little matchmaking. He probably thought John needed some R and R, and since he had admitted being attracted to Niema—well, why not? Except Frank hadn't been in Iran, and he hadn't watched Niema's face while he ordered her husband to kill himself, or he would have known why not.

"Ah . . . we're very interested in the work you've been doing. An undetectable surveillance device will be invaluable. As it happens, we have an urgent need for it now. You know more about the device than anyone, since you designed it. You also have some field experience—"

"No," she interrupted. "I don't do fieldwork." She was pale again, her jaw set. She got to her feet. "If that's the only reason you wanted to talk to me, I'm sorry you wasted our mutual time. A phone call would have sufficed, and you could have saved yourself the trouble of bringing me here." She paused, then murmured ironically, "Wherever *here* is."

"You haven't heard all the details," Frank said, shooting another quick look at John. "And you are, might I add, an employee of the Agency, not a freelance contract agent."

"Are you going to fire her if she turns you down?" John

asked interestedly, just to pin Frank down and make him squirm some more.

"No, of course not—"

"Then we have nothing more to discuss," she said firmly. "Please have me taken home."

Frank sighed, and gave up. "Of course. I apologize for the inconvenience, Mrs. Burdock." He wasn't a man accustomed to apology, but he did it well.

John let him reach for the phone before he interrupted. "Don't bother," he said easily, abandoning his lazy sprawl against the desk. "I'll drive her home."

CHAPTER
SIX

Niema got into the car and buckled her seat belt. "Shouldn't I be blindfolded or something?" she asked wryly, and she was only half joking. The garage door in front of them slid up and he pulled out, then turned left onto the street.

Tucker—no, she had to get used to thinking of him as Medina—actually smiled. "Only if you want. Don't tell me they blindfolded you to bring you here."

"No, but I kept my eyes closed." She wasn't kidding. She hadn't wanted to know where the deputy director of operations lived. She had lost her taste for adventure five years ago, and knowing where Frank Vinay lived came under the heading of information that could be dangerous.

Medina's smile turned into a grin. He was really a very

good-looking man, she thought, watching his face in the dim green glow of the dash lights. In the past five years when she remembered him it had been in terms of what happened, not in how he looked, and his face had faded from her memory. Still, she had recognized him immediately, even without the heavy stubble of beard.

Seeing him was a bigger shock than she had ever thought it would be, but then again, she'd never imagined she *would* see him again, so there was no way she could have prepared for it. Tucker—no, *Medina*—was such an integral part of the worst thing that had ever happened to her that just hearing his voice had thrown her five years into the past.

"I should have known you were regular CIA, instead of a contract agent." In retrospect she felt like a gullible idiot, but then things were always clearer in the mind's rearview mirror.

"Why would you?" He sounded interested. "My cover was as a contract agent."

Looking back, she realized that Dallas had known, which was why he had urged Medina to stay behind rather than risk capture. And Dallas, an ex-SEAL accustomed to top security clearances and need-to-know, had kept the information to himself, not even telling her, his wife. But she worked for the Agency now, and she knew that was how things were. You kept things to yourself, you didn't tell friends or neighbors what you did for a living; discretion became second nature.

"Dallas knew, didn't he?" she asked, just for affirmation.

"He knew I wasn't a contract agent. He didn't know my real name, though. When I worked with him before, he knew me as Tucker."

"Why did you tell me? It wasn't necessary." She wished he hadn't. If even half the rumors she had heard whispered about the elusive, shadowy John Medina were true, then she didn't want to know who he really was. Ignorance, in this case, was safer than discretion.

"Perhaps it was."

His voice was reflective, and he didn't explain further.

"Why did you have a cover with us? We were a team. None of us were out to get you."

"If you didn't know my real name, then, if any of you were captured, you couldn't reveal it."

"And if you were captured?"

"I wouldn't be."

"Oh? How would you prevent it?"

"Poison," he said matter-of-factly.

Niema recoiled. She knew that some operatives, back in the tense Cold War days, had carried a suicide pill, usually cyanide, that they were to swallow rather than allow themselves to be captured. To know that John Medina did the same made her feel sick to her stomach.

"But—"

"It's better than being tortured to death." He shrugged. "Over the years, I've pissed off a lot of people. They would all like to have a turn removing my body parts."

From what she had heard about his exploits, he was understating the case. It was even rumored he had killed his own wife, because he discovered she was a double agent and was about to expose a highly placed mole. Niema didn't believe *that* particular rumor, but then neither had she believed John Medina was a real man. Not one of the people who talked about him had ever met him, seen him, or knew anyone who had. She had thought him a kind of . . . urban myth, though one restricted to intelligence circles.

She couldn't quite take in that not only was he real, but she knew him. And even more astounding was how *accepting* he

was of everything entailed in being who he was, as if his noto-
riety was simply the price he had to pay to do what he wanted.

"Given your circumstances," she said with asperity, "you
shouldn't have told me now, either." The fact that he had
made her suspicious.

"Actually, I was so surprised to see you that I blurted it out
without thinking."

The idea of him being taken off guard was so out of character that she snorted, and stretched out her left leg. "Here, pull
this one, too."

"It's true," he murmured. "I didn't know you were going to
be there."

"You had no idea Mr. Vinay wanted me to . . . whatever it
was he wanted me to do? And you just happened to show up?
How likely is that?"

"Not very, but unlikely things happen every day."

"Does he expect you to talk me into taking the job?"

"Maybe. I don't know what he was thinking." Irritation colored his voice now. "I suspect, though, that he's working two
angles. You'll have to ask him what those angles are."

"Since I'm not taking the job, whatever it is, it doesn't matter what the angles are, does it?"

He grinned suddenly. "I don't think he was expecting to be
turned down, especially not so fast. Not many people can tell
him no."

"Then he needed the experience."

He said admiringly, "No wonder Dallas was so crazy about
you. Not many people stood up to him, either. He looked as
tough as he was."

Yes, he had. Dallas had been almost six-four and weighed
two hundred and thirty-five hard-muscled pounds. His biggest
strength hadn't been his body, though, as superbly condi-

tioned as it was; his mind, his determination and focus, were what had made him . . . extraordinary.

She had never been able to talk about Dallas to anyone. For the past five years her memories of him had stayed bottled up inside; they hadn't been married very long, hadn't *known* each other very long, so they hadn't had time to develop a circle of friends. Because of their jobs they had traveled a lot; they had gotten married in a hurry in Reno, had that wonderful honeymoon in Aruba, then Dallas had been gone for six weeks and she had been in Seattle working on surveillance for Customs. With one thing or another, they hadn't even met each other's families.

After Dallas's death she had gone to Indiana and met his folks, held hands, and cried with them, but they had been too shocked, still too involved in the whys and hows to reminisce. She had written to them occasionally, but they hadn't had time to develop a relationship before Dallas's death, and after he was gone neither party seemed to have the spirit to develop one now.

Her own family, her nice, normal suburban family in Council Bluffs, Iowa, had been sympathetic and caring, but neither were they completely able to hide their disapproval of her and Dallas being in Iran in the first place. Her entire family, parents, brothers Mason and Sam, sister Kiara, wanted nothing more than the familiar routine of nine-to-five, marriage, kids, living in the same town from cradle to grave, knowing everyone in the neighborhood, shopping at the same grocery store every week. They hadn't known what to do with the cuckoo in their nest, hadn't had any idea of the restlessness to see *more*, the urge to do *more*, that had driven Niema to leave her hometown and seek out adventure.

She had paid penance for the last five years and lived alone with memories that no one else shared. She might whisper Dallas's name in her thoughts, or sometimes when she was alone the grief would well up and she would say his name aloud, an aching, unanswered cry, but she hadn't been able to talk about him with anyone.

But Medina had known him, had been there. He would understand. He was, of all people, the only one who would fully understand.

She hadn't resisted letting him drive her home; her guilt wasn't his fault. Maybe she needed to talk to him, to put this part of the past behind her. She might have already done it, had she known how to contact him, but after they reached Paris he had vanished.

Lacing her hands in her lap, she stared out the windshield as the dark streets wound by. She wondered if Dallas would love her now, if he would even recognize the woman she had become. He had fallen in love with a gutsy young woman who'd had a taste for adventure. Those days were over, though. She was through taking risks.

"I never thanked you," she murmured. "For what you did."

His eyebrows lifted in surprise, and he slanted a quick look at her. *"Thank* me?"

She got the impression he wasn't just surprised, but astounded. "For getting me out of Iran," she explained and wondered why she needed to. "I know I was a liability coming out." *Basket case* was actually a better description. Long patches of those days were lost from her memory; she couldn't remember leaving the hut at all. She did remember walking through the cold, dark mountains, her emotional misery so intense that she hadn't felt any physical pain.

"I promised Dallas."

The words were simple, and ironclad.

It hurt to hear Dallas's name spoken aloud. In five years, not a day had gone by that she hadn't thought about her husband. The terrible pain was gone, replaced sometimes by an ache, a loneliness, but mostly she remembered the good times she'd had with him. She regretted that they hadn't had more time together, that they hadn't had the chance to learn all the little things about each other. Hearing his name brought back the ache, but it was softened now, gentled into something bearable, and she could hear the regret in Medina's voice. What time hadn't softened was her own guilt, the knowledge that Dallas wouldn't have been on that job if she hadn't wanted to take it.

And perhaps she wasn't the only one who felt guilty. Medina, under whatever guise, struck her as a man who would do what was expedient and then forget about it, but he hadn't. He had taken care of her, just as he had promised Dallas, when leaving her to freeze to death in the mountains would have been much easier. She couldn't imagine what had motivated him, but she was deeply grateful all the same. "Do you think I blamed *you?*" she asked softly. "No. I never did."

Again she had surprised him. Looking at him, she saw the way his jaw tightened. "Maybe you should have," he replied.

"Why? What could you have done?" She had relived that night a thousand times on the hard journey to accepting reality. "We never could have gotten him out of the plant alive, much less out of Iran. You knew it. He knew it too. He chose to complete the mission and chose a quick death over a slow, terrible one." She managed a crooked smile. "Like you with your cyanide pill."

"I'm the one who told him to push the button."

"He would have done it no matter what you said. He was my husband, and I knew when I married him that he was a damn hero." She had known the type of man Dallas was, known that he would feel he had to complete the job at all costs, and that cost had included his life.

Medina fell silent, concentrating on his driving. She gave him directions on the next turn; she lived in McLean, on the same side of the river as Langley, so the commute was easy.

Once before she had sat beside him as he drove through the night, and he had been silent then, too. It was after Hadi had "liberated" a 1968 Ford Fairlane from the Iranian village, and they had driven into Tehran together. Then Hadi had split off, and she and Medina had gone on alone. She had been feverish and aching, battered by grief and guilt, barely functional.

Medina had taken care of her. When the nail wound in her arm became infected, from somewhere he procured a vial of antibiotic and gave her an injection. He made certain she ate and slept, and he got her across the border into Turkey. He had been there during the first awful paroxysm of grief and hadn't tried to comfort her, knowing that weeping was better than holding it in.

All in all, she owed this man her life.

Blaming Medina would have been easy, much easier than blaming herself. But the inner steel that had attracted Dallas to her in the first place made it impossible, after his death, for her to do anything but face the truth: When Medina approached her and Dallas about the job, Dallas wanted to decline. She was the one who wanted to take it. She could tell herself that the job had been important, and it had been, but there had been others Medina could have recruited if she and Dallas had turned him down.

Yes, Dallas had been very good at explosives. She was very good with electronics, whether it was putting together a functional radio or detonator or bugging a phone line. But other people were also good at those things, and they would have done the job just as well. She had wanted to go, not because she was indispensable, but because she craved the adventure.

As a child she had always been the one to climb highest in the tree, to tie bed sheets together and use them to slide down from a second-story window. She loved roller coasters and white-water rafting and had even toyed with the idea, during high school, of working on a bomb squad. To her parents' relief she had instead begun studying electronics and languages, only to find that her expertise took her farther away from home and into more danger than she ever would have gone with the local bomb squad.

Niema knew her own nature. She loved the thrill, the adrenaline rush, of danger. She had been seeking that thrill, though in pursuit of a legitimate goal, and she had gotten Dallas killed. If not for her, they would have been looking for a home on the North Carolina coast, as Dallas had wanted.

If not for her, Dallas would still be alive.

So she had given it up, that high-voltage life she had so loved. The cost was too high. Dallas's last thought had been for her, and that knowledge meant too much for her to carelessly put her life in jeopardy again.

Medina pulled up to the curb just past her driveway, then reversed into it so the car was heading out. House key in hand, she got out of the car. Dallas had also parked so the car was heading out, too, a simple precaution that allowed for faster movement and made it more difficult to be blocked in.

Funny how she hadn't thought about that in years; she simply pulled into the garage, as millions of other people did. But Medina's method of parking brought so many things back to her in a rush: the sudden alertness, the clarity of her senses, the quickened pulse. She found herself looking around, examining shadows and searching with her peripheral vision for movement.

Medina had done the same thing, his surveillance much faster and routine.

"Damn it," Niema said irritably and marched up the sidewalk to the curved archway that sheltered her front door.

" 'Damn it,' what?" He was beside her, moving silently, positioning himself so that he reached the archway first. No assailants lurked there, not that she had expected any. She just wished she hadn't noticed what he was doing.

"Damn it, I spend half an hour with you and already I'm looking for assassins in the bushes."

"There's nothing wrong with being alert and aware of your surroundings."

"Not if I were Secret Service, or even a cop, but I'm not. I just fiddle with gadgets. The only thing likely to be lurking in my bushes is a cat."

He started to reach for her house key, but she stopped him with a look. "You're making me paranoid. Is there any reason for all this?" she asked as she unlocked the door herself and opened it. Nothing sinister happened; there were no shots, no explosions.

"Sorry. It's just a habit." She had left a couple of lights on and he looked inside, his expression interested.

"Would you like to come in? We didn't get around to drinking any of the coffee at Vinay's house." Until she heard the words, she hadn't known she was going to invite him in. They weren't exactly on easy terms, though to tell the truth she was surprised at how easy it had been to talk to him. Still, he was John Medina, not a steady, reliable, respectable bureaucrat who had just taken her out to dinner.

He stepped inside, his head up and alert, his gaze moving

around, absorbing details, watching as she opened the hall closet door and disarmed the security system. She had the sudden impression that he could describe everything he had seen in that brief sweep, and perhaps even tell her the security code.

She started to close the closet door and he said, "Humor me. Reset the alarm."

Because he had good reason to be acutely security conscious, she did.

Niema had bought the house three years before, when a hefty raise had given her the means to buy instead of rent, even with the outrageous property values around D.C. It was too big for one person, with three bedrooms and two-and-a-half baths, but she had justified the size by telling herself she would have space for her family to come visit, though they never had, and that the three bedrooms would make it easier to sell if she ever decided she wanted something else.

The house was vaguely Spanish in style, with arched doors and windows. She had painted the interior walls herself, choosing a soft peach for most of the house while her furnishings were dark green and turquoise. The carpet was an undistinguished beige, but it had been in good shape, so instead of replacing it she had covered it with a large rug in a geometric pattern of greens, blues, and peaches. The effect was cool and welcoming, feminine without being fussy.

"Nice," he said, and she wondered what conclusions he had drawn about her by seeing the way she had furnished her house.

"The kitchen is this way." She led the way, turning on the overhead light. She loved her kitchen. The room was long, with a bank of windows on the right wall. A long, narrow island topped with a mosaic of blue and terra-cotta tiles provided a wonderful work area for any cooking project, no matter how ambitious. Small pots of herbs grew on the window sills, lending their fragrance to the air. The far end of the room was a cozy breakfast nook, the small table and two chairs flanked by lush ferns.

She began making coffee, while Medina went to the windows and closed all the blinds. "Doesn't it get old?" she asked. "Having to always be on guard?"

"I don't even think about it now, I've done it for so long. And you should close the blinds anyway." Hands in his pockets, he strolled around the kitchen. Pausing in front of the block of oak that held her knife set, he pulled out the chef's knife and tested its edge on his thumb, then returned it to its slot. His next stop was the back door, the top half of which was glass; he closed the blinds there too and checked the lock.

"I usually do. I don't believe in inviting trouble." As soon as the words were out, she realized her own lie. Trouble didn't come any bigger than John Medina, and inviting him in was exactly what she had done.

"You need a stronger lock here," he said absently. "In fact, you need a new door. All anyone has to do is pop out one of these panes of glass, reach in, and unlock the door."

"I'll see to it first thing in the morning."

The dryness of her tone must have reached him, because he looked over at her and grinned. "Sorry. You already know all that, right?"

"Right." She took down two cups from the cabinets. "The crime rate in this neighborhood is low, and I *do* have the security system. I figure if anyone wanted in, they could break any number of windows and get in through them, not just the ones in the door."

He pulled one of the tall stools away from the island and

propped one hip on it. He looked relaxed, she thought, though she wondered if he ever truly was, given who he was and what he did. She poured the coffee and set one cup in front of him, then faced him across the tiled island top. "Okay, now tell me why you drove me home, and don't say it was for old time's sake."

"Then I won't." He seemed to be lost in thought for a moment as he sipped his coffee, but whatever distracted him was quickly gone. "How undetectable is this new bug you've developed? Tell me about it."

She made a face. "Nothing is totally undetectable, you know. But it doesn't cause a fluctuation in voltage, so an oscilloscope can't pick it up. If anyone swept with a metal detector, though, that's a different story."

"Frank seemed excited about it."

Niema was immediately wary. "It isn't that big a deal, because like I said, it's good only in certain situations. If you know how someone routinely sweeps for surveillance devices, then you can tailor the bug to fit. Why would he even mention it to you?" The bug had useful applications, but it was far from being an earth-shattering discovery that was going to change the face of intelligence gathering. Why would the deputy director of operations even know about it, much less call her to a meeting at his private residence?

"I asked how you were doing. He told me what you've been working on."

Her wariness turned into outright suspicion. Okay, it was feasible that Medina would ask about her, but that didn't explain why Vinay would know anything at all about her, much less anything about her current project.

"Why would the DDO know anything about me? We work in totally different departments." The vast majority of CIA employees were not the glamorous operatives of Hollywood fame; they were clerks and analysts and techno nerds. Until Iran, Niema had craved the thrill of fieldwork, but not now. Now she was content to work on the electronics side of intelligence gathering and come home to her own house every night.

"Because I asked him to keep tabs on you."

The bald admission astonished her. "Why would you do that?" She didn't like the idea of someone constantly checking up on her.

"I wanted to know if you were all right, plus I never lose track of someone whose expertise I might want to use again."

A chill ran up her spine. Now she knew why he'd driven her home; he wanted to draw her back into that world she had walked away from when Dallas died. He was going to figuratively wave a shot of whiskey under an alcoholic's nose, lure her away from the straight and narrow. He couldn't do it unless she still had the old urge to find that adrenaline rush, she thought in growing panic. If she had truly changed, nothing he could say would entice her away from the safe life she had built.

She thought she had changed. She thought the hunger for excitement was gone. Why, then, did she feel so panicky, as if the smell of adventure was going to make her fall off the wagon?

"Don't you dare ask—" she began.

"I need you, Niema."

CHAPTER SEVEN

Damn it, why hadn't she remarried? John thought savagely. Or at least gotten herself safely involved with some steady, nine-to-five bureaucrat?

He had stayed away from her for a lot of very good reasons. His job wasn't conducive to relationships. He had brief affairs, and nothing resembling an emotional attachment. He was away for months at a time, with no communication during those times. His life expectancy sucked.

Moreover, he had thought he would be the last person on earth she'd ever want to see. He was staggered to realize she didn't blame him for Dallas's death, had never blamed him. Even though she had never trusted him, she didn't

lay that at his door. It took a person of excruciating fairness
to absolve him of all blame as she had done.

He had learned not to agonize over the choices he had to
make. Some of them were hard decisions, and every one of
them had left their mark on his soul, or what was left of it. But
other people seldom saw things the same way, and that, too,
he'd learned to shrug off. As his father's old friend Jess
McPherson once said, he was hell on people. He used them,
exploited them, and then either betrayed them or simply disappeared from their lives. The very nature of his job demanded that he not let anyone get close enough to touch him
emotionally. He had forgotten that once and let a woman get
close to him; hell, he had even married her. Venetia had been a
disaster, both professionally and personally, and in the four-
teen years since he had been strictly solo.

Several times during the past five years he had been relieved
that Niema Burdock probably hated his guts. That put her
safely out of his range and killed the occasional temptation to
get in touch with her. It was better that way. He would just
check on her now and then, make certain she was all right—
after all, he'd promised Dallas he would take care of her—and
that would be that.

He had expected her to find someone else. She was young,
only twenty-five when she was widowed, and both smart and
pretty. He had *wanted* her to find someone else, because that
would put her forever out of reach. But she hadn't, and he was
through with being noble.

He wasn't giving her any more chances.

But she would run like hell if he simply asked her out. He
would have to play her gently, like taking a world-record trout
on gossamer line, never letting her feel the hook that was reel-
ing her in until it was too late for escape. On his side was her

own nature, the adventurousness she seemed determined to bury, and a very real situation that needed to be finessed. Weighed against him was the fact that, despite the uneasy bond forged between them in Iran, she didn't trust him; he'd always known she was smart.

Frank had asked her to his house on a bogus excuse, in a well-meant but awkward attempt to do a little matchmaking. Well, maybe it had worked. And maybe the excuse wasn't so bogus after all. John's mind raced, weighing risks and benefits. He decided to go for it.

"Delta Flight 183 was sabotaged. The FBI labs have turned up traces of explosive, but no detonator. The stuff seems to be a new, self-detonating compound, probably based on RDX and developed in Europe."

She put her hands over her ears. "I don't want to hear this."

John moved around the island and took her hands down, holding her with his fingers wrapped around her slender wrists. "Anything in Europe goes through an arms dealer named Louis Ronsard. He lives in the south of France."

"No," she said.

"I need you to help me get into his files and find out where the stuff is made and who has already gotten a shipment of it."

"No," she said again, but with a touch of desperation in her voice. She didn't try to pull away from him.

"Ronsard is susceptible to a pretty face—"

"Good God, you want me to *whore* for you?" she asked incredulously, dark eyes narrowing in dangerous warning.

"Of course not," he snapped. No way in hell would he let Ronsard, or anyone else, have her. "I want you to get an invitation to his villa so you can put a bug in his office."

"There are probably a thousand people in this city alone who could do that. You don't need me."

"I need *you*. Of those thousand people who could do the work, how many of them are women, because I can guarantee you no guy is going to catch Ronsard's interest and get invited to his villa. How many? Twenty, maybe? Say a hundred. Ronsard is thirty-five; how many women out of that hundred are roughly his age? And out of that number, how many of them are as attractive as you?"

She jerked on her wrists. John merely tightened his hold, while taking care not to hurt her. She was so close he could see the velvety texture of her skin. "You speak French—"

"I'm rusty."

"You'd pick it up again in no time. I need someone who's young, pretty, speaks the language, and has the skill. You meet all the qualifications."

"Get someone else!" she said furiously. "Don't try to tell me you couldn't find a contract agent who met all your criteria, someone who wouldn't know your real name. You make it sound like I'm some Mata Hari, but I've never done any undercover work at all. I'd probably get us both killed—"

"No you wouldn't. You've been on other ops—"

"Five years ago. And I just did technical stuff, not any role-playing." She added coldly, "That's your forte."

He let the slam roll off his back. After all, she was right. "I need you," he repeated. "Just this once."

"This once until something else comes up and you decide you 'need' me again."

"Niema . . ." He rubbed his thumbs over the insides of her wrists in a subtle caress, then released her and stepped away to pick up his coffee cup. He had pushed her enough physically; now was the time to back off and give her back control of herself, so she wouldn't feel as threatened. "I've seen you work.

You're fast, you're good, and you can build a transmitter from pieces of junk. You're perfect for the job."

"I went to pieces on the last job."

"You had just heard your husband die." He didn't mince words and saw her flinch. "You're allowed to be a little shell-shocked. And you kept up anyway; we didn't have to carry you."

She turned away, absently rubbing her wrists.

"Please."

Of all the words he could have used, that was the least expected. He saw her spine stiffen. "Don't try to sweet-talk me."

"I wouldn't dream of it," he murmured.

"You're so damn sneaky. I knew it the first time I saw you. You maneuver and manipulate and—" She stopped, and turned back to face him. Her throat worked, and her big dark eyes looked haunted. "Damn you," she whispered.

He was silent, letting the lure entice her. Danger was as addictive as any drug. Firemen, cops, special forces personnel, field operatives, even the emergency department staff in hospitals—they all knew the rush, the incredible thrill when your senses are heightened and your skin feels as if it won't be able to contain all the energy pulsing through your muscles. SWAT teams, DEA agents—they were adrenaline junkies. So was he. And so was Niema.

He did what he did partly because he loved his country, and someone had to be in the sewers taking care of the shit, but also because he loved walking on the knife edge of danger, continually poised on the brink of disaster, with only his skill and his wits to keep him alive. Niema was no different. She wanted to be, but she wasn't.

"Do you know how prevalent terrorism is?" he asked conversationally. "It isn't something that happens in other countries; it happens here, all the time. Flight 183 is just the latest episode. In 1970, Orlando, Florida, was threatened with a nuclear device if it didn't cough up a million bucks. In 1977, Hanafi Muslims took hostages in the D.C. City Council offices, and a couple of other places. In 1985, the FBI caught three Sikh Indians sent over here with a list of assassination targets. There was the World Trade Center bombing. Lockerbie, Scotland. Hell, I could give you a list three feet long."

She bent her head, but he had her undivided attention.

"We catch most explosives because of the detonator, not the explosive itself. If the bastards have come up with an explosive that begins as a stable compound, then degrades and becomes unstable and detonates, we have a big problem. One bridge taken out can foul shipping over the entire eastern seaboard. A blown dam threatens our entire power grid. Airplanes are particularly vulnerable. So I need to find out where the stuff is being manufactured, and Ronsard is my best bet. I'll find out some other way, eventually, but how many people will die in the meantime?"

She still didn't respond. He said briskly, as if she had already agreed to work with him, "I'll be there under a different cover, using an identity I've been building for quite a while. I would take you in with me as an assistant or a girlfriend, but Ronsard doesn't issue 'invitee and guest' invitations. You have to get invited in separately."

"No. I won't do it."

"Once we're in, I'll have Ronsard introduce us. I'll pretend to be smitten. That'll give us an excuse to be together."

She shook her head. "I'm not going to do it."

"You have to. I've already told you too much."

"And now you have to kill me, right?"

He put his hands in his pockets, his blue eyes alive with amusement. "I wasn't thinking of anything quite that James Bondish."

"That's what this whole thing sounds like, something out of a James Bond movie. You need someone trained in cloak-and-dagger stuff, not me."

"You'll have time to brush up on basic handgun skills. That's all you'd need, though if everything goes right, you won't even need that. We get in, you place the bug, I get into his files and copy them, and we get out. That's it."

"You make it sound as easy as brushing your teeth. If it were that easy, you would already have done it. He—what was his name? Ronsard?—Ronsard must have a pretty good security system."

"Plus a private army guarding the place," John admitted.

"So the job would be a lot trickier than you're trying to make it sound."

"Not if it goes right."

"And if it goes wrong?"

He shrugged, smiling. "Fireworks."

She wavered. He saw it, saw the temptation in her eyes. Then she shook her head. "Get someone else."

"There is no one else with quite your qualifications. The fact that you haven't been active in five years is a plus, because no one is likely to know you. The intelligence community is a fairly small one. I can build you an identity that will stand up under any investigation Ronsard does."

"What about you? You haven't exactly been inactive."

"No, but I go to a lot of trouble to make sure no one knows what I look like, or who I am. Trust me. My cover is so deep sometimes I don't know who I am myself."

She gave a little laugh, shaking her head, and John knew he had her.

"Okay," she said. "I know I'm going to regret it, but . . . okay."

"John," Frank Vinay said carefully, "do you know what you're doing?"

"Probably not. But I'm doing it anyway."

"Ronsard isn't anyone's fool."

John was relaxed in one of the big leather chairs in Frank's library. He steepled his fingers under his chin while he studied the chessboard. They had resumed the game that had been interrupted two days before, when an agent brought over the preliminary report on the crash of Flight 183. "You're the one who brought her into it," he pointed out.

Frank flushed. "I was being an interfering fool," he grumbled.

"And a sneaky one, or are you going to tell me you didn't have it in mind that I'd be a lot more willing to step into your shoes if I had an incentive to retire from field ops?" He moved a knight. "Check."

"Son of a bitch." Frank glared at the board for a minute, then looked up at John. "You have to retire some time, and I can't think of a better place for you to use your expertise than in my office."

" 'Some time' isn't now. Until I'm compromised, I can do more good in the field."

"Taking Niema Burdock into the field might make that sooner rather than later. For one thing, she knows who you are. For another"— Frank gave him a shrewd look—"could you leave her behind if necessary?"

John's eyes went flat and cold. "I can do whatever I have to do." How could Frank ask him that, after Venetia? "And Niema is probably the best choice I have available. I wouldn't use her if she wasn't. I need someone else in there with me, and she's the one most likely to get an invitation from Ronsard."

"What if he doesn't fall for it? What if he doesn't invite her?"

"Then I'll have to do what I can, but the risks go up. With her, I have a good chance of getting in and out without being detected."

"All right. I'll arrange for her to have an unspecified leave." Frank nudged a bishop into place.

"That's what I thought you'd do," John said, and moved a pawn. "Check and mate."

"Son of a bitch," Frank muttered.

"I'm crazy," Niema muttered to herself as she rolled out of bed before dawn. Yawning, she dressed: sweat pants and a T-shirt, then socks and athletic shoes. "Certified loony."

How had she let herself be convinced to help Medina on this job, when she had sworn she'd never let herself be sucked back into that life? Hadn't losing Dallas taught her anything?

But Medina was right about terrorism, right about the applications of such an explosive, right about the innocent people who would die. He was *right*, damn it. So, if she could help, then she had to do it.

She went into the bathroom and washed her face, then brushed her teeth and hair. The face that looked back at her from the mirror was still puffy from sleep, but there was color in her cheeks and a brightness to her eyes that made her hate herself. She was looking forward to this, for God's sake. Dallas had died, and she still hadn't learned anything.

"Niema! Get a move on."

She went rigid. Not quite believing what she'd heard, she opened the bathroom door and looked out into her bedroom. No one was there. She crossed over to the hall door and opened it. Light, along with the smell of freshly brewed coffee, spilled down the hall, coming from the direction of the kitchen.

"What in the *hell* are you doing in my house?" she snarled, stomping toward the kitchen. "And how did you get in?"

Medina sat at the island, a cup of coffee in his hand. He looked as if it were nine A.M. instead of four-thirty, his eyes alert, his lean body relaxed in black sweat pants and black T-shirt. "I told you that you needed a new lock on the back door."

"What about the alarm? I *know* I set the alarm."

"And I bypassed it. With a pocketknife and six inches of wire. Have some coffee."

"No thanks." Furious, she contemplated dumping the coffee on him. She had always felt safe in her house, and now, thanks to him, she didn't. "Do you know how much I paid for that alarm system?"

"Too much. Get a dog instead." He stood up from the stool. "If you aren't going to have coffee, let's take a little run."

Thirty minutes later, she was still matching him stride for stride. Talking while jogging wasn't easy, but they hadn't even tried. They had run down the street to the park half a mile from her house, then along the silent path lit only by the occasional street light. The mood she was in, she almost hoped someone tried to mug them, not that muggings were a common occurrence in this neighborhood.

Gravel and dirt crunched under their pounding feet. The early morning air was cool and fragrant. She was still breathing easily and there was still plenty of spring in her legs. She loved the feel of her muscles bunching and relaxing, and gradually she began to cool down and concentrate on nothing but the running.

Beside her, he ran as if they had just started. His stride was effortless, his breathing slow and even. Dallas had run that way, she remembered, as if he could go on at this pace for hours.

"You run like a SEAL," she said, irritated that she was panting a little.

"I should," he said easily. "If I don't, then I wasted the toughest six months of my life."

She was so surprised she almost stopped. "You went through BUD/S?"

"I *lived* through BUD/S," he corrected.

"Is that where you met Dallas?"

"No, I was a few classes ahead of him. But he . . . ah, recognized some of the stuff I did the first time we worked together."

"Did you use your real name during training?"

"No. The Navy didn't do me any favors, either. They agreed to let me take the training only if I made the physical conditioning cut, and then I was in only as long as I could make the grade."

"What was the criteria for being accepted into the class?"

"A five hundred yard swim using a breast or side stroke, in twelve and a half minutes or less, then a ten minute rest, then forty-two pushups in two minutes. There was a two minute rest after the pushups, then fifty sit-ups in two minutes. Another two minute rest, then eight pull-ups, with no time limit. After a ten minute rest, then came a mile and a half run, wearing boots and fatigues, in eleven and a half minutes.

Those were the *minimum* requirements. If a guy wasn't in a lot better shape than that, he didn't stand much chance making it through the real thing."

He had said all of that without gasping for breath. Impressed despite herself, she asked, "Why did you do it?"

He was silent for about fifty yards. Then he said, "The better I was trained, the better my chances were for staying alive. There was a particular job where I needed every edge I could get."

"How old were you?" He couldn't have been very old, not if he was a few classes ahead of Dallas, which meant he had begun black ops work at an early age.

"Twenty-one."

Twenty-one. Not long out of his teen years, and already so dedicated to his job that he had put himself through BUD/S, a training program so tough only about 5 percent of the men who began it made it all the way through. Now she knew why he and Dallas had been so much alike in so many ways.

"How much longer are we going to run?"

"We can stop whenever you want. You're in great shape; I don't have to worry about that."

She began slowing. "Are we likely to have to run for our lives?"

He dropped into step beside her. "You never know."

That was when she knew she was crazy for real, because she wasn't scared.

CHAPTER
EIGHT

How did you know I run every morning?" she asked as they returned to the house. The run had mellowed her considerably; early morning was her favorite time of the day. The sky was beginning to turn shades of pearl and pink, and the birds were awake and singing. She felt tired but also energized, the way she always did after a run.

"I told you, Frank kept tabs on you over the years."

"Bullshit."

He burst out laughing. She gave him an irritated look as she fished the house key out of her pocket and unlocked the door. "What's so funny?"

"Hearing you curse. You look like such a madonna—"

"What!" She stared at him in amazement.

"Angel, then. It's that sweet face of yours." Grinning, he stroked one finger down her cheek, then deftly maneuvered past and stepped into the house ahead of her. She hadn't seen him reach for it, but a pistol was in his hand. "You look as if you wouldn't understand most swear words if you heard them." He was moving, examining the house, as he spoke.

She rolled her eyes and followed him inside. "I'll try to stick to 'gosh' and 'darn,' then, so I won't shock you. And don't think you can change the subject. Mr. Vinay hasn't just 'kept tabs' on me, has he? I've been under pretty close surveillance. Tell me why."

"The surveillance isn't constant. It was at first, to establish your routine. Now it's just often enough to make certain you're okay and to see if anything's changed."

"Tell me why you've wasted Agency time and manpower like that." She had to raise her voice because he was down the hall checking the bedrooms.

"I haven't. Frank used a private agency."

Before, she had been irritated and disbelieving; now she was downright astounded. She slammed the door with a thud. "You paid for a private agency to watch me? For God's sake, Tucker, if you wanted to know, why didn't you just pick up the phone and call?"

He was coming back up the dark hall toward her. Because he was wearing black, he was difficult to see; only his face and bare arms and hands made him visible. Part of it was the way he moved, she thought absently. He was fluid, noiseless; you had to rely only on your eyes to detect him, because he was utterly silent.

"John," he said.

"What?"

"You called me Tucker. My name is John."

He stood directly in front of her, so close she could feel the animal heat generated by their run, smell the hot odors of sweat and man. She took a step back and tilted her head so she could look at his face. "I haven't quite adjusted yet. You were Tucker to me for five years, whether or not I ever saw you. You've been Medina for less than twelve hours."

"Not Medina. John. Call me by my first name."

He seemed strangely intent on this name business, standing motionless, his gaze fastened on her face. "All right, 'John' it is. I'll probably slip, though, especially when I get pissed at you—which so far is averaging at least once an hour."

He grinned, and she wondered if it was because he so easily irritated her or because she had said 'pissed.' What did the man think she was, a nun? He was going to make her uncomfortable if he kept laughing every time she said something the least bit blue.

She poked him in the chest with one finger. It was like poking a steel plate, with no give beneath the skin. "Since you'll be using another name when we get to France, shouldn't I be getting used to calling you that? What if I slip up then?"

"I'll be careful not to piss you off."

"You aren't going to tell me?" she asked incredulously.

"Not yet."

She pushed past him. "I'm going to take a shower. Lock the door behind you when you leave."

She fumed as she showered. There was no reason for him not to give her his cover name. He just loved being contrary and secretive, though it was such a habit for him now he probably didn't realize—no, of course he realized. He did everything deliberately; she had noticed that about him in Iran.

It followed, then, that he had intentionally revealed his own name, rather than being so surprised to see her that he blurted it out. John Medina didn't blurt out anything. He couldn't have lived this long if he did. The question was—why? He could have posed as Tucker, and she would never have known any differently. Mentally shrugging, she put the question aside. Who knew why Medina did anything?

She took her time in the bathroom, indulging in her morning ritual of moisturizing her skin, then smoothing on a body oil with a subtle scent that lingered all day. She didn't have to be at work until nine, so she didn't have to hurry. That was one reason she got up so early; she didn't like rushing around and arriving at work already frazzled. Of course, she usually got more sleep than she had last night, but Medina hadn't left until well past her normal bedtime.

Going into her bedroom, she took out a matching navy blue set of underwear, but only put on the panties. She wore a bra while she was jogging and at work, but didn't bother while she was at home. She put on her terry-cloth robe and snugly belted it, pulled her wet hair out from under the shawl collar, and walked barefoot down the hall to the kitchen to see if the coffee Medina had made was still drinkable.

He was sitting at the island bar, drinking coffee, much as he had been before. She checked only briefly, then went to the coffee pot and poured herself a cup. "I thought you were leaving."

"Why?"

She turned to face him, leaning against the cabinet and cradling the cup in her hand. His hair was wet, she noticed.

"I used your other bathroom for a shower," he said. "Hope you don't mind. I had to put these clothes back on, though."

"No, I don't mind. But I still thought you were leaving. I have to go to work."

"No, you don't. You're on indefinite leave."

She sipped her coffee, hiding her shock—and, yes, her irritation. "That's news to me."

"Frank took care of it last night. Until this job is finished, you're mine."

She didn't know if she liked the sound of that. A funny little pang tightened her stomach. She took refuge in her coffee again, hiding her expression.

He looked so pantherish and male, dressed all in black, lounging at his ease in her cheerful kitchen. The T-shirt he wore clung to him, revealing the breadth of his shoulders and the flatness of his stomach. He was tall and lean, but more muscular than he looked when wearing street clothes. He had meant his words one way, but his physical presence was so strong she couldn't stop herself from a brief sexual speculation. Did his stamina extend to lovemaking? If so . . . wow.

Immediately she pulled her thoughts away from that direction; nothing but trouble there. "So what am I supposed to do with my time until we're ready to leave? When *do* we leave, anyway?" she asked briskly.

"About a week. It takes time to set up a cover as foolproof as yours will be. In the meantime, we train. How are you with a handgun and self-defense?"

"Rusty."

"Have you had any formal self-defense training?"

"No. Just a rape-prevention course, the usual self-defense stuff." And the rudimentary training Dallas had begun with her, but that was five years ago, and she hadn't kept it up.

"Okay. We won't have time for anything in-depth, but in a week's time I can have you at a level where you can hold your own with most men. You're in good shape already, so that helps."

Great. It looked as if she was going to be in his company

nonstop for a week. She sighed and took a skillet out of the cabinet. "I'm not doing anything else until I eat. What do you want for breakfast?"

"Take your pick," Medina said, indicating the small arsenal he had laid out on a bench. They were in a private firing range, used by CIA personnel. The huge, barnlike building was empty except for the two of them.

It wasn't anything fancy, having been built more for use than looks. The far wall of the range was stacked with sand bags and bales of hay, so no rounds of ammunition went through the walls to do damage to anything or anyone out-side. The walls themselves were lined with what looked like pegboard, to contain the noise. Big industrial lights hung over-head, but they were individually controlled so that the lighting conditions could be adjusted

He indicated the first weapon. "This is a Colt .45. It's a heavy-duty cannon, with a lot of stopping power. The next one is a Smith & Wesson .357 revolver. Again, it's pretty heavy. But they're both as reliable as the sun, so you might want to prac-tice with them. I wouldn't recommend them for regular use, though, because of the weight. You need something lighter."

He indicated the other weapons. "The next one is a SIG Sauer P226, 9mm. It's my personal favorite. The other auto-matic is an H&K P9S. It's half a pound lighter than the Colt, and H&K makes a fine weapon. You can't go wrong with either one."

Niema studied the handguns, then picked each one up in turn. The two revolvers were so heavy she could barely aim them. The H&K was more manageable, but for sheer ease of handling the SIG suited her much better.

"Looks like the SIG is going to be my favorite, too." She

wasn't an expert with firearms, but neither was she a rank beginner. Dallas had been constitutionally unable to bear a wife who didn't know how to fire a weapon, so he had taught her the basics and insisted she practice. But that was five years ago, and she hadn't been on a firing range since.

"The SIG doesn't have a thumb safety," he said. "That lever on the left side of the frame is the decocking lever. Never, ever lower the hammer except with the decocking lever. Some SIGs are double-action and won't have the lever, but you need to get used to using it."

"It's awkward," she said after a minute spent familiarizing herself with the lever. "I can't work it without shifting my grip."

"Try using your left thumb. I learned to shoot it left-handed because I ran into the same problem."

She slid a glance at him. "Accurately?"

"Of course," he said coolly. "Or I wouldn't do it."

"Pardon me for insulting your manhood."

"My manhood isn't connected to my weapon, honey."

She bit the inside of her lip to hold back any rejoinders. That particular subject could rapidly get into dangerous waters.

A surprising amount of expertise returned as soon as she handled the weapon. She put a clip in the SIG, and Medina set the first man-shaped target at ten yards.

"Is that all?" she asked, wondering whether or not she should be insulted.

"Most situations where you would use a handgun are fairly close quarters, and things happen fast, in five seconds or less. Work on your accuracy before you start worrying about distance. Anything much over thirty yards and you'd be better off with a rifle or shotgun, anyway."

"How do we get our weapons on board the plane?"

"We don't. I could, but it would attract too much attention. I'll get them once we're in France. By the way, we won't be traveling together."

She nodded, put on her headset, and raised the pistol. Dallas had taught her the point-and-shoot method; studies had found that people were very accurate in pointing at something, but when they tried to aim a weapon the mechanics of doing so somehow interfered with that natural ability. The idea was not to aim, but simply to point.

Medina's arms came around her from behind, his hands closing over hers and making minute adjustments in her grip. "Gently squeeze the trigger," he murmured, his voice coming through the headset.

She took a deep breath and slowly let it out, the way Dallas had taught her. When she had exhaled about half, she stopped and squeezed the trigger. The weapon jumped in her hands as if it was alive, the barrel recoiling upward from the released energy. With the headset protecting her ears, the shot was a flattened crack, like a board popping. Smoke and cordite burned her nostrils. Without a word she steadied the weapon, took a breath, and shot again.

This time Medina braced her wrists with his own hands, but this time she was more prepared for the recoil. She didn't fight it, but let her forearms absorb the shock.

"Good," Medina said, and let his arms drop from around her.

Taking her time, not rushing her shots, she emptied the clip at the target. When the clip was empty, per Medina's previous instructions, she removed the empty clip and slapped a new one in. While she was doing that he called up a new target and set this one at twenty yards. She shot all the bullets in that clip, too.

Afterward he pulled the targets up for examination.

On the first target, out of a fifteen-shot clip, she had scored two rounds in the head, one in the neck, and five in the chest. "Only eight," she said in disgust. "Barely over fifty percent."

"This isn't a marksmanship competition, so don't try to be Annie Oakley. And look at it this way: With the other seven bullets, you probably scared the hell out of whoever was standing beside the target."

She had to laugh, even if it was ruefully. "Thanks a lot."

"You're welcome. Take a look at the second target."

The second target made her feel better. With both targets she had tried to divide her shots equally between the head and chest. It hadn't worked very well with the first target, and in one way she didn't approve much: only three shots went into the head. But eight shots were clustered in the chest area, meaning she had made all of those shots.

She told John what she'd been trying to do. "Forget the head," he advised. "In a tense situation, the chest is a much bigger target. You don't have to kill someone, just stop him. Now let's switch to another weapon."

"Why?"

"Because you never know what will be available. You need to be able to use whatever is at hand."

He made it sound like she was going to make a career of this, she thought grumpily. But she moved to the H&K as instructed and went through the same exercise. She ran into trouble with both the Colt and Smith & Wesson, though. The pistols were so heavy it took all her strength, using both hands, to hold her wrists steady. The first shot with the .357 jarred her teeth.

Medina stepped behind her then, wrapping his hands around her wrists and adding his strength to hers. "Unless you're with me, I'm not going to be much good with these," she said between gritted teeth.

"You're doing okay. Just take your time between shots."

She not only had to take her time, she had to work up her nerve. Now she knew why the big pistols were called hand cannons. She didn't make all her shots with them, either, but the ones that hit tore impressive holes in the cardboard targets. Afterward she had to massage her forearms to relax the muscles.

"That's enough for today," he said, taking note of her action. "Your arms will be sore if you keep on."

"Stopping suits me fine," she muttered. "I guess I'm not Rambo, either."

"Who is?" he asked dryly.

She laughed as she worked the kinks out of her shoulders. "What's next?"

"A workout, if you're up to it."

She gave him a wary look. "What kind of workout?"

"The kind where I teach you how to take care of yourself."

"I'll have you know I already take vitamins and moisturize my skin."

"Smart ass." He chuckled as he looped a companionable arm around her shoulders. "We're going to make a great team."

"A great *temporary* team," she corrected, ignoring the sudden thumping of her heart. No way was she going back into this full-time, or even part-time. This was a one-shot deal.

He let her have the last word, but she saw the self-satisfied quirk to his mouth, quickly smoothed out, that told her he planned otherwise. And that was almost as worrying as the job itself.

* * *

To her relief, he took it easy on her during the workout. The gym he took her to wasn't a gym at all, but an abandoned barn thirty miles south of D.C. Nevertheless, it was equipped with both weight machines and free weights, punching bags, what looked like gymnastic equipment, and a big, blue, three-inch thick foam mat.

"That isn't thick enough," she pronounced.

"It's thick enough. I'm not going to be dropping you on your head." He kicked off his shoes.

"It's my butt I'm worried about." Following his example, she took off her own shoes.

"I promise I'll take good care of your butt."

He was as good as his word. The workout didn't involve getting tossed around or twisted into a pretzel. "Rule one: Don't try to take anyone down," he said. "You aren't good enough. The best you can hope to do is get away, so that's what we'll concentrate on. You have the advantage of surprise on your side, because you're small—"

"I am not."

He cast his eyes toward the cavernous ceiling. "You're smaller than most men," he amended.

"But I'm wiry."

He laughed then. "Okay, you're wiry. Where, I don't know, but I'll take your word for it. But you look—"

This time she was the one who rolled her eyes. "I know, like an angel."

"You don't like that, huh? Then let's say you look like a lady. You look as if you've never been dirty, never sweated, never swore."

"Strike three, you're out," she muttered.

"And you don't look nearly as contrary as you are."

"I'm not contrary, I'm *accurate*."

"As I was saying . . ." He grinned down at her. "You look like a cream puff. An angelic, ladylike cream puff. So any guy who grabs you isn't going to be expecting you to do anything except maybe cry."

Deciding she'd bedeviled him enough for now, she shrugged her shoulders back and forth, loosening them. "Okay, so teach me how to make *him* cry."

"I'll be satisfied with just teaching you how to get away."

Courtesy of the rape-prevention class she'd taken, she already knew some of the basic stuff. John refreshed her on many of the moves: how to break the hold of someone who grabbed you from the front—you brought your arms up hard and fast inside your assailant's. A quick, stiff-arm jab of the palm up and into someone's nose might not kill him, though it could if done hard enough, but it would certainly cause him pain. So would slapping your cupped palms over his ears, a move designed to rupture the ear drums. A jab of stiffened fingers into the eyes or throat was disabling.

He showed her the most vulnerable place on the throat for crushing the trachea. Without immediate help, someone with a crushed trachea would die. Even if she couldn't manage crushing power, the blow, done properly, would disable.

They moved around on the mat, into different positions and scenarios. By necessity, the drill was close contact. Niema forced herself to ignore the sensations generated by having John's tall, hard-muscled body against hers, his arms wrapped around her in various holds as he patiently instructed her on how to break those holds.

They both worked up a sweat, and he kept at it until she was panting for breath.

"Would it help if I cried uncle?" she finally asked.

"We can stop any time you want," he said, surprised.

"Great. Now you tell me."

"I don't want to make you sore. We need to train every day, to build up your strength and stamina, and we can't if your muscles are too sore to work."

He actually looked worried, so Niema said, "No, I don't think I'll be sore, but I'm still ready for a break."

"There's some water in the fridge over there. I'm going to work with the weights while you rest."

She fetched a bottle of cold water from the rusty refrigerator standing in the corner and settled down on the mat to watch. He stripped off his T-shirt and tossed it aside. Quickly she looked away and drank more water. Seeing a man without his shirt was nothing out of the ordinary, but still . . . this was John Medina, and he wasn't ordinary.

She stretched out on the mat and closed her eyes, so she wouldn't give in to the temptation to stare at him. There couldn't be anything between them except the job. He was black ops, she was nine-to-five, two totally opposite lifestyles. Still, for a dizzying moment she thought of indulging in a brief affair with him.

What would it be like? She had enjoyed being with him today, even when he annoyed her. He challenged her, just by being himself. She was tired, but she could feel life coursing through her veins in a way it hadn't done in a long, long time. Had he done that, or was it the prospect of being back in action? Or was he irrevocably bound up in that action, so that she couldn't separate the two?

Her entire body felt sensitized after that workout with him. His forearms had brushed her nipples several times. His hands had been on her legs, her hips. His body had slid against hers, and several times, while they grappled, one of his legs had been between hers.

She rolled over onto her stomach and cradled her head on her arms. John Medina had "Danger Zone" written all over him, and for her own sake she should pay attention to the sign. She was already risking more than she could afford to lose.

"Time to get back to work, cream puff," he called from where he was doing bench presses.

"Cream puff, my ass," she snapped, and rolled to her feet.

CHAPTER NINE

Villa de Ronsard, the South of France

Louis Ronsard trusted in nothing he couldn't see, and very little that he could. Trust, in his experience, was a commodity with too high a price.

Even when he trusted, there were degrees: He trusted his sister, Mariette, to never deliberately do anything to hurt him, but she could sometimes be as foolish as she was lovely, so he trusted her with nothing that concerned his business. By necessity, he trusted a select few of his employees with some details of the business, but he made frequent checks on their financial and personal lives to detect any weakness that might pose a danger to him. His employees were forbidden to use drugs, for example, but Ronsard was under no delusion that just because he said it, it was so. So . . . drug tests for all the employees, from the lowest to the highest.

He was aware that he walked a knife edge of danger. The people with whom he dealt on a daily basis were not upstanding citizens. In his opinion, they were either fanatic or psychotic, or both. He had yet to be able to tell which was the most unstable.

There was only one way one could deal with such people: very cautiously.

He would not accept commissions from just anyone. The maniac who wanted to explode a bomb in a school as a protest for world peace was not going to purchase that bomb or the materials through him. Even in the world of terrorists there must be standards, no? Ronsard required an established organization, which would need his services again and so was not likely to turn on him.

For his part, he was absolutely scrupulous in delivering what he had promised. He took nothing for himself except the agreed payment. His own value, he knew, depended on his reliability. To that end, he went to extraordinary lengths to make certain nothing went wrong with any shipment, no matter how small. His business had flourished as a result, and his bank accounts in Switzerland and the Cayman Islands were . . . healthy.

Because he was so careful, anything out of the ordinary made him wary. Such was the phone call he received that morning on his private line, the number only a very few people knew.

"So," he murmured to himself as he leaned back in his chair and rolled a fragrant cigar, taken from an inlaid sandalwood box on his desk, in his fingers.

"So?" Cara Smith, his secretary and aide—his first aide, as

she liked to call herself—looked up from the computer she was using to track his various investments. He had been surprised, when he had her investigated, to discover her name really was Smith, and that she was from the unlikely named Waterloo, Kansas, which had given her the opportunity over the years to make some dreadful puns at his expense.

"We have a request from an . . . unexpected party."

Cara, of all people, knew how much he disliked the unexpected. But she also knew *him*, better than was sometimes comfortable, and immediately saw his interest. Something intrigued him, or he would have immediately refused the commission.

She swiveled her chair toward him and crossed her long legs. Since Cara was six feet tall, they were very long legs indeed. "And the name is . . . ?"

"Temple."

Her cornflower blue eyes widened. "Wow."

She was so *American,* he thought, so adept in the inelegant phrase. "Wow, indeed."

Temple, known only by the one name, was a shadow in the already murky world of terrorists. His name had been whispered in connection with some assassinations, with certain bombings. He did not choose his targets at random, for the sake of creating terror. He might bring down an airplane, but one person on that flight was his specific target. It was unknown whether he belonged to some even more shadowy organization or if he worked for himself. If for himself, no one knew what his agenda was. Temple was an enigma.

Ronsard didn't like enigmas. He liked to know exactly with whom, and what, he was dealing.

"What does he want?"

"The RDX-a."

To his relief, she didn't say "wow" again. Nor did she ask the obvious: How did Temple even know about RDX-a? It had been tested only a week before, and though the compound had performed as it was supposed to, its existence was still known to only a few. There were a few problems in production that were currently being eliminated, such as the tendency of some batches to decompose at an accelerated rate, with unpleasant results for the handler. It was a delicate balancing act, to stabilize an unstable compound just enough to be able to predict its rate of decomposition, without rendering it *too* stable to perform.

"Find every available bit of information on Temple," he said. "I want to know what he looks like, where he was born—everything."

"Are you going to accept the commission?"

"It depends." Ronsard lit the cigar, dedicating himself, for a few pleasurable seconds, to the ritual. When the end was glowing to his satisfaction he savored the subtle vanilla taste on his tongue. He would have to change his clothing before seeing Laure; she loved the smell of his cigars, but the smoke wasn't good for her.

Cara had already turned back to her computer and was rapidly typing in commands. Computers were something else he didn't trust, so none of his records were on the one Cara used, which was connected to that invisible electronic world the Americans called the Web. There were encryption programs, of course, but they were constantly being broken. Teenagers hacked into the Pentagon's most secure files; corporations spent billions in computer security that leaked like a sieve. The only secure computer, in his opinion, was one that wasn't connected to anything else—like the one on his desk, where he kept his records. As an added precaution he regularly changed his password, to a word chosen at random from the dog-eared volume of Dickens's *A Tale of Two Cities* that he always kept on his desk. He actually read the thing from time to time, though more to keep Cara from being suspicious about its presence than from any actual interest in the book. He would turn down the page from which he had chosen his password and leave the book lying out in the open as if it were of no importance.

His system wasn't perfect. He changed the password so often that sometimes he forgot which word he had chosen, hence the turned-down page. He could always recognize the word once he saw it, if he was on the correct page.

"Where's Temple from?" Cara asked. "I'm not finding anything on him using a broad search. I need a closer focus."

"America, I think, but I've heard rumors he had lived in Europe for at least ten years. Try Scotland Yard."

She sighed as she tapped keys. "This is going to get me arrested some day," she grumbled.

Ronsard smiled. He did enjoy Cara; she knew exactly what his business entailed but managed to maintain the same attitude as if she worked in a corporate office somewhere. Nor was she intimidated by him, and though a certain amount of intimidation was necessary in his chosen field, sometimes it was wearying.

Nor had she fallen in love with him, which was fortunate. Ronsard knew women, knew the effect he had on them, but Cara had bluntly told him that though she liked him she wasn't interested in sleeping with him. That, too, had been a relief.

She slept with other men, most recently his Egyptian bodyguard, Hossam, who had been obsessed with the tall blonde woman from the day he first saw her. Ronsard only hoped

Hossam wouldn't lose control of his Middle-Eastern temperament when his American Norse goddess lost interest in him.

"Damn," she muttered and typed furiously. The Scotland Yard computer was giving her problems, he concluded.

"Damn!" she shouted a minute later and slapped the monitor. "The bastards have added a wrinkle—"

She began muttering to herself as she tried to electronically wriggle into the Scotland Yard database. Ronsard waited, puffing on his cigar. Cara's mutterings were only half intelligible, thank God, because as she worked her language deteriorated alarmingly.

"Shitpissfuck—"

His eyebrows rose as she got up and stalked around the office, swearing under her breath and waving her hands in the air as she appeared to be having a conversation with herself.

"Okay, what if I try this," she finally muttered and resumed her seat to pound out another series of commands.

Ten minutes later she sat back with a blissful expression on her face. "Outsmarted the sons of bitches," she crowed. "Okay, let's see what you have on 'Temple, first name unknown.' "

A file popped on the screen. Cara hit the print button, and the printer whirred to life, spitting out a single sheet of paper.

"That isn't much," Ronsard murmured as she got up and brought the sheet to him. "Try the FBI; if he's American, they may have more on him."

He began reading. Scotland Yard didn't have many hard facts on Temple. "Believed" to have worked with Baader-Meinhoff in Germany. "Believed" to have been associated with Basque Fatherland in Spain. "Believed" to have had contact with the IRA. Evidently Scotland Yard "believed" a lot of things about Temple and knew very little.

Temple was either American or Canadian, believed—that

word again—to be between the ages of thirty-five and forty-five. No known place of residence.

As sketchy as the information was, at least it gave him a place to begin, Ronsard thought. He had contacts throughout Europe. If anyone in either of the three organizations mentioned had any knowledge of Temple, he—Ronsard—would shortly be in possession of the same.

Cara was muttering and swearing her way through the process of gaining access to the FBI's database. When he heard the triumphant "Aha!" he knew she had succeeded.

"Well, kiss my ass, we got us a photo!" she said in astonishment. "Not a good one, his face is half-hidden, but it's something."

Ronsard left his desk to cross the room and lean over Cara's chair, peering at the computer screen. "Can you enhance it?" he asked, studying the grainy, blurred picture that showed a dark-haired man about to get into a car.

"I can enhance what we have, but nothing will show what the camera didn't get, which is half his face."

"He's wearing a ring on his left hand. A wedding band?" Interesting, Ronsard thought. Not that Temple might be married; things like that happened, even in the terrorists' world. But for him to wear such a conventional symbol as a wedding band was amusing.

The photo showed a dark-haired man, fairly tall, given the scale of the car beside him. His face was turned partially away from the camera, giving a good view of his left ear. The photograph could have been taken anywhere; no license plates were visible on any of the cars; even the make of the car was impossible to tell. The red brick building in the background was equally anonymous, without any helpful lettering or a convenient sign to give a hint of the location.

"I'll print out the information for you to read while I work on enhancing this," Cara said and set the printer to working.

The FBI had more information than Scotland Yard, which illustrated exactly how closely the two bureaus worked. What information the FBI had on an international terrorist, Interpol was supposed to have. What Interpol had, Scotland Yard should have. That was the whole purpose of Interpol. The FBI had been holding back, and he wondered why.

"Temple," he silently read. "First name Josef, or Joseph. Birthplace unknown. First identified in Tucson, Arizona, in 1987. Disappeared, resurfaced in 1992 in Berlin. Brown hair, blue eyes. Identifying marks or scars: left scapula, a diagonal scar approximately four inches long, believed to have been made by a knife or other sharp object."

Knifed in the back, Ronsard thought. Mr. Temple had indeed lived an interesting life.

"Subject wanted for questioning regarding 1987 bombing of courthouse in Tucson, Arizona; 1992 hijacking of NATO munitions truck in Italy—" Ronsard's eyebrows rose. He thought he had a sure finger on the pulse of his chosen world, but he hadn't heard anything about the NATO hijacking. The list went on. In all, the FBI wanted Temple for questioning in fifteen separate incidents.

Temple was thought to be an independent, with no known affiliation with any one organization. He was a hired weapon, Ronsard thought; he didn't kill for pleasure or for himself, but for whoever bought his services, which would not be cheap. From the list of incidents for which he was the main suspect, none of the targets were "soft." All of them were difficult, and the more difficult, the more expensive.

Who was paying him this time? Who had heard of RDX-a and hired Temple to procure it? Why hadn't he—or they—

simply approached him themselves, instead of using Temple as a go-between? It had to be someone with a lot to lose if they became known.

"It isn't a wedding ring," Cara announced, printing out the photo.

Ronsard picked up the sheet as soon as the printer spat it out. She was correct; the ring seemed to have a peculiar braided design, like a dozen tiny entwined gold ropes. No, not ropes—snakes. That looked like a snake head on the ring.

And Mr. Temple's left ear was pierced. The gold hoop in it was discreet, but the photo enhancement plainly revealed it.

The people or person behind Mr. Temple were careful, sending him out to do their work while they remained safely in the background.

But Ronsard was just as wary, just as cautious. He didn't deal with anyone he didn't know.

"I think I want to meet the elusive Mr. Temple," he murmured.

CHAPTER TEN

McLean, Virginia

Niema hit the alarm on the clock before it could go off, got up, and dressed in her running outfit, did her usual routine in the bathroom, and sauntered into the kitchen. As she expected, Medina was sitting at his usual place at the island bar, sipping coffee.

"Very funny," he growled, and she laughed.

"Don't pout. You got in anyway, didn't you?"

"Yeah, but I had to climb in through the laundry-room window. Very undignified."

And very silent, she thought; she was a light sleeper, but she hadn't heard a thing. "I suppose you bypassed the alarm on the window, too."

"No, I disabled the entire thing. Get one that works off infrared or motion, not contact."

She scowled at him. The alarm system had set her back over a thousand bucks, and now he was proposing she spend another two thousand. "Why don't I just do the same thing to all my windows and doors that I did to the back door? Low tech seems to work where high tech doesn't."

"Both would be good." He grinned and lifted his cup in salute. "That was a good idea."

"Low tech" was a good description of what she had done to her back door. She bought two ordinary hook and latch sets at a hardware store, installed the first one in the usual manner with the eye screwed into the frame while the hook was mounted on the door. Then she had turned the second one upside down, butted it up against the first one, and installed it with the eye screwed into the door and the hook mounted on the frame.

With only a single hook latched, anyone with a credit card, knife, or any other thin object could slip it in the crack and force the hook up, freeing it from the eye. With two hooks, one upside down, that method wouldn't work. If you slid the credit card up from the bottom, you hit the upside down latch and pushed the hook into the eye, instead of out of it. If you came down from the top, you were pushing down on the upper latch, with the same results.

Of course, someone who was very strong or who had a battering ram could knock the door off its hinges, but that wasn't a very quiet way of breaking and entering. She was inordinately pleased that her simple solution had stymied him.

When they left the house, instead of turning right, toward the park, Medina turned left.

"The park's in the other direction," Niema said as she caught up and fell into step beside him.

"We ran there yesterday."

"Does this mean you never run the same route twice, or just that you're easily bored?"

"Bored," he said easily. "I have the attention span of a gnat."

"Liar."

His only response was a grin, and they ran in silence then, down the deserted street. There were no stars visible overhead, and the weather felt damp, as if it might rain. Her forearms were a little sore from all that shooting the day before, but other than that she felt great. Her thigh muscles stretched as they ran, and she felt her blood begin to zing through her veins as her heartbeat increased.

They had been running for half an hour when a car turned a corner onto their street, heading straight for them. It was rolling slow, as if looking for something.

John looped his right arm around her waist and whirled her behind a tree. She bit back her instinctive cry and barely got her hands out to brace herself before he crushed her against the tree trunk, holding her there with the hard pressure of his body. She saw the dull glint of metal in his left hand. She held her breath and pressed her cheek even harder into the rough bark of the tree.

"Two men," he said in an almost inaudible whisper, his breath stirring the hair at her temple. "They're probably from the private agency Frank hired."

"Probably? Don't you know?"

"No, I don't know your surveillance schedule, and they don't know I'm here. They're probably looking for you since you aren't on your usual route."

The thought of having a "surveillance schedule" was annoying. Equally annoying was the realization of how many times over the past few years cars had passed by her in the early morning hours and she hadn't thought anything of it, except to watch, with a woman's natural wariness, until the cars had turned the corner and disappeared. She had been so oblivious she was embarrassed. She should have been more alert.

The bark was scratching her cheek, and her breasts were being crushed. "Ease up," she panted. "You're squashing me."

He moved about an inch, but it helped. He remained behind the tree until the car was a block away, then lifted himself away from her. She grunted as she pushed away from the tree. "If they're ours, why don't we just let them see us?"

He resumed his steady stride, and she took up her place beside him. "Because I'm not positive they're ours, for one thing. For another, I don't want them to see me, much less see me with you."

"Some bodyguards they are anyway," she grumbled, "letting you break into my house two mornings in a row."

"They weren't there when I arrived. They must be on a drive-by."

"Why don't you just tell Mr. Vinay to call off the surveillance for now? That would be the most logical thing to do. Then, if anyone drove by, we'd know they aren't ours."

"I may do that."

The car must have just circled the block. It turned onto the street again. "Pretend to chase me and let's see if they'll shoot you," Niema said, and put on a burst of speed, knowing the car's headlights couldn't yet pick her out. She barely contained a giggle at Medina's soft curse behind her. She had taken three steps when a heavy weight hit her in the back and two arms wrapped around her, dragging her down. They landed on the soft grass beside the sidewalk, with her on her stomach and him on top of her. In the pre-dawn darkness, no one was likely to see them unless they were moving.

He held her down, despite her wriggles and erupting giggles, until the car had passed by again. "You little *witch*," he said breathlessly, as if he were trying to hold back his own laughter. "Are you trying to get me killed?"

"Just keeping you on your toes, Medina."

"On my belly is more like it," he grumbled, climbing to his feet and hauling her upright. "What if someone looked out their window and called the cops?"

"We'd be long gone. And if we weren't, I'd just say I stumbled and you tried to catch me. No problem."

"I hope you're having fun," he growled.

A little startled, she realized she *was* having fun. For the first time in a long while she felt as if there was some purpose to her life, as if she had something important to do. No matter how interesting her work with surveillance devices was, benchtesting circuits didn't give her a kick.

But she felt alive now, rejuvenated, as if she had been existing in some sort of half-life for the past five years. She had kept up her running all this time, but until yesterday she hadn't been aware of the workings of her muscles, the pumping of her blood. She enjoyed sparring with Medina, both verbally and physically. She wasn't a gun fanatic, but she had also enjoyed learning about the different handguns, learning how they felt in her hand, learning her own limits and then stretching those limits. She wanted to know more, do more, *be* more.

This was the danger of fieldwork. She had known the lure, resisted it for five years, but now the excitement was flowing through her veins like a potent drug. She didn't know whether to hate Medina or thank him for dragging her back into this.

Was five years' penance enough? Would a hundred years be enough to empty the guilt and anguish she felt over Dallas? Her stride faltered as she thought of the times they had jogged together; afterward they had showered together, then fallen into bed and made love.

Would Dallas have been attracted to the woman she had been for those five years, the woman she had made herself become? Or would he have been bored by the insistence on structure and security, the lack of risk? She was afraid she knew the answer. Dallas had been a risk taker; for all his low-key persona, he'd been a man who thrived on challenge and danger. Why else would he have become a SEAL, then a contract agent? What had attracted him most to her, and she to him, was the instinctive knowledge that they were alike.

Medina was the same type of man, only more so. Alarm bells, suddenly loud and clear, shrilled in her head. It was one thing to allow herself to be sucked back into the heady world of espionage and contract work, but letting herself develop feelings for another man in that same world was something else entirely.

She would have to keep her guard up, because emotions could boil over in such high-stress situations. And Medina was an attractive man; more than attractive, really. If he ever let his guard down, he'd be devastating. He seemed relaxed with her, but not once had he let any personal details slip. She knew nothing about him.

She had already felt warning twinges of physical attraction during the close contact required by training. A woman would have to be dead not to notice that lean, rock-hard body, especially when he was pressed against her.

Was that why she had teased him about making the surveillance team think he was chasing her, so he would catch her and hold her? In a flash of self-awareness, she realized she had been *flirting* with him. Uh-oh, she thought. She'd have to be more careful in the future.

What future? This was a one-time thing, wasn't it? They would work together briefly just this once, then she would return to her safe, familiar job and he would disappear again.

"Are you ready to pack it in?"

She glanced at the luminous dial of her wristwatch; they had already been running for over an hour. Luckily they hadn't gone in a straight line, or it would have taken them another hour to get back to her house; they had circled blocks and backtracked several times, so they were no more than half a mile from home. Dawn was close, so close that details were clearly visible now. "What if the surveillance team is still looking for me?"

"They had better be, or—" He didn't finish the sentence, but she could guess what he had meant to say: Or they would be looking for another job.

"They'll see you," she pointed out.

"I'll split off and let you go home alone. Once they see you're safely home, they'll break off surveillance."

"What else is on the agenda today? More target practice?"

"That and more self-defense training."

With her new insight into herself, she didn't know if close-contact training with him was such a good idea. "I thought only the basics were necessary."

"We might as well do something with our time. Who knows? It may come in handy some day. By the way, some boxes will be delivered to you today. It's a new wardrobe, jewelry, things you'll need."

"Why do I need a new wardrobe?"

"It's part of the cover. You'll be attending embassy parties, posing as the daughter of old friends of the ambassador."

She would be playing dress-up, Niema thought with amusement. She looked forward to that part of the job. Like most women, she liked good clothes and the thrill of knowing she looked good.

"Try everything on," he continued. "The clothes have to fit perfectly. What doesn't will be replaced or altered."

"They can't be returned if they're altered."

"Don't worry about it, you can keep them." He looked around. "This is where I leave you. See you in five minutes." He peeled off to the right, his stride lengthening as if he hadn't already been running for over an hour. He cut between two houses, jumped a fence, and disappeared from view.

Niema turned on the afterburners. Her thighs ached from the effort, but she pushed harder, her feet pounding. It was silly to compete with him when they weren't racing; all she had to do was leisurely jog back to her house and let the surveillance team see her, so they knew she was all right. She knew it was silly; she did it anyway. She fought to suck air deep into her lungs as she raced down the sidewalk. Anyone seeing her would think she was running for her life, she thought, except there was no one behind her.

Up ahead she saw the surveillance car, or at least she thought it was. She hadn't gotten a good look at it in the dark, but the tail lights looked the same, and there were two men in it. The car was parked at the curb; she blew by it in a dead run, without giving the men so much as a glance. When she was twenty yards past them, she heard the car engine start.

She was two blocks from home. She ignored the messages her thigh muscles were screaming at her and forced herself to maintain her speed. When she reached her house she pounded across the small front yard and to the front door. Out of the corner of her eye she saw the car cruise past. She unlocked the door and practically fell inside, gulping in huge breaths.

She leaned against the wall beside the door, wondering if the goal had been worth the effort. Her heart was pounding so hard there was a roaring in her ears.

Or was there? She forced herself to breathe regularly, her head tilted as she listened.

The shower in the second bath was running.

Muttering to herself, she stomped off to take her own shower.

Niema faced Medina across the blue foam mat. "Today I'm going to show you some strike points," he said. "Done properly—and it takes a lot of practice to do them properly—these are death blows."

She drew back and put her hands on her hips, eyeing him suspiciously. "Why would I need to know anything like that? Am I going to be in hand-to-hand combat?"

"If I thought you were, I wouldn't take you. This is partly just in case and partly because I have time on my hands." He motioned her forward. "Come on."

"You want to turn me into a trained killer because you're bored?"

That drew a flashing smile. "You won't be a trained killer. At most, you'll be able to stun someone so you can get away. I told you it takes years of practice to do this properly. The only way you'll kill someone is if you accidentally get it right." Again he motioned for her.

Warily she approached, but still remained out of his reach.

"Relax, there's no hitting in this session. I'm just going to show you some of the points and the striking motions." He took a quick step forward, grabbed her wrist, and dragged her to the middle of the mat before she could retreat.

"This is part of t'ai chi. Actually, it's the basis. Dim-Mak is death-point striking, and it involves acupuncture points.

Never, never use it unless it's a life and death situation, because like I said, you might accidentally get it right." He brought her hand up and caught her fingers, then held them against the outside corner of his eye.

"Here. This exact spot. Feel it."

"I'm feeling."

"Even a slight blow here can do major damage—nausea, memory loss, sometimes death." He showed her how to do the strike, using her fingertips. Positioning was important, to get the right angle. He made her go through the motion over and over, using himself as a dummy for her to aim at; she actually hit him once, nothing more than a touch. He whirled away from her, bent over from the waist, gagging.

"Oh God, I'm sorry!" She rushed over to him and put her arms around his waist as if she could hold him up. Panic surged in her as she remembered what he'd said about a slight blow. "Should I call 911?"

He shook his head and waved off that suggestion. He pressed under his nose, and rubbed from the corner of his eye back toward his ear. His eyes were watering a little. "I'm okay," he said, straightening.

"Are you sure? Maybe you should sit down."

"I'm fine. Things like this happen all the time in training."

"Let's do something else," she suggested uneasily.

"Okay, let's move on to the temple—"

"I meant like judo."

"Why, are you going into professional wrestling?" His blue eyes were like lasers, pinning her to the spot. He caught her hand and brought it to his temple. "Here. Hit hard, straight in. It's a knock-out point, and if a vein is ruptured the attacker will die in a day or so. CPR might revive him, but he could still die from the hemorrhage.

"Here." He moved her hand to just under his nipple. He showed her the exact spot, and the positioning of her hands. "This is instant death—"

"I'm not doing it," she said hotly. "I am *not* going to practice on you again."

"Good." He pressed her hand in the center of his chest, between the nipples. "A blow here makes the lower body spasm and go stiff, and the attacker falls down. Here—" He pulled her hand lower, just below his sternum. "A correct blow here stops the heart."

He was relentless. The gruesome lesson went on and on. He made her perform the motions until her hand positioning was correct, but she was adamant about not using him as a dummy again. She was still shaken that such a light touch had been able to produce such a strong reaction; what if she actually *hit* him?

Finally, he called a halt. He had just shown her a couple of strikes that caused instant diarrhea, and she thought she really should practice those on a live target. Medina stepped back, shaking his head and grinning.

"No way. You're mad enough at me to do it."

"Damn right I am."

"You'll thank me if you're ever in a tight spot and need to know how to bring someone down."

"*If* that ever happens, I'll make it a point to find you and let you say 'I told you so.' But I think I'll practice the diarrhea strikes instead of the death strikes."

He walked over to get one of the bottles of water they had brought with them. He twisted off the cap and tilted it up, his strong throat working as he swallowed. Helplessly, Niema watched him. Even though she knew she should be wary and keep a mental, if not a physical, distance, he was a fine specimen of masculinity and everything in her that was female appreciated the scenery. His sweat pants were soft, clinging to his ass and thighs like a second skin, and that black T-shirt didn't do a thing to hide the muscular contours of his chest and arms.

Her nipples tingled an alert, and a wave of heat swept over her. Clearing her throat, she tore her gaze away from him and turned her back to do some stretching exercises. Her legs especially needed the stretching, after that run this morning. She would have stretched even if they hadn't, just to give herself something to do besides think about John Medina's body.

I have to be careful, she thought. Very, very careful.

"Ready for target practice?" he asked behind her.

She groaned and straightened. What on earth had she gotten herself into?

Later that night, after a stop at the hardware store where she purchased their entire stock of hook and eye latches and spent a couple of hours installing them—except on the window in the second bathroom, which was high and small and she wanted to see if he could get in that way—she tried on the boxes of clothes that had been delivered.

Everything had a designer label. The underwear sets were silk, the hosiery was gossamer. Each pair of shoes had to have cost upward of two hundred dollars, and there were over a dozen pairs. There were cocktail dresses, evening gowns, smart little suits that showed more leg than she normally revealed; shorts, camp shirts, lacy camisoles, jeans, cashmere sweater sets, skirts. And there was the jewelry: pearl earrings and a matching necklace, a web of small diamonds that hung on an illusion chain, gold bracelets and chains, and an enormous, breathtakingly lovely black opal pendant with matching earrings. She carefully put the opal set back in its box and reached for a yellow diamond solitaire ring.

The phone rang. She stretched to reach the receiver, holding the opal pendant in her hand. "Hello."

"Have you looked at the clothes yet?"

"I'm going through them now." Funny how he didn't need to identify himself, she thought. Though she had never talked to him on the phone before, she recognized his voice immediately.

"Do they fit?"

"Most of them."

"I'll have that taken care of tomorrow. Have you gotten to the opal pendant yet?"

"I just put it away. It's the most beautiful thing I've ever seen." There was a touch of awe in her voice.

"There's a transmitter behind the stone, hidden between the prongs of the set. Be careful and don't jostle it. See you in the morning."

The phone clicked as he hung up. Slowly she replaced the receiver. His last words could be taken as a warning, considering his penchant for breaking into her house. She smiled, thinking of that small bathroom window.

"Oh, yes, Mr. Medina. I'll definitely see you."

CHAPTER
ELEVEN

B ingo," John said softly, and hung up the phone. Ronsard had taken the bait. The message had gone to a computer in Brussels, as per his instructions; the message had then been relayed to a computer in Toronto, which he had accessed using a calling card. Calling cards were untraceable, assuming Ronsard would even make the effort. He wouldn't expect Temple's name and number to pop up on caller ID, or for the number to be traceable.

Now he had to finesse the timing. First he had to bring Niema to Ronsard's notice and see if she was invited to the villa. If not, he would have to adjust his plan. But if Niema bagged the invitation, he didn't want to arrive at the villa until after she was already there.

Niema. As much as he had enjoyed these past few days with her, she was driving him crazy. Teasing her, touching her during her self-defense "lessons"—he had to have lost his mind to subject himself to such torture. But she delighted him on so many levels, he couldn't bring himself to stop. She was so quick to learn, and so competitive she automatically rose to any challenge. He had quietly laughed to himself that morning while he showered in her guest bath, knowing she had raced full out in an effort to beat him back to the house—after already running for over an hour.

She was aware of him now, where she never had been before. She hadn't had a clue, in Iran, how much he had envied Dallas. But he had seen her watching him when he took off his T-shirt, seen the effort she made not to stare. It was still too soon to make a move, though, so he'd had to fiercely concentrate to keep from getting an erection every time he got close to her. She had just today fully realized her attraction to him, so she was nowhere ready for him to do anything about it.

It wasn't as if they had just met and begun seeing each other. Under those circumstances, he would have felt free to move at his own pace, or at least as free as he ever felt with a woman. But they had baggage in common, the two of them; the manner of Dallas's death was something that both linked them and stood between them. No other man had been able to scale that wall because no other man had been able to understand it; *he* was the one who had been in that cold, dirty little hut with her, the one who watched her white, still face as she listened to her husband's last words, saw the screaming in her eyes. *He* was the one who held her when she at last was able to cry.

And he was the one who was going to break down that barrier of disinterest she had installed between herself and the male sex. He could do it because he understood her, because he knew that beneath her ladylike exterior beat the heart of an adventuress. He could give her the excitement she needed, both professionally and personally. God, the way she had come alive these past few days! She literally glowed. It took all his willpower not to grab her and let her know exactly how he felt.

But there was a time for that, and it wasn't now. She still wasn't comfortable with the idea of wanting anyone who wasn't Dallas, in general, and him in particular. But she would be; he would see to it.

Restlessly he got up and paced the room, automatically avoiding the window. He couldn't remember any woman's response being so important to him, not even Venetia's—

He stopped and stared sightlessly at the unremarkable framed print on the wall. After what had happened with Venetia, maybe he didn't deserve Niema. And maybe Niema wouldn't want anything to do with him, if she knew about Venetia. Maybe, hell; it was almost guaranteed. If he were honorable, he'd tell her about his dead wife.

His mouth quirked in a humorless smile. If he were honorable, he wouldn't have done a lot of the things he'd done in his life. He wanted Niema, wanted her with an intensity that continually took him off guard. And he was going to have her.

Ville de Ronsard

"Could you trace the message?" Ronsard asked Cara, who was staring at her monitor while she tapped out commands on the keyboard.

Absently she shook her head, her attention focused on the monitor. "Only to the first relay; after that, it disappeared into the ether. Temple has a damn good encryption and switch system."

Ronsard strolled around the office. The hour was early, very early, but he didn't need much sleep, and Cara adjusted her hours to his. "I thought you told me that everything on a computer leaves its print."

"It does, but the print may be a dead end. He could have programmed the first relay with a self-destroy code after the message went through. The first relay may not even be a relay; it could be the destination, but you don't seem to think Temple would be that easy to find."

"No, he wouldn't be," Ronsard murmured. "Where was the first relay, by the way?"

"Brussels."

"Then he is likely in Europe?"

"Not necessarily. He could be anywhere there's a phone line."

Ronsard tilted his head, considering the situation. "Could you tell anything if you had the actual computer in your possession?"

Her eyes gleamed with interest. "You betcha. Unless the hard drive is destroyed."

"If this is his usual means of contact, then he wouldn't destroy the link. He would safeguard it with encryption, but not destroy it. If you can discover the location of the computer, I will have it brought here."

She turned back to the monitor and began typing furiously.

Satisfied that he would soon have the computer in his possession—or rather, in Cara's possession—Ronsard returned to his desk. Laure had had a difficult night, and he was tired. He had staff who saw to her care, of course, but when she was upset or didn't feel well she wanted her papa with her. No matter where he was or what he was doing, if Laure needed him he dropped everything and went to her.

He hadn't yet gone through the mail from the day before, though Cara had opened it and put the stack on his desk. He began leafing through the bills and invitations; as usual, the latter outnumbered the former. He was invited everywhere; connections were everything in the world of business, even when that business was not of the approved sort. A great many hostesses were thrilled to have him at their functions; he was single, handsome, and carried an air of danger about him. Ronsard was cynically aware of his own attractions, and of the use they could be to him.

"Ah," he said, taking a cream-colored vellum invitation from the stack. The prime minister cordially invited him to . . . He didn't bother reading what function was involved, merely checked the date. Such social gatherings were invaluable. He had ceased being amazed at how many of the world's business, social, and political leaders found a need for his services. They felt free to approach him at a charity ball or political dinner, for after all that was their world, and they felt safe and comfortable there. Once that had been his world too; he was still comfortable there, but now he knew that nowhere was safe, not really.

"Got it," Cara said and gave him the address.

Brussels

The middle-aged man looked like any other in Brussels; he was average in height, weight, coloring; there was nothing about him to cause interest. He walked at a normal pace, seemingly paying more attention to the newspaper in his hand than to where he was going, until he came to a certain apartment building. He mounted the two stone steps and let him-

LINDA HOWARD

self in the door, then took the stairs instead of the creaky elevator, so he wasn't likely to meet anyone.

On the top floor, the third one, he unlocked the door to a certain room. It was empty except for the computer humming quietly on a wooden crate, cables hooking it to the electrical outlet and phone jack. There was no printer.

The lights were programmed to go off and on at random times. The window was covered with shutters. Sometimes he came in the mornings and opened the shutters, then returned in the afternoon to shut them, so it looked as if someone was living there. He didn't think anyone ever had; there was only the computer.

Per that morning's instructions, he walked quickly over to the computer and tapped a few keys on the keyboard, entering the program called Norton Utilities. On that program was a feature called "government wipe." He pressed a few keys, waited a moment, then pressed another one. He watched briefly as the computer performed as instructed.

He took his handkerchief and wiped off the computer keyboard, then the doorknob as he was leaving. He wouldn't be back to this empty room with its electronic inhabitant.

No one saw him arrive or leave, but then, he was so very average looking.

Later that afternoon, a white van stopped down the street from the apartment building. Two men got out and walked up the narrow street; they were dressed as laborers, in paint-stained coveralls, though their van bore none of the accouterments of painters.

They went into the apartment building and took the stairs up to the third floor. Once in the narrow, dingy hallway, they each took heavy automatic pistols from inside their coveralls

132

and quietly approached the closed door to one of the apartments. One positioned himself to the side of the door, his pistol held ready. He nodded to his companion, who cautiously reached out and tried the knob. Surprise etched both their faces when the door swung open.

Quickly they peeked around the frame, automatically jerked back, then relaxed; the room was empty. Still, they held their pistols ready as they entered the room and quickly searched it. Nothing. Not only was the room uninhabited, it showed no signs that anyone had lived there in quite some time.

On the other hand, there was that computer. It sat on the crate, quietly humming. The screen was a pure blue.

The two men were professionals; they got down on their knees and inspected the computer, following the power and telephone cords to their outlets, looking for anything unusual. Not finding anything, one of them finally reached out and turned off the computer. The screen went blank and the quiet hum died.

They briskly unplugged the computer and carried it downstairs to their van. They didn't bother closing the door behind them when they left.

Ville de Ronsard

Cara was swimming when Ronsard sent word the computer had arrived. She hauled herself out of the pool and bent over from the waist to wring the water from her hair. She knew Hossam was watching her, his dark eyes hot with excitement. She ignored him and wrapped a towel around her head and another around her torso.

Poor Hossam. All that jealous lust was getting tiresome. *Hossam* was getting tiresome. Cara was quickly bored with her lovers, because once they got her in bed they all seemed to get possessive and territorial. Why couldn't they just be satisfied with good sex, the way she was? She didn't like hurting them because she cared for them all, just not the way they wanted. On the other hand, she wasn't going to spend her life with a man she didn't want just because she felt sorry for him.

Extricating herself from the relationship with Hossam could be tricky. She was well aware of the cultural differences; in the beginning, they had even been exciting. Now she felt stifled whenever she was with him.

What she needed, she supposed, was a nice boy toy for *her* to keep, someone who knew she was the boss, at least of herself. She wasn't into dominance, just independence.

The truth was, no man she had ever met, with the exception of Ronsard, was as interesting as her computers—and she was smart enough to know Ronsard wasn't the settling-down type. Not ever. She liked him, but he wasn't for her. Maybe no one was. Maybe she was going to end up one of those eccentric, world-traveling old ladies. She kinda liked the image that brought to mind.

Hossam approached and laid his hand on her arm. "You will come to my room tonight?"

"Not tonight," she said, moving away as casually as possible. "Mr. Ronsard has brought in a computer he wants me to investigate, so I'll be working all night."

"Tomorrow, then."

"You know I can't promise that when I don't know what my schedule is."

"Marry me, and you will not have to work."

"I like working," she said. "Good night." She hurried away before he could stop her again. Yes, this situation with Hossam was definitely getting tricky. Perhaps she would ask Ronsard to reassign Hossam, though she hated to do that; after all, Hossam was only being himself. He shouldn't be punished for that.

She stopped in her room to get dressed and pin up her hair. In the States she would have hurried to the office in her bathing suit, but Ronsard was very European in his dress standards. She liked that, actually. It was nice to have standards.

He was waiting for her, his long dark hair pulled back in its usual style, giving his lean face a more exotic slant. He was dressed in black trousers and a white shirt, which was as informal as he got. "Your gift," he said, nodding to the unit that now occupied her desktop.

Quickly she hooked up the machine and sat down in front of it. She turned it on and waited for it to boot. Nothing happened. She tried it again. The screen still remained a blank blue.

"Uh-oh."

"Is something wrong?" Ronsard asked as he approached.

"It's been wiped."

"Erased?"

"Yeah. Maybe he just used a C-prompt command. If he did, there should still be some information on the hard drive."

"And if he didn't?"

"If he used a government wipe, then there's nothing left."

"A government wipe . . ."

"It's just what it sounds like. If there's anything you don't want the government to see, you use a government wipe. It's in Norton Utilities—"

He held up a hand. "Details aren't necessary. How long will it take you to find out which type of erasure he used?"

"Not long."

He waited patiently while she got into the hard drive and began searching for bits of data. There was nothing. The drive was as pristine as the day it came off the assembly line.

"Nothing," she said in disgust.

Ronsard put a comforting hand on her shoulder. "That is what I expected, really."

"Then why get the computer?"

"Because I want to know Mr. Temple. If he were careless enough to leave data on the computer, then perhaps I shouldn't deal with him. As it is—" Ronsard hesitated and gave a thin smile. "I've learned that he is almost as careful as I."

"Almost."

"I'm not going to him," Ronsard said gently. "He is coming to me."

CHAPTER
TWELVE

Y our name is Niema Jamieson," Medina said, handing over a passport, driver's license, and social security card.

She looked down at them in both interest and disbelief. "Niema?" she questioned.

"Your name is so unusual you'd probably slip up if you had to answer to anything else. It's always best to stay close to your real name."

"Is that so, Mr. Darrell Tucker?" she murmured.

He gave a faint smile in acknowledgment of the hit. "I've used so many names, I ran out of similars."

She opened the passport. Her photo was there, as well as several pages of stamps. According to her passport, within just the past year she had been to Great Britain twice, once to

Italy, once to Switzerland, and once to Australia. Niema Jamieson was certainly well-traveled.

The driver's license looked just as authentic. She was a resident of New Hampshire, evidently. Niema Price Jamieson.

"My middle name is Price?" she asked in disbelief.

"That's your maiden name. Your family is old friends with the ambassador's wife's family."

"So I'm married?"

"Widowed." He gave her a steady, unyielding look, as if expecting her to object to a cover line so close to her own life. "Your husband, Craig, was killed in a boating accident two years ago. The ambassador's wife—her name is Eleanor, by the way—persuaded you to join them in Paris for a vacation."

She was silent. Of course so many of the details paralleled her own life; that way the story was easy to remember.

"And if Ronsard does invite me to his home and does a background check on me, he'll find . . . what?"

"He'll find that you're exactly who you say you are. He'll find society page articles mentioning you. He'll find an article on Craig Jamieson's death that mentions his grief-stricken widow, Niema. Don't worry; your cover will stand up to any scrutiny."

"But what about the ambassador and his wife? They obviously know I'm not an old family friend."

"Yes, but they're accustomed to covers. You know how many Agency personnel are in our embassies. It's standard."

"Then why won't Ronsard suspect me?"

"Because you aren't staff. Believe me, they know, or have a good idea, who is Agency and who isn't."

She took a deep breath. "When do I leave?"

He pulled a ticket folder from the inside pocket of his jacket. "Tomorrow, on the Concord."

"Cool." Her eyes lit. She had always wanted to fly on the supersonic jet. "When will you get there?"

"You won't see me until we're both at Ronsard's villa. If he doesn't invite you—" He broke off and shrugged.

"Then I won't see you again." She tried to keep her tone matter-of-fact, but inside she didn't feel that way. In just a few days he seemed to have become the central element of the excitement she felt. But she had known from the beginning how things would be, known that he would leave as abruptly as he had appeared.

"I didn't say that."

"No, but I've worked with you before, remember? When the job's finished, you disappear. And now that I know who you are, I know why."

"Niema . . ." He put his hands in his pockets, looking oddly ill at ease. Medina was always in such control of himself that his expression diverted her. "I'll be back. That's all I can say now."

She was immediately intrigued, and alarmed. Did he mean he wanted to use her on another job? Part of her wanted to shout "Hell, no!" but deep inside was a yearning, a craving for more.

Common sense took the upper hand. "This is a one-time deal, Medina; don't bank on sucking me into another job. I don't get hazardous-duty pay, you know."

"Of course you do."

Taken aback, she warily eyed him. "What do you mean?"

"I mean you get a hefty bonus for this."

"Oh, great! That means anyone in payroll—"

"Nope. This is black ops, remember? Everything comes out of an off-books account. And try to call me John, instead of Medina. John's a fairly common name, but there are a lot of people in this town who would perk up their ears if they heard you call me Medina."

Reluctantly she said, "John." She preferred thinking of him and referring to him as Medina; that kept him at a certain distance, at least in her mind. She was having a difficult enough time battling her attraction to him as it was. "Back to my original statement: This is a one-time deal. It has to be."

Hands still in his pockets, he wandered over to the kitchen window and absently fingered the hook and eye latches she had installed. For the past two mornings he had been reduced to wriggling through a damn small bathroom window, and the fit was so tight he had to do some major contortions to get in. She was so pleased with those little latches that he didn't tell her he'd figured out a way to unlatch them. The average burglar wouldn't have the means of doing it, and anyone who really, really wanted to get into the house would simply break a window anyway. The ordinary citizen usually couldn't afford the safety measures that would make a house truly burglar-proof, but then the ordinary citizen didn't need to go to that effort and expense.

"Don't think you can ignore me," she warned.

He gave her a brief, warm smile as he turned away from the window. "I've never thought that."

Both the smile and the statement rattled her. Deciding to change the subject, she took a deep breath. "Let's get back to the plan. What happens when—if—I wrangle and invitation to Ronsard's home? What if you aren't invited for the same time?"

"I've already received an invitation. Ronsard is hosting a formal party in ten days. He does it annually, as sort of a repayment to all the people who look the other way when delicate situations arise concerning his occupation. The security is extremely tight, even tighter than normal, because of so many people in the house. He would consider the meeting with me more controlled. If Ronsard invites you to the party, accept. If he merely invites you to his house for a visit, decline. That will only whet his interest."

"What I know about whetting interest would rattle around in a peanut shell," she muttered.

He grinned. "Don't worry, Mother Nature took care of that. We men are easy. We don't require much more than that a woman be breathing, and we're interested."

She tried to take umbrage, but instead found herself laughing. "That simple, huh?"

"Compared to women, we're amoebas. Our brains only have one cell, but it's dedicated."

So said the most complicated man she'd ever met. She shook her head. "I think we need to get to work, before your one cell goes completely haywire. What's on the agenda for today?"

"Nothing," he said. "Get some rest, pack, brush up on your French. I just came by to give you your papers."

She had become so accustomed to working out with him that the prospect of a day without that challenge seemed flat. "So this is it, huh? If I don't get that invitation, I won't see you again."

He hesitated, then reached out and lightly touched her cheek with his fingertips. He started to say something and stopped. Something like regret, only more complex, flickered briefly in his blue eyes. Without a word he turned and left, letting himself out the back door, his movements so silent she wouldn't have known he was there if she hadn't been looking at him.

She stood in the kitchen, fighting the chill that raced over her at his touch. No, she wasn't cold. She was shivering, but she wasn't cold. Just that light touch of his fingertips had set her nerve endings to tingling. Holy cow. What would it be like to actually—"No," she ordered herself aloud. "Don't go there." Don't imagine what it would be like to make love with him. Men like John Medina didn't make love, they had sex; they didn't have relationships, just encounters.

Though one couldn't tell it from the way she had lived her life for the past five years, she had sometimes thought, in a vague way, of remarrying and having children. That was always in the nebulous future, and even though there hadn't been any candidates for the position of husband, still she had expected her life to eventually take that route. If she became involved with John, though, she could kiss that dream good-bye. She wouldn't be able to settle for an ordinary Joe if she ever let herself indulge in an affair with him.

He might pass himself off as a sheep to most of the world, but she knew him for the wolf he was. And she knew her own nature, knew her craving for excitement. She'd never be able to get herself back, because sleeping with John would be going one step too far. That was the ultimate kick, and nothing else would ever equal it. But if she didn't let herself taste him, she would never know what she missed. She might suspect, but she wouldn't know, and she would still be capable of happiness with that ordinary Joe who had to be somewhere in her future.

What difference did it make? she wondered, pressing a fist to the pit of her stomach in an effort to squash the butterflies that were fluttering there. He was gone. If this plan didn't work, she probably wouldn't see him again. Though he'd said he would be back, she didn't quite believe him. She couldn't let herself believe him, because if she did, she might start dreaming he was coming back for her, and that was the most dangerous fantasy of all.

Niema packed in the battered Vuitton luggage that had been delivered the day before. The luggage was a nice touch, she thought; it was expensive and fit with her supposedly well-heeled background, but still looked far from new. It looked, in fact, as if it had been around the world several times. The name tags carried her fictitious name and address.

She dressed in a stylish linen and cotton blend sage green dress for travel, a simple chemise style that she topped with a lightweight cardigan. On her feet were sensible taupe flats. For all its simplicity, or perhaps because of it, the ensemble shrieked "money." Old money, at that.

The day was bright and sunny; there wouldn't be any bad weather delays. She felt jittery and couldn't tell if it was due to anticipation or dread. But she felt ready; she wanted to be in Paris right now. She wanted to meet this Louis Ronsard and see if breathing was, indeed, all she had to do to be come-hitherish. John needed her inside Ronsard's villa; he would continue on his own, but the job was less risky if he had backup. She had to get that invitation.

Uneasily she thought of a precaution John had insisted she take: birth control pills. It was standard for female operatives, he'd told her. Did he expect her to sleep with Ronsard? She knew that sex was often the route women used to get to the men they targeted, in real life as well as in espionage. Well, her devotion to the job didn't go that deep; she would not, could not, sleep with the arms dealer, no matter how good-looking he supposedly was.

The cab arrived on time, and the driver came to the door to carry her bags. As he went back down the sidewalk she looked around at her comfortable home, wondering at the weird sense of disconnection, as if she would never see it again. This wasn't much different from going on vacation. A week, two weeks at the most, and she would be home again, once more settled into the routine of work and chores. This episode wouldn't be repeated.

She carefully locked the door and set the alarm, which John had reactivated. He had definitely made her more safety conscious, though; even with the alarm, she found herself going around to every window and door and hooking the latches. She had bought a timer for the lamps and television, to give the house at least the appearance of being lived in. And John had promised that Agency people would keep an eye on the house for her, so she wasn't really worried.

The cab driver was looking impatient, so she hurried down the walk, and with every step her spirits lifted. She was finally in action again!

She was met in Paris by a uniformed chauffeur who loaded her luggage and solicitously handed her into a large Mercedes-Benz. She sank into the leather seats and closed her eyes with a sigh. Did the Concord eliminate jet lag, she wondered, or did the body automatically note the position of the sun and know something was wrong? The supersonic flight was much faster than a regular jet, but she was still as exhausted as if the flight had taken the normal length of time. All she wanted was a long bath and a quiet place to lie down.

The Marine guards at the embassy checked the car and her passport before allowing her into the embassy grounds. As the car stopped out front, a tall, slender woman in her early sixties, with striking silver-white hair, came down the steps, her hands outstretched and her face wreathed in smiles.

"Niema!" she cried. "It's *so* good to see you!"

This must be Ambassador Theriot's wife, Eleanor, the old family friend. The chauffeur opened the door, and Niema climbed out, going straight to Mrs. Theriot with a warm hug.

"You look exhausted," Mrs. Theriot said, patting her cheek in a motherly way. "Jet lag is terrible, isn't it? Supposedly it's worse going west—or perhaps that's east, I can never remember which it is, but it doesn't matter because I get jet lag no matter what direction I'm traveling."

Mrs. Theriot was giving her recovery time by chattering, Niema realized. She managed a smile. "I *am* tired, but I don't want to waste my visit lying around."

"Don't worry about that," Mrs. Theriot cooed as she led her up the steps into the embassy. "A nap will do you a world of good. There's nothing you have to do, nowhere you have to go."

From that, Niema deduced that her presence not only wasn't expected at dinner that night, but for some reason would be a definite problem. "In that case, I would love a nap."

Still smiling, still chatting as if they had known each other for years, Eleanor Theriot led Niema to an elevator. They exited on the third floor. "This is your room," she said, opening the door to a spacious bedchamber decorated in a gorgeous combination of antique and modern pieces, and in a soothing pale turquoise color with touches of peach and white. The bed was so high there was a footstool beside it, and the mattress looked thick enough for her to sink out of sight.

"There's a private bath through here," Mrs. Theriot continued, opening a white paneled door and giving Niema a glimpse of gleaming brass bathroom fixtures—or were they gold? "Your bags will be brought up, and if you'd like a maid will unpack for you."

Niema started to say that wasn't necessary, then realized that Niema Price Jamieson was probably accustomed to such help, even if Niema Burdock wasn't. "A nap first, please," she said. "My bags can be unpacked later."

"Of course, dear. I'll tell everyone you're not to be disturbed." As she talked, Mrs. Theriot walked over to the desk and scribbled a brief note, which she gave to Niema. "When you're awake, we'll have a long talk just to catch up on gossip. I simply don't have the time to call all my friends the way I used to. Just tell me Jacqueline and Sid are all right, and I'll leave you to your nap."

"Jacqueline" and "Sid" were her make-believe parents. "Mom and Dad are fine," Niema replied. "They're in Australia now, for an extended vacation."

"How I envy them! But I won't ask any more questions now. Have a nice rest, dear." She gave Niema another hug, then let herself out.

Niema looked down at the note. "Don't assume you can trust everyone who works in the embassy," Mrs. Theriot had written. "Stick to your cover at all times."

She wadded up the note and started to toss it into the wastebasket, but on second thought tore the paper into tiny pieces and flushed it. She yawned mightily; that nap was becoming more necessary by the moment.

Her luggage arrived, carried by a serious young man who called her "ma'am." Once he was gone and the bedroom door was locked, Niema pulled the curtains closed, then stripped off her clothes and took a quick shower. Fighting to keep her eyes open, she toweled dry and stumbled to the bed, not bothering with a nightgown or pajamas. Using the two-step stool, she climbed upon the bed and stretched out between the cool, fragrant sheets. She groaned in relief as her tired muscles relaxed.

When was this ball at which she was supposed to meet Ronsard? She couldn't remember. Not tonight, for certain. Tomorrow?

Was she ready? She went over the details of her cover, even repeating "Niema Jamieson" to herself over and over, to make certain she responded when someone addressed her by that name. She couldn't just pretend to be Niema Jamieson, she had to become that person. Ronsard was sharp; he would notice if she appeared not to recognize her own name.

John had been thorough in building the cover identity. The documents would stand up to any inspection and investigation. She didn't have to worry about that aspect of her cover. No, what she worried about was her own ability; John might not have doubts about her, but she did. She had never played a role before, unless it was when they were in Iran, if wearing a chador and not speaking was the same as playing a role.

She didn't, however, doubt her ability to plant a listening device in Ronsard's office. When it came to that part of the job, she was confident she could handle it.

"Let the games begin," she murmured to herself, and went to sleep.

PART
THREE

CHAPTER THIRTEEN

L ouis! It is wonderful to see you. You are looking as handsome as always." The prime minister's wife beamed up her toothy smile at him as she took both his hands and planted kisses on each cheek.

Louis carried her hands to his lips and returned the salute, briefly kissing her knuckles. He was actually fond of Adeline, who was good-natured and inherently kind. Her strong features bore an unfortunate resemblance to a horse, but in the Parisian way she made the most of her best features, her eyes, and after one got to know her, one saw only her nature and didn't think of the long boniness of her face. "I would never miss the opportunity to see you, my dear."

"Flatterer." She beamed at him. "I must continue greeting
the guests, but promise me you won't leave without speaking
with me again. I don't see enough of you, you rogue."

He promised, an easy thing to do, then left her to the receiving line and mingled with the throng of guests crowding the
ballroom and adjacent rooms. A small orchestra was discreetly
installed in an alcove and partially blocked from view by a
gauze curtain.

Black-clad waiters carried trays of delicate flutes half-filled
with golden champagne, while others offered a dazzling array
of hor d'oeuvres. Ronsard plucked a glass of champagne from
one passing waiter and a delicate pastry from another. He had
just taken his first sip of the rather mediocre wine—it was
always mediocre at such parties—when he heard his name
being called.

He turned to see his sister, Mariette, bearing down on him
with her husband in tow. Eduard Cassel's expression was
indulgent, as always. Mariette was a bubbly froth of a woman,
as giddy and harmless as a butterfly. She was three years
younger than Ronsard and he had always been protective of
the pretty creature. When she married, she had chosen a man
fifteen years her senior, and Eduard had taken over as her
protector.

Eduard had been beneficial to Ronsard on several occasions.
Positioned as he was in the Ministry, he often knew interesting
little details about the government, the economy, and some
high-ranking officials' personal lives, which he passed along to
his brother-in-law. In return, Ronsard had set up and regularly
added to a substantial trust in Mariette's name, allowing the
Cassels to live in a level of comfort that far exceeded Eduard's
salary.

"Louis!" Mariette flung her arms around his neck and kissed

his cheek. "I didn't know you would be here tonight. This is wonderful. How is Laure?"

"She is well." Louis's voice was flat, his tone pitched so his words didn't carry. He didn't discuss Laure in public. Many of his acquaintances had no idea she existed.

Mariette wrinkled her nose in apology. "Forgive me," she said contritely. "I forgot."

"Of course," he said gently and kissed her forehead as he held out his hand to her husband. "How are you, Eduard?"

"Well, thank you." Eduard was slightly heavy, balding on top, and his features could best be described as "not ugly." His expression was usually bland, disguising the shrewdness that lurked in his eyes. "And you?"

"Well." Those social niceties out of the way, Ronsard settled his arm around his sister's waist. "You look stunning. That gown is very becoming."

She beamed and smoothed a hand down the shimmery pink fabric that brought out the color in her cheeks. "You don't think it too young?"

"My dear, *you* are young."

"And so I tell her," Eduard said. "She grows lovelier every day." As saccharine as the compliment was, he meant it. His devotion to Mariette always weighed heavily in his favor, in Ronsard's estimation.

"Oh, there is Juliette," Mariette cried, her attention instantly diverted. "I must speak to her." She darted away, her full skirt fluttering around her as if she would take flight.

Ronsard and Eduard drifted away from the crowd, strolling casually as if they had nothing more important to do than idly chat and look for acquaintances in the throng. "I think everyone in government is here tonight," Ronsard observed. "There must be something interesting in the air."

Eduard shrugged, his heavy lips set in a benign smile. "Elections, my friend. Everyone is courting everyone else. And commerce is always interesting, is it not? The Iraqis wish to buy a very expensive, sophisticated computer system from us, but the Americans, as always, are having a tantrum at the idea. Their economy is healthy, so they can't comprehend difficulty in other countries. Our industrial leaders don't like having the Americans intrude on their business. But if we tell them to leave—" He spread his hands. "The Americans have so many lovely dollars. What does one do?"

"Whatever one must, on the surface," Ronsard said dryly. No Frenchman liked the American presence that seemed to permeate the world. France was French, and would remain so. Whatever agreements the Americans forced, they could not be everywhere and oversee everything. France agreed, then did whatever was in France's best interests. Pragmatism was the cornerstone of the French character.

"The Russians, of course, are desperate for technology. Unfortunately they have no means to pay. Perhaps the Americans will pay for them. These are interesting times, are they not?"

"Very interesting." In the past ten years, old boundaries had been completely obliterated. Politics was in a state of flux, and such an atmosphere was very favorable to his business. Instability was the greatest of motivators to a certain type of person.

"The American ambassador is here, of course," Eduard continued. "His aide is drifting around with his ears on alert."

The ambassador's aide was an employee of their Central Intelligence Agency. Everyone knew who everyone was, but still an astonishing amount of information was passed around at these functions. Intelligence officers were often conduits of information that governments wanted to dispense to other governments, but by back channels. No one, after all, wanted to precipitate a crisis.

"A family friend is visiting the ambassador and his wife. She is the daughter of one of Madame Theriot's oldest friends. A lovely young woman, if I may say so. One always sees the same faces at these things, you know; anyone new is a welcome change."

Ronsard was a man. He was always interested in a lovely young woman, provided she wasn't too young. He had no interest in giggly adolescents. "Point her out to me," he said idly.

Eduard looked around. "There," he finally said. "By the windows. Brunette, dressed in white. She has the loveliest eyes."

Ronsard located the woman in question. She was not, he saw, an adolescent. She was standing beside Madame Theriot, a smile that managed to be both polite and warm on her face as she tilted her head, listening to a minister of finance who was probably expounding on his favorite subject, horse racing.

Ronsard exhaled in appreciation. Eduard had not exaggerated; she was indeed lovely. Not beautiful, not spectacular, but . . . lovely. She wasn't dressed in a manner calculated to draw attention, but somehow she did. Perhaps it was the quiet dignity of her manner, coupled with those stunning eyes. Even from there, Ronsard could appreciate Eduard's comment about her eyes. They were huge and night-dark, the type of eyes a man could look into and forget what he was saying.

Her gown was a simple, unadorned white, relying on its exquisite cut for its charm. Her complexion was pale, so pale he wouldn't have thought she could wear white without looking washed-out, but instead the color seemed to accentuate the faintest of pink flushes that made one think one could see the warmth of her blood under that delicate skin.

She was slender without being thin, as so many fashionable women were these days. The gown skimmed over nicely rounded hips, and her bosom, though not large, was enticingly shaped. She wore a single, gracefully long strand of pearls, which matched the bracelet on her right wrist and the earrings on her lobes. She turned as he watched, and the strand of pearls swung sideways to curl under and frame her left breast.

Unconsciously she touched the strand, restoring it to is previous graceful drape, but the brief image made Ronsard's loins pleasurably tighten.

"Is she married?" The French were sophisticated about such matters, but Americans remained, for the most part, annoyingly prudish.

"Widowed," Eduard supplied.

The orchestra at that moment began playing a gently stirring movement from Beethoven, as the dancing had not yet begun. As Ronsard watched, the lovely widow's head turned toward the orchestra, her expression arrested as she listened to the music. She became very still, and her eyes seemed to fill with an aching sadness. She turned to the ministry employee and said a few words, then inclined her head to Madame Theriot and seemed to whisper something. Madame Theriot looked sympathetic and touched the young woman on the arm. Then the young woman slipped out the open patio doors into the night.

Ronsard had no idea how long she had been widowed, but obviously the music had just brought a painful memory to mind. Sad young women, in his opinion, should always be comforted. "Pardon me," he murmured to Eduard and strode across the ballroom floor.

It was a tedious passage; everyone wanted to speak to him. Women called his name and gave him slumbrous smiles. He shook hands, kissed cheeks, and made graceful escapes while he kept his eye on the patio doors. The minister of finance to whom she had been speaking seemed to dither, but finally found the courage to approach the doors. By that time Ronsard was there, and he deftly stepped in front of the man. "Your solicitude is much appreciated," he murmured, "but won't be necessary."

"Ah . . ." The man blinked at him as Ronsard's identity registered. "Yes, of course."

Ronsard went outside into the warm Paris night. The flagstoned patio was lit only by indirect light, from the windows behind him and by the lights strung in the ornamental trees in the garden. Small tables and chairs had been scattered about the patio, providing guests with an opportunity to take fresh air and escape the noise of the ballroom.

The widow sat at one of those tables, her hands quiet in her lap as she looked out over the garden. She hadn't wept, Ronsard saw when he drew near, his footsteps slow and purposeful. She had kept her composure, though he thought he detected a sheen of tears in her eyes, and her mouth had that soft, sad curve that made him want to kiss a smile onto it. A mouth that delectable should always smile.

"Hello," he said gently in English, and the slight start she gave told him that she hadn't been aware of his approach. "Forgive me, I didn't intend to startle you."

She turned those big dark eyes on him, and again he felt that surge in his loins. She looked so sad, so alone and vulnerable. Even as he watched she gathered herself and sought refuge in the social face she had probably been taught to assume from the time she was out of the cradle.

"That's perfectly all right," she said, beginning to stand. Her voice was low and feminine, without the annoying nasal tones of so many Americans. "I was just about to return to the party—"

"No, don't let me displace you," he said quickly, reaching out to gently touch her arm. He was always gentle in his dealings with women, and so many of them were endearingly susceptible to that tenderness, as if they didn't get enough of it in their lives. The widow, however, looked mildly shocked that he had touched her, and she drew back just a little.

"I saw you come out and thought you looked . . . upset." He had to be cautious here and ease her wariness.

For a moment she didn't say anything. She turned her head to look out into the garden, and he admired the graceful line of her neck, the curve of her cheekbone. Then she said, "The music reminded me of another time."

That was all. There were no forthcoming details, no expounding. He sensed her reluctance to give him any personal information. He was accustomed to women responding to him, trying to hold his attention; this woman's very lack of response was intriguing.

"My name is Louis Ronsard," he said, settling into the chair beside her.

"I'm pleased to meet you," she said politely. "I'm Niema Jamieson."

"Niema." He said the name slowly, tasting the sound of it. "What a lovely, unusual name."

She gave a small, quick smile. "Too unusual, sometimes. People seldom know how to pronounce it if they see it spelled out—they usually pronounce it 'Neema' instead of 'Nye-ema,' and if they hear it they don't know how to spell it. When I was a child I often wished my mother had named me Jane, or Susan, or anything straightforward."

"Is it a family name?"

"Nothing so dignified," she said, and the smile became a chuckle. He was delighted by the transformation of her face, from sadness to humor. "She liked the rhythm of the name Naomi, but not the name itself. So she substituted vowels until she found a combination she liked, and"—she spread her hands—"Niema was invented."

"I think it's lovely."

"Thank you. I've become accustomed to it." She glanced over her shoulder into the ballroom. "It's been nice talking to you. I think I should—"

"Of course," he said, getting to his feet. "You don't know me, and you're uncomfortable being alone with me." He paused a beat to give her an opportunity to demur, but she didn't, and he was amused. "Will you reserve a dance for me, Mademoiselle Jamieson?" He purposefully called her mademoiselle, to give her an opening to tell him she was widowed.

"Madame," she corrected, and he was pleasantly surprised by her accent. He was less pleased when she left it at that, withholding the fact of her widowhood; a woman who was interested would have made her marital status clear.

His own interest increased. Ronsard seldom had the opportunity these days to enjoy the chase. Women were all too willing, which was a nice state of affairs, but sometimes a man wished to be the predator.

His question hung in the air between them. Finally she said, "Yes, of course," but her tone held only politeness, not any eagerness for his company.

He was both piqued and amused. Perhaps he had become spoiled, but he knew he wasn't repulsive. Far from it, in fact. This woman, though, seemed totally unaware of him as a man.

Politely he offered his arm, and she laid a graceful hand on it. Her touch was barely perceptible; she didn't cling, didn't actually hold him. Together they walked back into the ball-room, drawing more than one pair of eyes. Ronsard saw Madame Theriot frown and whisper something to her husband. So, she wasn't pleased that her young friend had become acquainted with the notorious arms dealer?

Ronsard smiled at Madame Theriot, then turned to his prey and made her a small, graceful bow. Something in his manner must have alerted her, because her eyes suddenly widened and her soft lips parted. Before she could pull away he pressed his lips to her hand, a brief salute that he didn't allow to linger, and caressed her with his eyes. "Until later," he murmured.

CHAPTER
FOURTEEN

Niema took a deep breath as she walked across the ballroom. A major hurdle had been crossed, and so swiftly, so easily, she was astounded. The plan had been for Eleanor to introduce her to people who had spoken with Ronsard, but not to the arms dealer himself. Eventually their paths would have crossed, but it would have looked odd for Eleanor to be the one who made the introductions, as she naturally would not have liked for her best friend's daughter to associate with someone like Ronsard.

None of that had been necessary. Out of the corner of her eye, she had seen him speaking with someone she had already met—his name escaped her—and both of them had been watching her. At that moment the orchestra had begun playing a particularly lovely piece of music and inspiration struck.

She allowed sadness to play across her features for a moment, then excused herself to the gentleman who was something boring in the French government. She leaned over and whispered to Eleanor, "He's watching. I'm going to slip out onto the patio."

Eleanor, whose acting skills were worthy of Hollywood, immediately saw the opportunity and what Niema was doing. She put on a concerned face and touched Niema on the arm— nothing dramatic, but a touch of sympathy that wouldn't go unnoticed.

Then Niema had simply sat on the patio and waited. Within five minutes, Ronsard joined her.

He was remarkably good looking. The photos she'd seen of him didn't compare to the man in the flesh. He was tall, with dark blue eyes set on a slant above his exotic cheekbones, and he wore his long dark hair loose on his broad shoulders. The hint of savage in an elegant tuxedo was a devastating combination.

His voice was smooth and low, his manners impeccable, and his eyes managed to convey both his interest and his concern over her sadness. A romantic, handsome Frenchman at a formal party was enough to give any woman weak knees.

As soon as she reached Eleanor, the older woman gripped her wrist and leaned over to whisper in Niema's ear, all the while frowning at Ronsard, as if she were informing Niema of his reputation. "Mission accomplished?"

Niema put a startled look on her face, then an alarmed one. She darted a quick glance at Ronsard. Yes, he was watching. She quickly looked away. "He asked for a dance," she murmured.

Eleanor, who knew only the basic story and that Niema was to draw Ronsard's attention, turned away with a practiced smile as the prime minister's wife approached, and Niema's attention was claimed by a young staffer from the embassy who was from New Hampshire and was evidently suffering from homesickness. Since Niema had never been to the state, she hoped he didn't start asking specific questions.

The only formal party she had ever been to in her life was her high school prom. This was far out of her league, but to her surprise she felt comfortable. The clothes were better, the food more exotic, the people more serious and aware of their own importance, but all in all the same dynamics applied: polite chitchat, polite laughter, the constant mingling. The politicians worked the room while the lobbyists worked the politicians. Everyone wanted something from someone else.

Her French had rapidly returned, once she heard it spoken again, but then French had been her best language. Ronsard had spoken in English, however, so that was how she had answered him. She doubted he was a man who ever let anything slip, but if he thought she didn't understand him he might be a little careless in what he said. It wasn't her intention to hide the fact that she spoke the language, though, as that was too easy to give away, and he would immediately be suspicious.

She had to avoid any appearance of being interested in him. Quite the opposite, in fact. He had to make all the moves, so he couldn't suspect her of maneuvering for an invitation to his villa. But at the same time she had to show she *liked* him, or she wouldn't have a reason for accepting.

In her favor was the fact that other women fawned over him. She would stand out in his mind because of her very lack of response. Men liked a challenge, and she was going to give him one.

The dancing started, and she let herself be steered around the floor by the first person who asked, who happened to be the boring gentleman she had been talking to earlier. He pumped her arm as if he expected her to spout water out of her mouth, and all the while he enthused about thoroughbred racing. She smiled and made an occasional comment, and he was happy.

Next the ambassador claimed a dance. He was a stately gentleman with silver hair and a sweet smile, a little shorter than his wife, but with a smooth tact that made her instantly comfortable. He spoke to her as if she were indeed an old friend of the family, chatting on about friends they supposedly had in common, a vacation their families had once spent together when she was a child. She wondered if one of the qualifications to an ambassadorship was to be a consummate liar, because he excelled.

After the dance with the ambassador ended, she excused herself and went to the ladies' room, where she killed as much time as she could. She didn't immediately return to the ballroom, but mingled in the other rooms, speaking to those people to whom she had already been introduced. If Ronsard really wanted to dance with her, he was going to have to find her.

He did. A warm hand closed around her elbow and he said, "You promised me a dance."

Niema hesitated. A small silence fell around them. Everyone knew who he was, of course, and waited to see if she would snub him. She saw his eyes begin to narrow, and into the silence she said, "Are you certain you want to risk your toes?"

Relieved chuckles rippled around them. His face relaxed, and a slight smile curved his lips. "My toes would be honored." He held out his hand, indicating the direction of the ballroom.

She walked calmly by his side, ignoring the hand that settled on the small of her back. The orchestra was just beginning a number slower than the others had been, and she realized that he had waited and chosen his moment—either that or bribed the orchestra.

"I thought you were going to refuse me," he said in a low voice as his arm closed about her waist and he swept her into a gliding circle. He held her closely enough that she could feel the warmth of his body, the movement of his legs against hers, but not so close that she would be alarmed and pull back.

"I was."

One dark eyebrow arched, his expression sardonic. "Why didn't you?"

"A dance won't hurt me," she said calmly.

"Neither will I." He looked down into her face, his tone gentle. "I assume Madame Theriot warned you against me."

"Understandable, don't you think?"

"Understandable, but unnecessary. I mean you no harm."

She didn't respond to that, her expression serene as he swept her around the floor. He danced with a grace that made the exercise effortless, and she thanked God that her parents had insisted she take dance lessons in high school even though she would much rather have learned how to hang glide; at least she wouldn't embarrass herself. A socialite would know how to dance, after all.

When she made no effort to pick up the conversational ball, he asked, "Are you just visiting, or have you been employed at the embassy?"

"Gracious, no!" She looked amused. "Visiting, only."

"For how long?"

"No definite time. A few weeks."

"That isn't much time," he complained softly, looking down at her with such apparent masculine interest that a woman would have to be blind to miss it.

"Monsieur Ronsard—"

"Please don't be alarmed. You're a lovely woman, and I would like very much to see you while you're in Paris. That is all."

"There's no point in it." She looked away, staring at a point over his shoulder. She made her tone gentle and faintly sad.

He firmed the guiding touch of his hand on her back, pressing his palm against her. Her gown was fairly low cut in back, and his fingers brushed her bare skin. "There is always a point to pleasure."

"I don't seem to be very good at pleasure these days."

"Then you must learn how to enjoy yourself again."

Her lips trembled, and a look of pain haunted her eyes. He saw it, as she had meant for him to. "Forgive my clumsiness," he murmured, dipping his head so his mouth was close to her temple. "I never intended to distress you."

She firmed her lips and lifted her chin. "The orchestra is very good, isn't it? I love this piece."

He allowed her to steer the conversation into mundane waters, but she felt his unswerving gaze on her face the entire time. Louis Ronsard was definitely a man on the hunt. So far, she thought, she had done a credible job of appearing reluctant without insulting him.

The dance ended, she thanked him for it, and turned to leave. He fell into step beside her. "Have you been to Paris before?"

"Yes, of course."

"Ah. I had hoped to show you the city."

"Monsieur . . ." She hesitated, as if groping for words. "Forgive me if I sound presumptuous, but I'm not interested in any sort of romance. Even if your occupation wasn't a barrier I wouldn't—"

"Forgive *me,*" he interrupted, "if I've made you in any way uncomfortable. I would like to spend time with you, yes. I would like to make you smile again, as you did out on the patio. A lovely lady should not have such sad eyes. And even if you say that, no, I may not kiss you, or delight myself in other ways, I would still like to take you out to dinner."

For a moment Niema was so diverted and charmed by the phrase "delight myself" that she couldn't stop herself from smiling.

"Aha! I have achieved one goal already." He touched one finger to the corner of her smiling lips. "Your smile is as lovely as I remembered. Please say yes to dinner. My reputation is greatly exaggerated, I promise."

She searched his face, as if looking for the truth. Finally she said, a bit hesitantly, "I haven't dated since my husband—" She broke off and looked away.

"I understand you're a widow," he said. "Yes, I asked about you. I'm sorry for your loss. It has been . . . how long?"

Five. The word echoed in her brain, and this time the sadness that flashed across her face wasn't an act. Five long years. "Two years," she managed to say, her voice constricted. "Most people think that's long enough to grieve, but . . . it isn't."

His expression was somber. "I think the heart has its own calendar. You mustn't let anyone rush you, including me. I give you my word I would attach no expectations to a dinner together. It would just be a meal in pleasant company, no more. Or perhaps you would prefer lunch?"

She let herself waver, then said softly, "Yes, lunch sounds . . ."

"Safer?" he suggested.

"More casual. Less like a date."

He chuckled. "I see. Then, Madame Jamieson, will you *not* go out to dinner with me? Let's just have lunch instead."

She smiled up at him. "That sounds very nice."

As soon as he was back in his town house, Ronsard placed a secure call to the villa. Cara answered immediately, though it was late, after one A.M.

"Consult that computer of yours," he said. "I want to know whatever you can find out about Niema Jamieson, from New Hampshire. She's a widow, a friend of the American ambassador, and she's visiting them now."

"How do you spell her name?"

Ronsard hesitated, then remembered what she had said about her mother modeling the name on 'Naomi.' "N-i-e-m-a," he said. "Late twenties, early thirties. Dark hair and eyes."

"Got it. When do you want this?"

"In the morning."

"I'll get right on it."

Ronsard hung up and paced slowly around his luxurious bedroom. It had been a long time since he had been so intrigued by a woman, but that didn't mean he was careless. If Niema Jamieson wasn't what she seemed, he'd know it soon enough. And if she was, then he looked forward to a pleasant chase and seduction. Most women could be had, eventually, and he doubted she would be any different.

He had forgotten how pleasurable it was to be the pursuer, to feel that triumphant thrill when she agreed to meet him for lunch. He laughed at himself; such a small victory, but he felt like a conqueror. He would put a satisfied smile on the widow's face yet.

She had been faithful to her husband's memory for two years. Such steadfastness was rare in his world. He found he respected her for that and envied her the love she must have known. Such a love had eluded him; he loved Mariette, of course, and Laure was his heart, but a sweeping, romantic love . . . no, he hadn't known one. Passion, yes. Lust. Possession. But not love. He suspected he never would love anyone in such a manner, that he wasn't capable of that depth of emotion. Or perhaps he was simply too wary, too guarded, with too much at stake to let himself become vulnerable.

Not even for a woman like Niema Jamieson.

CHAPTER FIFTEEN

T he telephone beside her bed rang at six A.M., jerking Niema out of a sound sleep. She rolled over and groped for the receiver. "Hello." She sounded as groggy as she felt.

She heard a stifled chuckle. "You certainly sound alert."

John. The sound of his voice did funny things to the pit of her stomach. She settled herself deeper into the pillow. "We social butterflies need our sleep."

"Has the fluttering attracted any attention?"

"It certainly has." She yawned. "Within minutes."

"Told you. We're amoebas."

"I hope this line is secure," she said in sudden alarm.

"If it isn't, then the Company isn't doing its job. All lines into the embassy are secure, and I'm on a secure phone. Tell me everything about last night."

How did he know she'd met Ronsard last night? she wondered in annoyance. "Are you keeping tabs on me? How? Where are you?"

"Of course I'm keeping tabs on you," he said calmly. "You didn't think I'd bring you into this and just leave you on your own, did you? I'm nearby, for the moment."

And that was all he intended to tell her, she realized. Still, it was enough. Until she heard his voice, she hadn't realized how much she had missed him, missed the constant challenge of his presence. If he was nearby, that meant she had to be on her toes, because he could pop up at any second. She didn't want to step out of the shower, stark naked, and come face to face with him. On the other hand . . .

Whoa. She backed away from that thought without finishing it. Instead she began a recital of the previous night's events. "He followed me onto the patio and introduced himself and asked for a dance later. When we danced, he asked me out to dinner. I refused. We're having lunch today at one, at Le Café Marly. Do you know where that is?"

"It's in the Richelieu wing of the Louvre. It's where you go to see and be seen."

"And here I thought having lunch with him would be more discreet than dinner."

"Not at Café Marly. Why are you trying to be discreet?"

"If I'm this fine upstanding citizen and an old family friend of the ambassador's wife, it would seem more reasonable to at least *worry* about seeing an arms dealer."

"Ronsard is seen by every influential person in Paris," John said dryly.

"Yes, but I'm different." She said that with an airiness that had him chuckling.

"When will you give in and have dinner with him? With enough time, I can arrange to have some of our people placed around you, the table wired, things like that."

"I don't think I will. I'll have lunch with him, but other than that I don't want to encourage him too much."

"Just make certain you encourage him enough to be invited to his estate."

"I'll be friends with him, but that's all."

A pause stretched over the line. "If you're trying to tell me you won't sleep with him, I never intended for you to," he finally said, his tone flattening out.

"That's good to hear, because sex was never an option. Even though I did go on those damn birth control pills the way you ordered."

Silence again. "The pills weren't in case you wanted to have an affair; they're in case something goes wrong."

She understood, then. If anything went awry and she was captured, she could be raped. "Got it," she said softly. The issue of birth control pills hadn't arisen on the job in Iran, because she had been taking the pills anyway. She and Dallas had wanted to wait a year or so, maybe longer, before starting a family.

"I'll be in touch," he said, and hung up.

Slowly she replaced the receiver and snuggled back in bed, but any chance of sleep was gone. Her brain felt alert, racing along the way it always did when she talked with John. What she needed was a good, long run. The more she thought about it, the better the plan sounded. She would ask Eleanor where the best place to jog was. She hopped out of bed and began digging out her sweats, which she had packed for a just-in-case occasion.

Not only did Eleanor know, she arranged for one of the off-duty Marines who was a dedicated jogger to run with her. Niema and the serious young man with the sidewall haircut raced side by side until they were both dripping with sweat. By the time they returned to the embassy, she had teased him out of his stiffness and he had spilled out his life story to her, as well as the details of his wedding, which would take place during his next long leave.

Feeling both energized and relaxed by the run, she showered and ate a light breakfast, then decided to get in a bit of shopping before meeting Ronsard for lunch. Eleanor gave her a list of interesting shops, and Niema ventured out into the French capital.

When the taxi let her out at Café Marly's terrace on Cour Napoleon at two minutes 'til one, she was carrying a large shopping bag. She looked at the café and for a moment a strong yearning swept over her. She would like to be meeting John for lunch in a place like this—*No*, she told herself sternly, cutting off the thought. She couldn't let herself lose focus on the job. She had to concentrate, not think about what John was or wasn't doing, and what it would be like to have lunch dates with him, and dinner dates—"I'm doing it again," she muttered.

Pushing all thoughts of him out of her mind, she entered the café and was immediately greeted. All she had to say was "Monsieur Ronsard" and she was whisked away to a table.

Ronsard was already there, smiling as he rose to his feet. He took her hand and briefly kissed it, then seated her in the chair beside him, rather than in the one across the table. "You're even lovelier today than you were last night."

"Thank you." She was wearing a classic red sheath with a single-strand pearl necklace. If he had a discerning eye, and he seemed to, he would recognize the style and quality of Chanel. She looked around, intrigued by the café. Glass walls were all that separated the café from the stunning works of art in the Louvre.

"You're glowing. Boosting a nation's economy must agree with you." He nodded meaningfully at the shopping bag.

"A woman can never have too many pairs of shoes."

"Really? How many do you have?"

"Not enough," she said firmly, and he laughed.

Today his hair was gathered at the back of his neck with a simple, round gold clasp. But even though he was dressed in trousers and a linen jacket instead of a tuxedo, and his hair was confined, every woman in the café seemed to be staring at him just as they had at the ball last night. He had a natural, exotic flamboyance that drew the eye.

Evil should show on the face, she thought. It should twist and mar the features, give some indication of its presence within a person. But if Ronsard was evil, she hadn't seen any sign of it yet. So far he had been unfailingly polite and charming, with a tenderness to his manner that didn't seem at all feigned.

"So," he said, leaning back, perfectly at ease. "Tell me: Did Madame Theriot warn you about me again?"

"Of course. Eleanor cares about me."

"She thinks I'm a danger to you?"

"She thinks you're an unsavory character."

Taken by surprise by her candor, he blinked, then laughed aloud. "Then why are you here? Do you have a yearning for danger, or do you think you can rescue me from my wicked ways?"

"Neither." She regarded him with somber, dark eyes. "I think you may be a very nice man, but I can't rescue you from anything. And you're no danger to me at all."

"I think I'm insulted," he murmured. "I would like to be a danger to you, in one particular way. You must have loved him very, very much."

"More than I can say."

"What was he like?"

A smile broke across her face. "He was . . . oh, in some ways he was extraordinary, and in others he was like most men. He made faces when he shaved; he left his clothes on the floor when he took them off. He sailed, he flew his own plane, he took CPR courses and regularly donated blood, he voted in every election. We laughed and argued and made plans, like most couples."

"He was a lucky man, to be loved so completely."

"*I* was the lucky one. And you? Have you been married?"

"No, I haven't been so fortunate." He shrugged. "Perhaps one day." But it was obvious from his tone he thought marrying was as likely as the sun rising in the west.

"I don't think your wicked reputation scares off many women," she teased. "Every female in here has been staring at you."

He didn't even glance around, as most men would have done, to see if that were true. "If I'm alone, it's because I choose to be. I was thinking last night that I'd never felt anything like what you obviously felt—still feel—for your husband. Part of me thinks it would be pleasant to love someone that much, but a part of me is very grateful that I don't. But why am I saying this?" he asked ruefully. "Telling you I don't think I'll ever love you is not a good way to convince you to have an affair with me."

Niema laughed. "Relax," she advised, patting him on the hand. "An affair wasn't on the books anyway."

He gave her a crooked smile. "But I would very much like for it to be."

She shook her head, amusement still on her face. "It can't be. All I can offer is friendship."

"In that case, I would be honored to be your friend. And I'll keep hoping," he said, his eyes twinkling.

Later that afternoon, Ronsard picked up the sheaf of papers Cara had faxed to him. He had quickly read through them when they arrived, but now he studied them more closely. There was nothing suspicious about Niema Jamieson. She was from New Hampshire, had attended an exclusive women's college, married at the age of twenty-four, and was widowed at twenty-eight. Her husband had been killed in a yachting accident. They had been mentioned a few times in society columns, usually with a descriptive tag such as "devoted couple." She was exactly what she seemed to be, a rarity in his world.

He liked her. She could be surprisingly blunt, but without malice. In a way, he even liked that she wasn't romantically interested in him. He still wanted to take her to bed, but there was no pressure from her, no expectations to be met. She had simply had lunch with him, and that was that. Afterward she had taken a taxi back to the embassy, without hinting for another invitation—which, of course, made him even more determined to see her again. He had asked her out to dinner again, only to be gently refused. He persisted until she at least agreed to another lunch.

The telephone rang, his private line, and he absently answered it. "Ronsard."

It was Cara. "Ernst Morrell has been in contact."

Ronsard's lips thinned. He neither liked nor trusted Morrell. Though by the nature of his business he dealt on a daily basis with fanatics, madmen, or plain murderers, Morrell was probably the most vicious. He was the head of a small but particularly virulent terrorist organization and had a particular fondness for bombs. He had set explosives in a hospital in Germany, killing six patients in retaliation for Germany's cooperation with the United States on a military action against Iraq.

"What does he want?"

"He's heard about RDX-a. He wants it."

Ronsard swore a lurid phrase. First Temple, and now Morrell. But Temple was one thing, and Morrell something else entirely; though he had expected information about RDX-a to leak, he hadn't expected it to happen quite so fast. He and the manufacturer had an agreement; he would be the lone conduit of the compound. Such exclusivity would be enormously profitable to both of them, at least until someone else was able to duplicate the compound. *He* had not told anyone, because the explosive still wasn't perfected; it would be much more in demand if it were reliable, rather than having an unfortunate reputation for early detonation. That meant the manufacturer was logically responsible for, as the Americans would say, everyone and his brother knowing about RDX-a.

But it seemed as if his partners had decided to sacrifice large future riches for immediate gain. He sighed. To hell with them. He would collect his percentage and issue a warning to the buyers that the compound wasn't yet reliable. He had to protect his business on that end, since the source had proven so short-sighted.

"When does he want it?" he asked in resignation, rubbing a sudden ache between his eyes.

"He didn't say. He wants to talk to you."

"Did he leave a number?"

"Yes, and he said you could reach him there only for another forty-five minutes."

That was common, at least among the more efficient organizations: They moved frequently and had only short windows of time during which they could be contacted. Such tactics greatly reduced their chances of being located.

Ronsard jotted down the number Cara recited, and as soon as their call was disconnected he began dialing. It was a London number, he saw. The rings *brrrd* in his ear, then stopped as the receiver was lifted. "Bakery." The one word was heavily accented.

Ronsard said only one word, his name. There was thirty seconds of silence, then a different voice said heartily, "You are prompt, my friend." Morrell was a stocky, barrel-chested man, but his voice was incongruously light. He always spoke as if he were throwing the words from his mouth, trying to counteract the lightness of his voice by sheer velocity.

He was not, and never would be, Morrell's friend. "You have an order, I believe."

"I hear such interesting rumors about a new recipe! I have use for one thousand kilograms."

A thousand kilograms! Ronsard's eyebrows arched. That was enough explosive to destroy London, not that Morrell would use it only in one place. No, he would wreak destruction all over the industrialized world, or perhaps sell some of it himself. "Such an amount will be very, very expensive."

"Some things are worth their cost."

"Did the rumors tell you that the recipe has not been perfected?"

"Not perfected, how?"

"The results are unreliable. Unstable."

"Ah." There was silence as Morrell processed this. No sane person wanted to work with an explosive that might go off during transport, but then, Ronsard thought with grim humor, sanity was not required with these people.

"What brings about these unfortunate results?"

"Rough handling. Being dropped, for instance."

Another "Ah." If one used RDX-a on an airplane, then it would have to be in a carry-on bag so one could control the motion—a suicide mission. Or one could always use an unsuspecting courier, as on Delta Flight 183.

"One must accept these risks," Morrell finally said, meaning that he himself would not be handling the explosive.

"There is one other problem."

"So many problems!" Now Morrell sounded petulant, as if a favorite toy had been broken.

"The recipe must be used within a certain amount of time or it will . . . perform unexpectedly. Timing must be precise."

"So I have heard, my friend, so I have heard! It is a most interesting recipe."

"A thousand kilograms is a considerable amount to be handled."

"But an organized person can handle such a task. When will the shipment be ready?"

From that statement, Ronsard deduced Morrell already had his targets selected, and that they would be hit almost simultaneously. He did not, however, have enough people in his organization to do it all himself. Different organizations occasionally cooperated with each other, especially if they had mutual enemies.

To Morrell he said, "I'm not certain. That's such a large amount; the manufacturer perhaps doesn't have that much available." In fact, Ronsard was certain of it.

"It is worth a great deal of money to me to have this recipe within two weeks."

"I'll give the manufacturer your order."

"Good, very good! I will call again tomorrow."

Ronsard hung up. He was extremely irritated; by precipitously putting RDX-a on the market, the manufacturer had increased not just their risk, but his. Such risk would have to be compensated, of course. *Highly* compensated.

Then he had an amusing thought. Production was, he knew, still very limited. An order of a thousand kilograms would be difficult to fill, and he didn't yet know how much of the compound Temple would want. Perhaps he should simply let Temple and Morrell settle between them who got the RDX-a. A showdown, as they said in the Westerns. Yes, that would definitely be amusing.

CHAPTER
SIXTEEN

I'm having a house party in three days," Ronsard said to Niema several days later as they
strolled in a small, quiet park. "At my home in
the Rhône-Alpes region, south of Lyon. The countryside is
beautiful, and my home is comfortable. I would like very
much for you to attend the party."

She was silent, her head dipped as she walked along beside
him. The canopy of trees shaded them from the warm summer
sun, and birds sang overhead. They were not the only people
enjoying the little park. Young mothers and nannies supervised
shrieking children of all ages as they dashed about, skipping
and jumping, rolling in the grass. Joggers pounded up and
down the paths, singly and in pairs. Lovers walked hand in
hand, sometimes stopping to kiss. Older people occupied the

benches, some of them playing board games, some of them just watching the activity that surrounded them. The sweet perfume of flowers lay on the warm air like the touch of a lover.

"You aren't saying anything," he observed after a moment. "Are you worried about Madame Theriot's disapproval?"

"That, and though you *say* you expect only friendship, somehow I don't think you've given up hope that . . . well, that I'll change my mind."

"Of course I hope," he said matter-of-factly. "I am a man—a Frenchman. I would like very much to sleep with you. But it's also nice just being with you. You don't want favors from me, and you don't want my money. Do you realize how few people like you I have in my life?"

"Your life is what you've made it." She glanced up at him. "I refuse to feel sorry for you."

Smiling, he caught her hand and swung it between them. "There, that is what I mean. You say what you think."

"Not always," Niema said. "I'm too polite for that."

The smile became a chuckle. "Are you insulting me?"

"Of course. You know what I think of your . . . profession."

Something closed in his eyes, some expression that was shuttered before she could read it. "We all do what we must."

"Not everyone. Some people do what they can."

"And there is a difference between 'must' and 'can'?"

"There seems to be. People say they do what they must when what they've done has hurt someone. People who do what they can are usually helping."

"A matter of semantics." He shrugged. "But perhaps you're right. I made a choice, when I was a young man, and now I mustn't whine. Perhaps I had other options, but at the time, at that age, I didn't see them. Given the same circumstances, I would make the same choice again."

There was no regret in his voice, only a pragmatic accep-
tance of who and what he was. He didn't despair over the mis-
takes he had made; there was no angst, no wrestling with his
conscience. He had set his feet on a certain path and never
looked back.

She wanted to ask him why he had made the choice he had,
but the answer seemed fairly obvious: money. He had needed
money, and that was the means he had chosen to get it. The
"why" didn't matter; by his own free will, he had put himself
across the line that divided legal from illegal. She couldn't help
liking him, but at the same time she had no qualms about pre-
senting herself to him under false pretenses. Ronsard was an
adversary, however friendly and charming he might be.

"My profession aside, I still want an answer to my invitation."

"A house party." That was exactly the function to which
John had wanted her to get invited, but there was no enthusi-
asm in her voice. "How large a party?"

That question had him smiling again. "Are you wondering if
it would be a party of two, which I would much prefer? I
believe there are about a hundred people invited."

"Then your house must be more than just 'comfortable,' "
she said dryly.

"Perhaps that was an understatement. But there are separate
guest quarters that house half that number, so not everyone is
staying under the same roof."

"That is still a large roof."

"Yes, it is. Don't hold my roof against me, please."

She laughed. "I'm sure it's a very nice roof. Would you mind
if I ask who the other guests are?"

His eyes gleamed. "You wouldn't ask unless you were considering accepting," he said with satisfaction. "You met many

of the same guests at the prime minister's ball that you'll meet at my home."

Many, but not all. Undoubtedly some of his guests were the sort who wouldn't be invited to government functions. It was a cynical world, when the lawmakers and the lawbreakers mingled together behind the scenes. John would be there, as one of the latter group. She wondered if he would be surprised at any of the other guests, then dismissed the idea. No, he wouldn't be surprised. He probably knew of them all.

"Please say yes," he cajoled. "I won't be in Paris much longer, and your visit may end before I return."

"Yes," she said, and sighed. "I'll probably go home afterward. It would be awkward for me to visit you, then come back to the embassy. I don't want to do anything that would damage Albert's career."

He was silent as they walked along. Perhaps he didn't like being told associating with him had repercussions for others, but she wasn't going to sugarcoat anything for him. She had a job to do, and so far her instincts had been on target; so many people sucked up to him, and he was pursued by so many women that the very fact she didn't made her memorable to him.

"So I won't see you again after you leave the house party," he finally said. He gave her a wry smile. "I don't think we normally travel in the same circles."

"No," she said. "We don't."

"Then it's all the more important for you to come. There's someone I'd like for you to meet."

"I got the invitation," she told John the next morning when he called.

"Good. When are you going?"

"Day after tomorrow."

"I won't be there until the next day. There's a fancy-dress party that night, and I'll probably schedule my arrival during the party."

"How do you know the schedule? And why in the middle of the party?"

"Everyone's attention will be splintered, including Ronsard's. It's just a small advantage for me, but every detail matters. We don't know his security arrangements, the floor plan, or his schedule, so we'll have to play that part by ear. Don't forget, I'll be smitten by you the first time I see you, so we'll have an excuse to be together."

"I'm turning into a love goddess," she muttered. "Men are being smitten left and right."

He laughed quietly. "Maybe you've found your niche in life."

"Smiting men?"

"I think you could get to like it."

"That depends on what I'm smiting them with."

"See you in three days, Mata."

Ronsard left that day for his villa, so she didn't have lunch with him for the first time since they had met. Glad of the downtime, she spent a good portion of the day assembling the things she would need once she got to Ronsard's house. The CIA station chief in the embassy was of great help in procuring the tiny transmitters, batteries, and wiring she needed. If he asked any questions, he didn't ask them of her. She knew he had to have cleared everything with Langley for him to be as cooperative as he was.

The station chief didn't know anything about the job she was doing, just that he was to get whatever she needed; the Paris-based CIA contingent didn't even know she had been meeting Ronsard, unless one of the case officers had taken it on himself to follow her one day, but she couldn't think why they would. So far as any of them had known until now, she had simply been a friend, visiting the ambassador and his wife.

Lyon was about three hundred kilometers from Paris, farther than she wanted to drive, so she booked a flight and called the number Ronsard had given her to arrange to be picked up at the airport.

She was eager to arrive, to look around and see what she had to deal with, so she could make concrete plans and decisions. Being a socialite, even a subdued one, wasn't her cup of tea. She wanted to do something besides shop and have lunch and attend parties.

The weather was beautiful the day she flew down to Lyon, the flight smooth. She was met at the airport by a man in a stylish gray suit, his blond hair cut military short and his eyes hidden by sunglasses. He didn't speak other than when it was necessary, but he was efficient. He collected her luggage and handed her into a silver Jaguar, and she settled back to enjoy the drive.

They went south on the expressway, then turned east, toward Grenoble. The region was beautiful, perhaps the most beautiful in France, with the French Alps rising in the east. The weather was warmer than it had been in Paris, the heat radiating through the expensive tinted glass of the Jaguar's windows.

Her first view of Ronsard's villa made her blink in astonishment, and she was glad she was wearing sunglasses to hide her expression. After all, she was supposed to be used to wealth and luxury. John should have warned her, she thought absently.

A sleekly paved drive, bordered with multi-colored flowers,

led up to massive gates set in a twelve-foot-high gray stone wall that completely encircled the estate. The stone in the wall alone had to have been an enormous expense. The gates slid smoothly open as the car approached; when they drove through, the gates started closing again almost immediately.

The estate itself was massive; she estimated at least forty acres had been enclosed, though the grounds had been so artfully landscaped there were sections where she couldn't see the wall at all. The house itself—though she doubted a structure that huge could be called a mere house—was four stories high, with wings stretching out on each side. It had been built with huge slabs of pale, luminous gray marble, with faint streaks of pink and gold running through the stone. The effect was stunning.

To the right was a long, two-story building that was rather barrackslike in style, though more of that incredible landscaping went a long way toward disguising it. To the left, set like a jewel on a picturesque pond, was what looked like another house. She guessed that this was the guest quarters Ronsard had mentioned. It was large enough to be a small hotel, and looked small only in comparison to the massiveness of the main building.

Illegal arms–dealing had to be a very, very lucrative business.

Until now she hadn't had any grasp of Ronsard's wealth, but now she had a better idea why he was pursued for his money.

There were men in shades everywhere—his private army. There seemed to be a system of dress to designate authority. Most of the men wore a dark green uniform-type pants and shirt, and these men carried weapons openly. Next in number were those wearing dark green pants, but white shirts, and

they wore only side arms. Fewest in number were those wearing light gray suits like her driver.

A number of guests had already arrived. They were wander-
ing in the formal gardens, casually but expensively dressed in
what she had always thought of as country-manor style. Some
sat on a side patio, indulging in cocktails. Six industrious indi-
viduals were on the tennis courts, batting the chartreuse ball
back and forth with increasing languor as the heat sapped
their strength.

Ronsard himself came down the broad, shallow steps to
meet her, smiling, and his hands extended as she got out of the
car. He took her shoulders in a light grasp and, bending,
brushed his lips across her cheek. Startled, she drew back and
blinked up at him. That was the first time he had done more
than kiss her hand, and she must have looked uneasy because
he rolled his eyes.

"One would think, from your expression, that I had
attempted to remove your dress," he said dryly. "If my ego had
been inflated, it would now be as flat as yesterday's champagne." He gave a rueful shake of his head. "And to think I've
missed this."

"I'm sorry, I was just startled."

"No, don't apologize and ruin the effect."

"Now you're making me feel guilty."

"I'm teasing." He smiled down at her, then said briefly to
the two young staffers who stood behind him like sentinels.
"Put Madame's luggage in the Garden room."

"The Garden room," she repeated. "That sounds lovely."

"It's actually a small suite. I want you to be comfortable.
And before your suspicious nature rears its ugly head, no, it is
not next to my private suite. None of the guest rooms are."

"Consider my suspicions headed off at the pass." She took

his arm, and he led her inside, where delicious coolness and airy space replaced the heat of outside.

Marble columns soared to a painted ceiling three stories high. The floor was granite flagstones, in a darker hue than the pale gray of the columns, and dotted by enormous, richly colored rugs with tight, thick weaves. Twin marble staircases curved to the left and right, coming together at the top of the arch with hallways opening off each side.

"I hope you're providing tour maps to everyone, so they don't get lost," she said as he escorted her up the stairs.

"The design is basically simple," he began, and smiled at the disbelieving look she gave him. "There aren't any cul-de-sacs. All secondary hallways lead directly back to the main hallway. If you have a sense of direction, you can find your way back to here without any difficulty."

As they mounted the stairs she looked up at an enormous tapestry hung on the left wall. "How old is your house?"

"It isn't old at all. It was built in the seventies by one of the Middle-Eastern oil billionaires. When the price of oil dropped, he needed to raise cash, and I was in a position to provide it."

Upstairs, the marble stairs gave way to dove-gray carpeting so thick her feet sank into it. Light streamed through Palladian windows; walking over to look out, she saw an enormous swimming pool in the courtyard below; the pool was irregularly shaped so that it resembled a lake, exquisitely landscaped, with a small waterfall sparkling over rocks before cascading back into the transparent turquoise water.

"The pool must be spectacular at night, like another world," she said.

"It's one of my pleasures. A long swim is relaxing after a difficult day."

He led her along the hallway, turned left down a secondary

hallway, then opened a door on the right. "Here is the Garden room. I hope you will be comfortable."

Niema stepped inside, and her eyes lit with pleasure. "It's beautiful."

The reason it was called the Garden room was obvious: It was filled with greenery. Besides the lovely arrangements of cut flowers, there were eight-foot tall areca palms in strategic locations, succulent jade, rhododendrons. They were in a small sitting room; double doors to the right were opened to reveal a sumptuous bedroom. Straight ahead, glass doors opened onto a private balcony that was lush with potted trees and flowers. The balcony was the width of both the sitting room and bedroom, perhaps forty feet wide.

Ronsard was watching her move around the suite, touching the plants, smelling the flowers. "This is a peaceful place. I thought you would enjoy it; an escape from the social whirl."

"Thank you," she said sincerely. His thoughtfulness in providing this retreat was touching. He was correct in thinking she enjoyed occasional solitude and serenity in which to recharge, but as she looked around she realized that the balcony would also provide an excellent means of clandestine entry, à la Medina. She would make certain the glass doors were always unlocked—not that they would provide much difficulty to someone as adept at breaking and entering as John was.

Her luggage had already been deposited on a padded bench at the foot of the bed. Ronsard took her arm. "A maid will unpack for you. If you aren't too tired, I have someone I'd like you to meet."

"No, I'm not tired," she said, remembering he had mentioned in Paris that he wanted her to meet someone. The electronic supplies she had brought were safely locked in her jewelry case, so she wasn't worried about the maid seeing them and reporting to Ronsard that one of his guests had brought some interesting equipment with her.

"My private wing is on the other side of the house," he said and smiled. "I wasn't lying when I said your suite wasn't next door to mine. I wish it was, but I deliberately remodeled so that the guest rooms were somewhat distant."

"For privacy, or protection?"

"Both." A tender look swept his face, an expression all the more astonishing because it seemed to be directed elsewhere. "But not my privacy, and not my protection. Come. I told her I was bringing someone to see her, and she has been excited all day, waiting."

"She?"

"My daughter. Laure."

CHAPTER
SEVENTEEN

H is daughter? John hadn't mentioned that Ronsard had a daughter. Niema tried to hide her surprise. "You've never mentioned her before," she said. "I thought your sister was your only family."

"Ah, well, perhaps I'm paranoid. I do everything I can to safeguard her. As you pointed out, I'm an unsavory character; I have enemies."

"I said *Eleanor* thinks you're an unsavory character," she corrected.

"She's right, you know. I'm far too unsavory for a woman like you."

She rolled her eyes. "Smooth, Ronsard. Women probably

fall all over you when you warn them that you're too dangerous for them."

"Have I ever mentioned you have this annoying habit of
seeing through my ploys?" he asked conversationally, and they
both laughed.

They weren't the only people in the hallway. They passed
several guests, all of whom had to speak to their host. One
gentleman looked familiar, and he swept her with a knowing
look. It took her a moment to place him as the horse-racing
afficionado she had met at the prime minister's ball. She
smiled at him and asked how his horse had finished in the
weekend's race.

"You have a slave for life," Ronsard said as they continued
down the hall. "He bores everyone with his talk of horses and
racing."

"I like horses," she replied serenely. "And it doesn't take any
more effort to be nice to someone than it does to be nasty."

Getting from one side of the huge villa to the other took
some time, especially when he was continually stopped. At
last, however, they passed into his private wing, which was
guarded by heavy wooden double doors. "My suite is here," he
said, indicating another set of double doors on the left. He
showed her a family dining room, a den that surprised her
with its coziness, a small movie theater, an enormous play-
room filled with all manner of toys and games, a library so
packed with books she doubted he could get another volume
on the shelves. The titles were both fiction and nonfiction,
with an amazing variety of children's books mixed in.

"This is one of Laure's favorite rooms," he said. "She loves
to read. Of course, she has outgrown fairy tales and Dr. Seuss,
but I make certain there is always a selection of reading material appropriate to her age."

"How old *is* she?"

"Twelve. It's a delightful age. She's hovering between child-hood and adolescence, unable to decide if she wants to play with her dolls or experiment with lipstick. I've forbidden the lipstick for another year, at least," he said, his lips quirking.

He turned to her, a smile still on his lips, but his eyes were somehow looking beyond her. "Laure is small for her age," he said. "Very small. I want to prepare you. Her health is . . . not good. Every moment I have her is a gift from God."

An odd thing for a man like Ronsard to say, but then again, perhaps it wasn't. He opened a door into a room so cheerful and charming Niema caught her breath, and they stepped inside.

"Papa!"

The voice was young, sweet, as pure as the finest crystal. There was a whirring sound and she came rolling toward them in a motorized wheelchair, a tiny doll with an animated face and a smile that lit the world. An oxygen tank was attached to the back of the wheelchair, and transparent tubing ran from the tank to her nostrils, held in place by a narrow band around her head.

"Laure." His voice was filled with an aching tenderness. He leaned down and kissed her. He spoke in English. "This is my friend, Madame Jamieson. Niema, this is my heart, my daughter, Laure."

Niema bent forward and extended her hand. "I'm very pleased to meet you," she said, also in English.

"And I you, madame." The young girl shook Niema's hand; her fingers were painfully fragile in Niema's careful clasp. Ronsard had said his daughter was twelve; she was the size of a six-year-old, probably weighing only about fifty pounds. She was so very, very thin, her skin a bluish white. She had Ronsard's eyes, dark blue and intelligent, and an angel's smile set in an alabaster face. Her hair was a silky light brown, brushed to a careful smoothness and tied back with a festive bow.

She was wearing lipstick.

Ronsard noticed it the same time Niema did. "Laure!" he exclaimed. He put his hands on his hips and gave her a stern look. "I forbade you to wear lipstick."

She gave him a long-suffering look, as if she despaired of ever making him understand. "I wanted to look nice, Papa. For Madame Jamieson."

"You are beautiful as you are; you don't need lipstick. You are too young for makeup."

"Yes, but you're my papa," she said with unassailable logic. "You *always* think I'm beautiful."

"I think the shade is very flattering," Niema said, because females should always stick together. She wasn't lying; Laure displayed an intelligence beyond her years by choosing a delicate shade of rose and using only a light application. Anything more would have looked garish in such an unearthly pale face. She ignored the girl's tiny size; what was important here was her mind, not her body.

Ronsard's eyebrows flew up in disbelief. "You're taking the part of this . . . this disobedient hoyden?"

Laure giggled at hearing herself described as a hoyden. Niema met Ronsard's accusing look with an innocent expression and a shrug. "Of course. What did you expect me to do?"

"Agree with him," Laure said. "He expects *all* of his women to agree with him."

This time Ronsard's astonishment wasn't feigned. Stunned at hearing such a statement issuing from his innocent daughter's lips, he stared speechlessly at her.

"But I'm not one of his women," Niema pointed out. "I'm just a friend."

"He has never brought any of the others to meet me. Since he brought *you,* I thought perhaps he wants you to be my *maman.*"

Ronsard made a little choking sound. Niema ignored him to grin at the child. "No, it's nothing like that. We aren't in love with each other, and besides, your papa is allergic to marriage."

"I know, but he would marry if he thought that was what I want. He spoils me terribly. He will get anything I ask for, so I try not to ask for very much, or he would be too busy to do anything else."

She was an alarming blend of childlike innocence and trust, and an astuteness far beyond her years. Whatever her physical problems were, they had forced her to look inward much earlier than young people usually learned to do. "While he is recovering," she said, briskly turning the wheelchair, "I'll show you my rooms."

Niema strolled beside the chair while Laure gave her a guided tour of her suite. Everything had been specially outfitted so she could reach it from a wheelchair, and attached to one side of the chair was a long pair of tongs so she could pick up anything she dropped. A middle-aged woman came forward, smiling, to be introduced as Laure's nurse, Bernadette. Her bedroom opened off Laure's, so she was available during the night if she was needed.

Anything that could possibly interest a young girl had been made available. There were books, movies, dolls, games, samplers she had made, fashion magazines. Laure showed all of them to Niema, while Ronsard trailed behind, bewildered and bemused at being made to feel unnecessary.

Laure even showed Niema her makeup case. Ronsard made choking noises again. This was not a little girl's pretend makeup, but the real stuff from Dior, stunningly packaged in a silver train case. "I ordered it," Laure said, unperturbed by her father's horror. "But nothing looks right when I put it on. Even the lipstick is too . . . too much like a clown. Today, I rubbed my finger on the stick, then on my lips."

"That's good. It's called staining," Niema said, pulling a chair over to sit beside the girl and taking the train case on her lap. She began pulling out the sleek containers of makeup. "Makeup is like anything else, it takes practice to use. And some things will never look good because they don't flatter your coloring. You learn by experimenting. Would you like me to show you?"

"Oh, please," Laure said eagerly, leaning forward.

"I forbid it," Ronsard said, with more desperation than sternness. "She is too young—"

"Louis," Niema interrupted. "Go away. This is girl stuff."

He didn't go away. He sat down, a charmingly helpless expression on his face, watching as Niema demonstrated how to use each item.

A pink blush was much too dark for that white face. Niema took a tissue and wiped most of it off, leaving only a delicate tint. "Remember, none of this sets into stone when you apply it. If it is too much, wipe part of it off. I always have a tissue and cotton swabs with me when I put on makeup, so I can make the effect more subtle. Do you see my eyeliner?" She leaned closer, and Laure nodded as she stared hard at Niema's eyes.

"I use a black pencil, like this—very soft, so it doesn't pull my skin. Then I use a swab to wipe most of it away, so it's barely noticeable. But my coloring is dark, while yours is fair, so black would be too harsh for you. When you are old enough to start wearing eyeliner, use a soft gray or taupe—"

The makeup lesson went on, with Laure hanging on every

word. Under Niema's tutelage, very little was actually applied to the small, skeletal face, just the merest hint of color. Laure peered in a mirror, studied herself, and smiled. "Now I don't look so ill," she said with satisfaction. "Thank you very much, Madame Jamieson. Were you watching, Papa?"

"Yes, I was watching. It looks very nice, but—"

"If I die, I want you to make certain someone puts makeup on me just like this. I do not want to look sick when I reach Heaven."

All the color drained out of Ronsard's face. Niema felt stricken on his behalf, but also for this little girl who had never in her life known what it was to enjoy good health, to run and play like other children.

"I won't wear it now, I promise," she said. "Not even lipstick, though I do like it. But . . . *if*. Promise me, Papa."

"I promise." His voice sounded hoarse, strained, unlike Ronsard's normal suave tones.

She reached over and patted his knee, the child comforting the parent. "You may take the case," she said, "and keep it safe for me. That way you will always know where it is."

He lifted her out of the wheelchair and settled her on his lap, taking care not to dislodge the oxygen tube. She was so frail, so tiny; her legs dangled like a kindergartner's. He couldn't speak for a moment, his dark head bent so that his cheek rested on the top of her head. "You won't need it for a long, long time," he finally said.

"I know." Her eyes, though, held a different knowledge.

She seemed to be tiring. He touched her cheek. "Do you want to lie down for a while?"

"On the longue," she said. "There is a movie I wish to see."

Bernadette came over and pushed the wheelchair and its container of oxygen while he carried Laure to the plush chaise longue and carefully placed her on it. Under the rose stain, the child's lips held a tinge of blue. He covered her legs with a soft blanket while Bernadette arranged the pillows just so, propping her in a comfortable position.

"There!" she said, squirming back against the pillows. "I am in the perfect position for watching movies." She gave him a sly look. "It is a romance."

He had recovered his aplomb. "You will give me gray hair," he announced, feigning a scowl. "A romance!"

"With sex," she added mischievously.

"Tell me no more," he said, holding up his hands as if to ward off anything else she might say. "I don't want to know. A papa can bear only so much. Tell Madame Jamieson good day, and we'll leave you to your romance."

Laure held out her hand. "Good day, madame. That was fun! Will you visit me again?"

"Of course," Niema said, smiling despite the ache in her chest. "I've very much enjoyed meeting you, mademoiselle. Your papa is lucky to have you as his daughter."

Laure looked up at her father, and again the expression in her eyes was far too old for her years. "I am the one who is lucky," she said.

He kissed her, touched her cheek, and left her with a smile. His grip on Niema's hand, however, was almost bone-shattering.

When they were out in the hallway, he said, *"Dieu,"* in a stifled tone, and bent over from the waist, bracing his hands on his knees while he took deep breaths.

Niema automatically reached out to offer him comfort. She hesitated, her hand in midair, then lightly touched his back.

After a moment he straightened and walked farther down the hall away from Laure's rooms before he spoke again.

"Sometimes it is more than I can bear," he said, his voice still constrained. "I apologize. I hadn't realized she—I've tried to keep from her how very ill she is, but she's so intelligent . . ." The words trailed off.

"What's wrong with her?" Niema asked gently. There was a decanter of liquor and a set of glasses on a side table. She went over to it and poured him a hefty portion of whatever liquor it was. He downed it without question.

"Too much," he said, turning the empty glass around and around in his hands. "If it was any one thing, there would be things that could be done. She has a defective heart, only one kidney, and cystic fibrosis. The CF seems to affect her digestive system more than her lungs, or she likely would have already—"

He broke off, his throat working. "There are new drugs that help, but it's still so difficult for her to get the nutrients she needs. She eats constantly, but she doesn't grow and doesn't gain weight. What growth she *has* had strains her heart. A heart transplant is out of the question because of the cystic fibrosis." He gave a bitter little smile that wasn't a smile at all. "Finding a suitable heart is almost impossible. She would have to have a young child's heart, because of her size, and donor hearts from children are rare. And her blood type is A negative, which narrows the chance of finding a heart almost to zero. Even if one came available, the opinion of the medical establishment is that a healthy heart shouldn't be wasted on someone who . . . who has so many other problems."

There was nothing to say. She couldn't offer meaningless phrases of hope when Laure's condition couldn't get much more hopeless.

"I've been trying to find a heart on the black market for years." He stared blindly at the glass in his hands. "I pour money into research on genetic treatments for CF, on new drugs, anything that will buy her some time. If I can fix just one thing—just one!" he said fiercely. "Then she will have a chance."

Realization slammed into her like a blow. "That's why you—" She stopped, not needing to finish the sentence.

He finished it for her. "Became an illegal arms dealer? Yes. I had to have enormous sums of money, and quickly. The choice was drugs or weapons. I chose weapons. If anything—*anything*—happens that will increase her chances, whether it's a heart miraculously coming available or a new treatment, I have to be ready immediately with the cash. The research is also hideously expensive." He shrugged. "She is my child," he said simply. "The devil may have my soul, but he's welcome to it if she can live."

She had known there were layers to him. Except for his occupation, he had seemed to be an honorable man, as if he completely separated the two halves of his life. What he did was abhorrent, but he did it out of his consuming love for his child. She ached for him, and for Laure.

"What of Laure's mother?"

"She was a . . . passing fancy. She didn't want to have the baby, but I convinced her to carry it to term. I paid all of her expenses and gave her a large lump sum for her trouble. I don't believe she ever saw Laure. The doctors told her the baby probably would not live, and she left. I brought Laure home with me.

"I wasn't poor. My family was more than comfortable. But it wasn't enough, not if I wanted my baby to live. So I used my entrée into the Parisian upper crust to both provide contacts and protect my efforts. Don't look at me with such heartbreak in your eyes, my dear. I'm not gallant or tragic, I'm ruthless and pragmatic. My one true vulnerability is my daughter, and for her I am putty, as you saw. She can be quite ruthless in handling me, a quality she doubtless inherited from me."

"The heartbreak is for her, not you," Niema said tartly. "You made your choice."

"I would make the same choice again, as I told you before. And you might do the same." He eyed her, a cynical smile hovering on his mouth. "You never know what you might do until your child is involved."

She couldn't argue with that, not if she were honest. She wasn't the type of person who could accept, without a fight, her child's death sentence. If possible she would move heaven and earth, and if it wasn't possible she would try anyway. That was what Ronsard had done. Though she didn't agree with his path, his reaction was the same as hers would have been.

He set the glass down with a decisive thunk and got to his feet. He ran his fingers through his loosened hair and worked his shoulders as if loosening tense muscles. "I have a hundred guests waiting for me," he said. "Perhaps I should begin fulfilling my duties as host. But I wanted you to meet Laure, and . . . know that part of me. Thank you for taking the time to show her about the makeup. I had no idea."

"How could you?" Niema's heart broke all over again, thinking of the young girl who wanted to look her best when she died.

"I forbid you to cry."

She squared her shoulders. "I'm not crying. But I will if I want to, and you can't stop me."

He held up his hands. "I surrender. Come, let's rejoin the party."

As they left his private wing, a tall, blonde Valkyrie of a woman approached. "I hate to disturb you," she said to Ronsard. Her accent was pure American. "But several details have come up that need your attention."

He nodded. "Niema, this is Cara Smith, my secretary. Cara, Niema Jamieson. Will you excuse me, my dear?" he asked Niema. "Duty calls."

"Certainly." Niema watched him stride off down the stairs, with Cara half a step behind him. She noted the direction in which he went; his office must be on the first floor, then, and in the west wing.

She ached with sympathy for both him and Laure. That would not, however, get in the way of her doing her job.

She walked casually in the same direction, but by the time she crossed the huge central foyer he wasn't in sight. They had disappeared through one of several doors, and it would be too obvious if she walked through the villa opening all the doors.

But at least she now had a general idea of his office's location. She would try to get him to give her a guided tour of the main floor, and surely he would indicate which room was his office.

Tomorrow, John would arrive. If she already had the location, they could possibly plant the bug and copy Ronsard's files tomorrow night.

Anticipation zinged through her. John would be here tomorrow.

CHAPTER

EIGHTEEN

It was ten o'clock at night when John drove up to Ronsard's estate. The grounds were so well-lit that he could see the glow from several miles away. The curving drive led him to a set of double gates, which remained closed as he approached. When he stopped, a uniformed guard came out to shine a flashlight in John's face, ask his name, and see his identity. Silently John reached inside his tuxedo jacket and produced his ID. He didn't give his name verbally, an omission that made the guard glance sharply at him, then step away to speak into the two-way radio he carried.

A moment later, he gave a signal and the gates swung open. The signal, John surmised, meant that the guard on the outside couldn't open the gates himself. He had to give the okay to someone else inside, which eliminated the chance that he could be overpowered and access gained to the estate.

He gave John another hard look as he leaned down to return the identification to him. John returned the look without expression, then drove through the gates.

He stopped the car in front of a massive curving entry and got out. Immediately a pair of red-jacketed valets approached; one got out his luggage, while the other gave him a ticket, got into the car, and drove it away. It would probably receive a thorough search while it was in their possession, John thought. His luggage, too.

Let them search. They wouldn't get any information from it, not even his fingerprints. He had carefully sprayed his fingertips with a clear-coat gel that hardened and provided a smooth finish. It was thin and very nearly undetectable to the touch and would come off when he washed his hands with hot water. A cold-water wash wouldn't disturb the gel.

The spray was a vast improvement over the methods he had used in the past; sometimes he would dip his fingertips into puddles of melted wax, but the wax wasn't very durable. For a brief job or an emergency, however, it would do. Another trick was to paint his fingertips with a thick application of clear fingernail polish, but he had to have time for it to dry or that was useless. Band-Aids wrapped around each finger were a quick and effective method of hiding his prints, but someone with bandages on every finger was noticeable—at least, if that someone was over three years old.

As he mounted the steps, a tall, tuxedo-clad man approached. "Mr. Temple," he said in a crisp British accent. "Mr. Ronsard will see you now. Follow me, please."

John silently followed, not inclined to exchange pleasantries. He could hear music, and people in formal dress stood in small groups, laughing and chattering in a mix of languages. The women glittered in jewels, and so did some of the men. His own tuxedo was severely cut, without a frill or ruffle in sight, but the cut and fit shouted that it was custom made for him. Several women glanced his way, then looked again. When he wanted, he could pass through a crowd completely unnoticed, but tonight he wanted people to notice. He walked with a silent, graceful saunter, like a panther that has seen its prey but knows there's no need to hurry.

The elegant flunky led him to a small anteroom off the foyer. The room was comfortably furnished with a sofa and two wing-back chairs, a cozy little selection of books, a small fireplace, and a selection of spirits. Considering that the room was no more than eight feet square, and that the door had a sturdy lock, John guessed that it was there more for quick and furtive lovemaking than it was for any other purpose. A good host always provided for his guests, after all.

"Monsieur Temple." Ronsard rose to his feet as John entered. He nodded a dismissal at the other man, who silently closed the door behind him as he left. "I am Louis Ronsard." He extended his hand, every inch a gracious host.

John let a fraction of a second lapse before he took Ronsard's hand. Not a flicker of expression crossed his face. "Why am I here?" he finally asked, his tone low and controlled. "This . . . meeting wasn't necessary."

"I think it is." Ronsard was slick about it, but he was carefully studying John's face. "I don't like dealing with unknown factors. Moreover, you knew about a compound that is very new and supposed to be unknown. Would you mind telling me how you came to hear of it?"

John regarded him silently, eyes at half-mast. "*I* don't like to be called by name in the middle of a crowd, and my definition

of a crowd is any number greater than two." Let Ronsard wait
for his answers; he wasn't in the mood to be cooperative.

"I assure you, no one here has any idea who you are."

"And I assure you, there's always at least one person at
parties like this who is making a list of names, to be sold
afterward."

"I deal harshly with betrayal," Ronsard said softly. Evidently
deciding Temple wasn't a man who could be charmed, impressed, or intimidated, he indicated the chairs. "Please, be
seated. Would you like a drink?"

John chose one of the wing-back chairs. "I don't drink."

Ronsard paused with his hand on a decanter, his eyebrows
lifted, then moved his hand to a bottle and poured himself a
small amount of wine.

"I apologize if you think coming here has jeopardized your
cover. But I'm a cautious man too, and handling this compound is not without its own risk. I do so only when I am
assured that this is a legitimate order and that I am not being
set up. So, given the secrecy surrounding the compound, I
think you understand why I am interested in learning how you
heard of it."

John steepled his fingers, staring unblinkingly at Ronsard
for a long moment. He saw Ronsard's gaze flicker to the ring
of entwined snakes on his left hand. "Flight 183," he finally
said.

"The plane crash? Yes, that was unfortunate. I suspected it
was a . . . test, shall we say? I wasn't aware beforehand."

"I don't care if it was a test or not. It worked."

"But how did you find what explosive was used?"

"I . . . obtained a copy of the NTSB preliminary chemical
analysis. I have access to a very good lab in Switzerland. The
chemical fingerprint was similar to RDX. The NTSB found no

evidence of a detonator. It's self explanatory," John said, his tone bored.

"Do you really think I would believe you put all this together by extrapolation?" Ronsard smiled gently. "No, someone told you. A second party has also approached me wanting to buy a quantity of the compound, someone who has no access to the NTSB. How could *he* know, unless by the same leak?"

"Ernst Morrell," John supplied. "I told him."

Ronsard stared at him a moment, then drank his wine. "You surprise me," he murmured.

"Morrell will provide a . . . distraction. Anything that happens will be laid at his feet."

"So he is a decoy." Ronsard shook his head, smiling. "Mr. Temple, I salute you. That is truly devious."

John relaxed, subtly but visibly. The stony expression on his face eased. He let himself blink. "If I'm lucky, the bastard will blow himself up. If I'm not lucky, he'll still bring so much heat down on himself he'll be caught. Either way, he won't step on my toes again."

"So you've met Morrell before?"

"No, but he's a blundering idiot. He interfered in a job."

Ronsard laughed, his handsome face lit with real amusement. "Monsieur Temple, I think it will be a pleasure doing business with you. We'll talk more, but I've been away from my guests too long, and I must get back to them. Come, I'll introduce you around."

"Introduce me as Mr. Smith."

"Smith," Ronsard repeated. He still looked amused. "That's my secretary's last name as well."

"Maybe we're related."

They drew more than one interested gaze when they left the

LINDA HOWARD

anteroom. John walked with his host across the huge foyer and into a glittering ballroom. They stopped at the top of three shallow steps, looking out over the crowd. Enormous crystal chandeliers hung overhead, glittering like diamonds, and a wall of French glass doors had been opened to the night. People moved around the room, out to the patio, back in, in a constant motion that reminded him of a hive.

He looked casually around, not letting his gaze rest on anyone in particular, but he spotted Niema almost immediately. An industrialist approached Ronsard and made polite chitchat for a moment, then waited expectantly for an introduction. John had met the man before, but he'd been using a different name at the time, and with his appearance altered; his hair had been gray and he had worn brown contacts. The industrialist thought he was shaking hands with a total stranger.

A voluptuous redhead, her breasts all but bared in a skintight emerald green gown, was the next to attach herself to Ronsard's arm and angle for an introduction. Ronsard, obviously amused, obliged. John became his most impassive, not responding to any of the woman's flirtatious remarks. For all her obviousness, she was no fool; after a few minutes she switched her flirtatiousness to Ronsard, who smiled and flattered her, all the while with that look of amusement still in his eyes.

After the woman left, they were briefly alone. John let his gaze sweep the ballroom once again, and he went still.

Ronsard noticed immediately, of course. "Do you see someone you know?" he asked, becoming subtly more alert as he looked around.

"No." The word sounded as if it were being dragged out of John's throat. "Someone I'm going to know. That woman—who is she?"

212

"Who?"

"Dark hair, blue gown. Wearing pearls. She's talking to the tall blonde woman."

Ronsard's search narrowed on Niema. His face hardened as he realized she was the woman John had noticed. "She's with me," he said in succinct warning.

John spared his host only a glance before once more focusing on her. He let himself greedily drink her in, admiring the way the soft light gleamed on her bare shoulders. "Are you going to marry her?" he asked almost absently.

Ronsard gave a short, hard laugh. "No, of course not."

"I am."

The soft words lay between them like stones. Anger darkened Ronsard's eyes. "She's a friend, one I've come to cherish. She isn't for the likes of us."

"Perhaps not for you. If you had some claim on her, I'd back off, but you've admitted you don't. She's free—but not for long."

Ronsard was a consummate businessman. He was also astute enough to realize the man called Temple wasn't someone who could be intimidated. He took a deep breath, reaching for control. "I don't brawl over women," he said. "But neither will I allow you to force yourself on her. I say this because she . . . isn't receptive. She is a widow, and still very much in love with her dead husband. Even if she wasn't, she is one of the few principled people of my acquaintance. She frowns on people such as you and I."

"She turned you down," John stated.

"Flat." For a moment humor quirked Ronsard's mouth. "I like her. I won't have her hurt."

"Neither will I."

Into the silence that fell between them Ronsard said,

"You've astonished me. I wouldn't have expected you to become enamored of any woman, especially at first sight. It seems out of character."

"It is." John drew a deep breath and let all the pent-up hunger of the past five years burn in his eyes. "It is," he repeated. "Introduce me."

"I think I will," Ronsard mused. "This should be amusing."

Niema saw the two tall, broad-shouldered men cutting their way through the crowd. Ronsard looked as dashing and debonair as usual, his long dark hair free on his shoulders, but it was the predator beside him who took her breath. John looked severe, dangerous, somehow different. His blue gaze was focused on her like a laser.

Startled, she actually took a step back, her hand lifting to the pearls around her neck.

She hadn't seen him in over a week. She wasn't prepared for the sudden impact of sensation, like a punch in the stomach. All the times before when she had seen him he had muted the dangerous power of his personality, she realized, because the full strength of it was blasting at her now.

His gaze swept down her and she felt as if he had stripped her naked, as if he were about to eat her alive. She tried to look away from him, tried to compose herself, but she couldn't. Excitement sang along her nerves. He was here, and the game had truly begun.

"Niema." They had reached her, so tall their shoulders blocked out the rest of the room, even though she was wearing heels. Ronsard took her hand and pressed a brief kiss on her knuckles. "My dear, this is Mr. Smith, who begged me for an introduction. Mr. Smith, Niema Jamieson."

"Niema." John said her name as if he tasted it.

"Mr.—Mr. Smith." She could barely speak. Her throat had inexplicably tightened. She flashed a helpless look at Ronsard, who didn't look at all pleased by her reaction. She couldn't understand it herself. She knew it played well with John's plans, but . . . she wasn't acting.

"Joseph," said John.

"I—I beg your pardon?"

"My name is Joseph."

"Joseph . . . Joseph Smith?" She blinked, trying to swallow the sudden bubble of laughter. At least he hadn't chosen Brigham Young for a name. "You're an American."

"Yes." Somehow he had her hand, his fingers hard and strong around hers. "Dance with me." It was more command than invitation.

She gave Ronsard another dazed, helpless look, but this one was over her shoulder as John led her onto the dance floor. He didn't just put his hand on her back, he put his arm around her waist and pulled her close, anchoring her to him. He clasped her hand in his free one, holding it against his chest. He began moving in a smooth rhythm and she had no choice but to follow.

He bent his head close to hers. "I fell in love with you on sight," he murmured.

"Did you?" She quivered as she fought back another laugh. *"Joseph Smith?"* She ducked her head against his shoulder to hide her expression. She had been bored, chatting with people with whom she had nothing in common, but now energy was flowing through every cell in her body.

"Joseph Temple, actually. I told him to introduce me as Mr. Smith."

"Temple," she repeated, burning the name in her brain cells. The one thing she couldn't do was slip up and call him John.

"Where's your room?"

"It's in the east wing. It's called the Garden room, and it has its own private balcony." She had counted the doors, so she could tell him exactly how to reach it. "Go up the stairs, take the hallway to the right. Go down ten doors, turn left, and it's the third door on the right."

"Leave the balcony doors unlocked."

"Why? Locks don't mean anything to you."

His arm tightened around her waist in a punishing squeeze for her teasing. Beneath the silk of his tuxedo, his chest was like iron. He was holding her so closely her breasts were flattened against him. The heat of his body seeped through the layers of clothing between them, and the scent of him wrapped around her, warm and masculine and flavored with some subtle cologne.

"You're holding me too close," she said, faint panic welling up in her, because the pleasure she felt was far from safe. Her hands pushed against his chest, not hard enough to be noticeable but enough to lever her upper body an inch away from him.

He simply gathered her back in, the strength in his arms overpowering her without effort. "I'm in love with you, remember? And you're helplessly fascinated by me."

How did he know? The question seared through her brain, a split second before she remembered the scenario they were enacting.

The pattern of the dance had brought them near the open French doors. He made a swooping turn and she found herself out on the patio. The night was warm, but still cooler, and much fresher, than the air inside, with so many people in one room. There were people sitting at the small tables scattered about the patio, talking and laughing, but the noise level dropped dramatically.

He stopped dancing and led her down the steps into the garden. The sweet, peppery scent of roses filled the air. Small gravel crunched under their shoes as they walked a little way down one of the paths. Though the grounds were too well-lit for there to be complete darkness, the garden provided at least some semblance of privacy.

"This is far enough," John said, stopping and turning to face her. "He can still see us." Before she had any idea what he was about to do, he framed her face with his hands and kissed her.

Automatically her hands came up and locked around his wrists. Her breath stopped for two long heartbeats, and her knees went weak. She felt as if he were supporting her only with the warm clasp of his hands on her face, though the pressure was too light to do any such thing.

His kiss was light at first, a tender tasting, an exploration. She stood motionless, dazzled by the pleasure of the simple caress, then returned it with gentle pressure. He slanted his head more and deepened the kiss, his tongue probing her mouth. Then something hot exploded inside her, and she sagged against him. He released her face and folded her in his arms, tighter than before, closer, so close she was welded to him from breast to thigh.

His mouth was ravaging, devouring. He kissed her the way he shouldn't, the way she hadn't let herself imagine: deeply, intensely, the way a man kissed a woman right before he rolled her on her back and slid between her legs. And she accepted those kisses, welcomed them, returned them. Her tongue played with his, her arms lifted to twine tightly around his neck. Her body reached to his, and she discovered he was rock hard, his erection pressed against her stomach.

The discovery so shocked her that she tore herself out of his arms, staggering back. He grabbed her arm to steady her, then immediately let his hand fall to his side. They faced each other in the scented garden, the dimness of the light not dim enough. She could see the cool, focused expression in his eyes, and the realization was another punch in the stomach. Those kisses had rocked her foundation, but John, despite the automatic response of his body, had only been doing his job. Working. Pretending to be smitten.

And Ronsard was watching them, weighing what had just happened. Niema swallowed, trying to decide what she should do. Slap John's—Temple's—face? She had been a willing participant, and Niema Jamieson wasn't a hypocrite.

Forget Niema Jamieson; she was too shattered to play a role right now. She reached down into who she really was, Niema Burdock, and found that the two women were much the same. Had John planned that deliberately, made Niema Jamieson's history so close to her own so she was essentially playing herself?

But it was Niema Burdock who gathered her dignity around her, turned, and walked quietly away. No histrionics. She made her way back up the path toward the patio and saw that Ronsard was indeed standing just outside the ballroom doors, watching them. With the bright light behind him, she couldn't read his expression, but she braced herself and approached him.

He was silent, looking down at her. She met his gaze, inwardly flinching at the cynical disillusionment she knew she would see there, but instead all she could find was concern. Her lips trembled, and suddenly tears blurred her vision.

"Oh, God," she whispered. *"How?"*

Ronsard extended his arm to her and she took it, and he walked her back inside as if nothing had happened. He didn't appear to hurry, but still their progress across the crowded room was mercifully fast. Her fingers dug into his arm as she clung for support. Her legs were shaking. Her entire body was shaking, fine tremors rocking her muscles.

A sumptuous buffet had been set out in another room, with tables set for those guests who wished to eat there, or they could take their plates out onto the patio or into the pool courtyard. Ronsard settled her at one of the empty tables and went to the buffet, where he loaded two plates and brought them back. At a signal from him, a waiter appeared with two glasses of champagne.

"I noticed earlier you weren't drinking," he said. "Try it; my champagne is infinitely superior to that swill the prime minister served. Besides"— he gave a crooked smile—"you need the sedative."

She drank the champagne and ate the strawberries on her plate. He cajoled her into trying the delicious pate, too, though her throat kept threatening to close.

"I see I was too much of a gentleman," he said, amusement rich in his voice and eyes. "I should have simply grabbed you and kissed you, overwhelmed you with my animal magnetism. But really, my dear, that isn't my style."

"I—I didn't think it was mine, either." She could barely speak.

"One can never predict chemistry, though somehow we always underestimate it." He patted her hand. "And now I'm going to do something I have never thought I would do. I'm so astonished at myself I may never recover."

"What?" Ronsard's humor had a steadying effect on her. So she had responded to John with a shattering intensity—that was what she was *supposed* to do. It was part of their scheme. John wouldn't, couldn't, know that there hadn't been anything deliberate about her response, that for a few searing moments she had been lost in the physical pleasure she had been trying to resist since the moment John Medina had reappeared in her life.

"Mr. Smith—"

"He told me his real name," she broke in, rubbing the spot between her eyebrows, partly to shield her expression and partly because tension was beginning to give her a slight headache.

"Then . . . you know he wouldn't be using a pseudonym if there wasn't good cause. He isn't a celebrity, my dear; quite the opposite. Every law enforcement agency in the world would love to have him in its custody."

She stared at him while she pretended to work it through. "He—he's a terrorist?" Her voice was almost soundless.

Ronsard let his silence answer for him.

She drank more champagne, but that didn't loosen the knot in her throat. "He's the only man I've kissed since my husband—" Five years. Five years since Dallas had died, and she hadn't been able to feel even a flicker of response to any of the very nice men she had occasionally dated. She hadn't been able to let any of them kiss her, not because it felt like a betrayal, but because it hadn't seemed fair to them to pretend even that much. The lines between role and reality had blurred again, with Niema Burdock speaking, trying to work her way through what had happened to her in John Medina's arms.

"I can't stay here," she said, surging to her feet. "I'm going to my room. Louis—"

"I understand." He rose too, his handsome face full of concern. "I can't tell you want to do, my dear; the decision is yours. But make it with all the facts in your possession, and no matter what your answer is, I'll always cherish your friendship."

God, how could he be so *nice* in so many ways, and still be what he was? The puzzle of Louis Ronsard wasn't any closer to being solved than it was the day she met him. But for all the vividness of his character, she was losing her focus on him, had been from the moment she saw him walking toward her with John beside him.

Blindly she groped for his hand, squeezing it hard. "Thank you," she said, and fled.

CHAPTER
NINETEEN

It was three A.M. when she saw the curtains by the balcony doors flutter. Niema was lying in the dark, unable to sleep, waiting for John to appear. She didn't hear anything; there was only that small flutter to signal his arrival, then his black shape silhouetted against the faint light coming through the glass behind him.

She sat up and tugged her robe, the most substantial one she had, more tightly around her. The room was dark and he couldn't see her any better than she could see him, but she felt she needed every bit of protection she could muster. He crossed the room with eerie stealth and accuracy, approaching the high four-poster bed. He leaned over and put his mouth against her ear. "Have you swept the room?"

"I checked it when I got here," she whispered back. "I figured if the place was wired, it was part of the security system rather than a patch job. It's clean."

"Mine wasn't."

"Permanent or patched?"

"Permanent. He wants to keep tabs on whomever he puts in that room. Probably other guest rooms in this place are wired, too, and he decides who he wants to stay in them."

The mattress dipped as he sat down on the side of the bed. She felt a brief flare of panic and fought it down. After all, there wouldn't be any point in kissing her now, when there wasn't anyone else around to see.

"Are you okay with what happened this evening?" he asked, an edge of concern in his voice. "You looked stunned. I thought you understood the plan."

"I guess I didn't quite get it," she managed to say and fought to keep her tone even. "Everything's okay, though; I can handle it." His face was a pale blur in the darkness, but still, now that he was this close, she could pick out his features and feel the heat from his leg even through the bed clothes as his thigh pressed against her hip.

"As it turned out, that was the perfect reaction. You played it just right."

Only she hadn't been playing. She had managed to keep her presence of mind, but she hadn't pretended anything. The power of her response to John had been real, and that was what was frightening. As long as he thought her distress was caused only by surprise, though, she didn't feel as exposed.

"Everything's okay," she repeated, and in quiet desperation changed the subject. "What's the plan for tomorrow?"

"Ronsard and I will talk business. If I'm lucky, it'll be in his office. If not, then I'll have to find it some other way."

"I can give you the general location. It's in the west wing, ground floor. And he has a secretary, Cara Smith, so she may be in the office even if he isn't."

"Then we'll have to keep track of both of them. I'll figure out some way to keep them occupied. I'll locate the office tomorrow, check out the security system, then we'll go in tomorrow night. You plant the bug, I copy the files, and we're out without anyone knowing."

If everything went according to plan, that is. Anything could happen, as she had already learned far too well.

"I brought you a little present." There was a faint rustle of clothing, then metal, warm from his body, was pressed into her hand. Automatically she closed her fingers around the grip of the pistol. "It's a SIG .380 caliber, smaller than the one you practiced with, but that just means it'll be easier to conceal."

"I'll tuck it in my bodice," she said dryly, because the thing still weighed over a pound and was at least six and a half inches long. Until the pistol was in her hand, she hadn't been aware of a nagging, low-level sense of alarm, but now she felt something inside her relaxing. She had never carried a weapon in her life, not even in Iran, because that would have given away her disguise; how had she become so rapidly accustomed to being armed?

He gave a low laugh. "That's my girl." There was warm approval in his voice. He patted her thigh. "I'll see you in a few hours. What are you doing tomorrow? What time do you get up?"

"I'm going to sleep as late as I can." Since she hadn't slept any yet that night, she figured she would need all she could get. "I don't have any plans beyond that, though."

"Meet me for lunch, then."

"Where?"

"The pool courtyard, one o'clock."

"Any reason for that particular place?" There had to be; John never did anything without a reason.

"See you, get in a swim, let Ronsard see the scar on my shoulder as a little extra reassurance."

"You don't have a scar on your shoulder," she said automatically, and wished she hadn't, because it revealed how closely she had looked at him when he took off his shirt that day they had been working out.

"No, but Joseph Temple does."

So he must have a fake scar, as part of his disguise. She remembered that he had looked different, too, when Ronsard introduced him, but she couldn't put her finger on exactly what the differences were. "What else have you done? You're not the same."

"I changed my hairline a little, made my brows straighter, put thin rolls of cotton in my jaw to change the shape."

"How long have you been building Joseph Temple's cover?"

"Years. At first he was only a name on a file, but gradually I circulated him more, and added a few details of description, a photo that didn't give away much. But it was enough to let Ronsard compare hairlines, and I imagine he has."

"But he'll have a photo of you now," she said. "You know he will. He wouldn't pass up an opportunity like this."

"It doesn't matter." He stood up. "Temple won't exist after he leaves here."

What was it like, she wondered, to build identities as if they were changes of clothing, putting them on for just a little while and then discarding them? Did he leave pieces of himself behind? Somehow lose just a little bit more of who he really was each time he became someone else?

As he moved toward the balcony, she thought of something. "How did you get up here?"

"I didn't. I got *down*. I came from the roof." With those words he slipped through the doors and disappeared.

Niema got up and locked the balcony doors, then returned to bed. She was so tired she ached, but despite her plans to sleep late she wasn't certain she could sleep at all. The next twenty-four hours were crucial, the reason she had agreed to this elaborate charade. She had to keep her mind on the job, and not on John. After this was over and she was back home, and he was gone from her life again, then she would let herself think about him because then it wouldn't matter—he would be gone.

Cara Smith always enjoyed Louis's house parties. She loved dressing up, loved the glitter and sophistication and sheer luxury. It was like something out of a fairy tale, watching men in tuxedos whirl women in jewels around a polished ballroom floor. Because she was so tall she seldom wore high heels, but for these posh occasions she put on three-inch pumps, which lifted her way over most people's heads, and eye-to-eye with Louis himself. Her legs looked as if they were six feet long, an illusion she heightened by wearing dresses that were slit up the side and exposed long, narrow strips of flesh when she walked.

But that was for night. During the day she still worked at keeping Louis's correspondence up to date, paying bills—it always surprised her that billionaires had bills, but she guessed some things were impossible to escape. She also had to handle the phones, and notify Louis of any business that cropped up, any problems that needed handling. But her hours were abbreviated, and for the most part she played with the guests. She swam, played tennis and billiards, and listened to gossip. She never failed to be amazed by the intimate details and government secrets people blabbed at parties, especially to tall, leggy blondes, as if she wasn't expected to have a brain in her head—which was, of course, why Louis let her play instead of work. She'd learned a lot of interesting stuff during these house parties.

She was fascinated by that Temple man. Few males compared with Louis in terms of elegance and sophistication. But *he* did. And he looked so damned cool and contained—he was a very *still* man, his few gestures controlled and minimal, with little expression on his face. With that kind of control over his body, she bet he could last for hours in bed. She thought of being the woman on the receiving end of all that control and went all shivery.

On the other hand, Cara was astute about which men were attracted to her, and Temple wasn't. She and a bunch of other people, including Louis, had seen him in the garden putting the move on the Jamieson woman. She had wondered how Louis would handle that, considering he had shown more attention to Mrs. Jamieson than to any other woman she could remember, but Louis was Louis—one woman didn't mean that much to him. She knew for a fact he hadn't slept alone last night, while Mrs. Jamieson had chickened out and left the party early, to hide out in her room. Boy, if she'd been in Mrs. Jamieson's place, *she* wouldn't have chickened out. She'd have grabbed that man by the bow tie and ridden him for all he was worth.

But she had her eye on another guy, as a consolation prize. He was rich, he wasn't bad looking, and he did something in the French defense department, or whatever they called it. He'd have lots of interesting things to tell her. From the way his wife hung on to him, he had something of interest in his pants, too. She had seen him eyeing her, so she figured he'd find a way to escape from the little woman for a while.

She couldn't wait. She hadn't had sex in—well, she couldn't remember exactly how long, but she knew it was too long. Damn Hossam and his jealousy! She'd been trying to wean him away, let him down gently, but he just wouldn't go away. She hadn't slept with him, but in the interest of keeping things calm she hadn't slept with anyone else, either. She didn't want to stir up trouble among the guys in Louis's security guard, because Louis wouldn't thank her for it.

She played a game of tennis at nine, and Mr. Defense Department showed up, sans wifey. Cara flirted outrageously with him, until she noticed a tall, mustachioed man, wearing a suit and sunglasses, watching them from the west patio. Hossam. Damn it, if she took him to her room now, which was really the only safe place *to* take him, Hossam would know and was likely to cause trouble. Louis would be majorly pissed if one of his guests was killed by her jealous ex-lover.

Fuming, she finished the game, then excused herself and stalked across the wide expanse of lawn to the west patio. She swished her racket angrily through the air, wishing it was connecting with Hossam's head. Why, he was *stalking* her. She had tried to be nice and not rub his nose in the fact that she was tired of him, but nice hadn't gotten her anywhere. It was time for some plain speaking.

He stood with his arms folded over his chest, stolidly watching as she steamed up to him. He was a big man, about six-five; she had enjoyed his size, because he wasn't big just in height, but now she wished he was normal sized so she could knock him on his ass.

"Stop it," she hissed, standing toe to toe with him and glaring up into his sunglasses. "It's over. Don't you get it? Over! O-v-e-r. Kaput. Finished. I would say it in Egyptian but I don't know the damn word. I had a good time but now I'm moving on—"

"Arabic." His voice was a deep rumble, reverberating in that big chest.

"What?"

"Egyptians speak Arabic. There's no such thing as an Egyptian language."

"Well, thank you for the lesson." She poked him in the chest. "Stop following me, stop spying on me—just stop. I don't want to cause trouble for you but I will if I have to, do you understand."

"I want only to be with you."

Gawd, she thought in despair. "Your head must be made of wood! *I* don't want to be with *you!* I've seen all your tricks, and now I want a new magician. Don't bother me again."

She pushed past him and went inside. She managed to smile at the people she passed on the way to her room, which was on the third floor facing the driveway, but inside she was furious. If Hossam messed up the best job she'd ever had, she would wring his thick neck with her bare hands. Men were enough to make a woman think of joining a convent, she thought, fuming. Maybe she didn't need another lover right now; maybe what she really needed was her head examined because she was even thinking about it.

If she saw Hossam so much as looking at her again, she'd tell Louis. Enough was more than enough.

Without appearing to, John studied the security system as Ronsard unlocked and opened the door to his office. The lock operated on a numeric code that translated to different tones, like a telephone. Ronsard was careful to keep his body between John and the control panel, so he couldn't see the numbers. John didn't even try to see them; he half-turned away, studying the hallway, noting the blinking eye of the camera that was mounted at the far end of the hall. Making sure his motion was hidden from the camera, he slipped his hand inside his jacket and triggered a powerful miniature recorder that picked up the small beep of the tones as Ronsard punched in the code.

"We won't be disturbed here," Ronsard said. "Please be seated. Would you like something to drink? Coffee?"

"No, thank you." Call him paranoid, but he was real careful about taking anything to eat or drink from someone else. A buffet was fine, if everyone else was eating, but when he was on a job he was always in control of his intake. If he had to set a drink down, he didn't pick it back up. It was a simple rule, but an effective one.

He looked around. There was a computer on Ronsard's large, antique desk, but no phone line going to it, which meant it was secure. If there were any files Ronsard didn't want compromised, they would be on that computer. Another unit sat on a Louis XIV desk across the room, and this one was hooked to a phone line, a printer, a scanner, the works.

Also on Ronsard's desk was a small monitor with an elaborate control attached to it, and from where he was sitting John could see just enough of the screen to tell it was surveillance of the hallway outside, so Ronsard knew in advance who was coming toward his office. There was probably a central surveillance control room somewhere in this massive building, but whether or not the entire building was under watch was something he'd have to find out. It could be that, like the listening devices, only certain rooms were involved. This part of the estate was, after all, Ronsard's private living quarters, and he probably wouldn't want his employees watching *him*.

"Who's making the compound?" he asked, deciding to at least ask. Sometimes people just blurted out what he wanted to know.

Ronsard smiled at him. "I have an agreement with the . . . ah, developers. They don't use anyone else to distribute the compound, and I don't tell anyone who they are. Once it's known, you understand, then they'll be under siege. Opportunists would try to get the formula, perhaps resorting to kidnap and torture in the process; the government might try to shut them down, but would at least take over the manufacturing. That's the way governments are, isn't it?" He sat down behind his desk. "I had thought they were dealing behind my back. Both you and Ernst Morrell were asking about the compound; what else could I think? But you've relieved my mind."

"I'm glad."

The total lack of expression in John's voice brought a smile to the arms dealer's face. "So I see. Well, Mr. Temple, shall we complete our business? I have guests, and you'll want to continue your pursuit of Mrs. Jamieson. Tell me—what would you do with a wife, assuming you succeed?"

John's eyes sharpened. "Keep her safe."

"Ah. Can you do that, though?" He indicated the computers in the office, specifically the fast, powerful one on his secretary's desk. "Computers have made the world very small. Eventually, one will be able to find out anything about anyone. It's almost possible now. You won't be able to disappear the way you do now."

"Information can be falsified or erased. If I need a social security number or a credit card, I use someone else's."

"Yes, but what about her? She can't disappear, you know. She has family, friends; she has a home, a routine, and a social security number, and those credit cards you disdain. I know the lady well enough to promise you she would balk at using a stolen credit card."

Still warning him away from Niema, John realized, inwardly amused. "If she doesn't want what I can give her, all she has to do is say no. Kidnapping somebody is too chancey; it draws a lot of attention."

"Something you want to avoid," Ronsard agreed. "But if she did go with you—what would you do?"

John regarded him silently, refusing to be drawn on the question. It was a nonissue, of course, but Ronsard didn't know that. Let him think that Temple was the most secretive bastard he'd ever met, and let it go at that.

He stonewalled every attempt Ronsard made to talk about Niema, though he was actually beginning to like the guy. There was something both absurd and touching about someone as ruthless as Louis Ronsard displaying this kind of concern for a friend. Niema had gotten to him too, John thought, just the way she had Hadi and Sayyed, and himself, in Iran. The situation was almost funny. He should have been able to express an interest in Niema, with her reciprocating, and that would have been that: a burgeoning affair. Instead Niema was rattled, Ronsard was protective, and he was having to pursue a reluctant target.

Of course, no one would ever think this was part of any plan. It was just too damn implausible, like a soap opera. Maybe that was why it seemed to be working so well.

Half an hour later, their business concluded—amount of explosive needed, when, how it would be delivered, how much it would cost him—John went to his room and changed into his swim trunks. The room had been searched again, he saw; he didn't know what they expected to find that they hadn't found the first time. The fact that they *hadn't* found anything probably disturbed Ronsard a little. Of course, they were looking in the wrong place. Since acquiring the weapons last night after arriving here, he had given one to Niema, taped another under one of the massive hall tables outside his room, and one was strapped to his ankle. The ankle holster would have to go in a secure place while he was swimming, though. Smiling, he stuffed it and the tiny recorder under the mattress. The maids had already been in and cleaned, and the room had been searched—twice. Looking in the most obvious place in the world was now the one place they were the least likely to look.

He pulled on a T-shirt and a pair of trousers over his swim trunks, then went down to the pool courtyard. It was a hot, sunny day, but still fairly early. The ladies didn't want to mess up their hair so close to lunch time, so they were sunbathing instead of swimming, and the pool wasn't crowded.

Rather than putting his clothes in the large cabana, he shucked his shirt and dropped it over a chaise, then took off his pants and did the same with them. He didn't have anything in his pocket other than his room key, but if by leaving his clothes in the open he frustrated anyone wanting to go through his pockets, so much the better.

He dove into the pool in a long, shallow dive and began swimming laps, his arms stroking tirelessly. He was as at home in the water as he was on land, courtesy of his BUD/S training. Swimming in a pool was child's play, after swimming miles in the ocean. It was nice of Ronsard, he thought, to provide him a means of keeping up his physical conditioning. There was probably a weight room somewhere in this place, too, but he doubted he'd have time to use it.

The only thing about swimming in public was, after a while people began to notice. Not many people could swim nonstop for that length of time, even though he'd only been at it half an hour. He could have kept on, using one stroke or another, for hours, but it wasn't wise to draw that kind of attention. Already people around the pool were watching him, and he was pretty sure one woman had been counting the laps as he turned them.

He hauled himself out of the water and took a fluffy towel from the stacks Ronsard had put out for his guests, and which were constantly being replaced, and roughly swiped it over his torso. Though it wasn't one o'clock yet, he saw Niema coming toward him. She was dressed casually, in loose, drawstring natural linen pants and a blue camisole, with a gauzy white shirt worn loose over the camisole. She had pulled her thick dark hair back and secured it with a silver clasp at the nape of her neck. Her dark eyes looked huge and luminous.

She checked a little when she saw him, as if she hadn't known he was there. He stood still, staring at her, then lifted his hand and beckoned her to him.

She hesitated for a long moment before obeying, just long enough for him to begin wondering if she was going to do something totally unexpected, like turning around and leaving, which would be taking the show of reluctance a little too far and might prod her unlikely protector into action.

But then she began walking slowly to him, and he knotted the towel around his waist to hide his response as he waited for her to join him.

CHAPTER
TWENTY

Niema faltered as she approached John and slid her sunglasses on her nose to hide her expression from him. Good God, the man should put on some clothes before she had heart failure. Greedily she drank in the strong lines of his torso, the well-defined muscles of arms and shoulders, the ridges down his abdomen. His legs were the most powerful she had ever seen, the long muscles thick and sinewy in the way that showed he did it all, running and swimming as well as strength training.

Water still sparkled on his shoulders and in the hair on his chest. He had roughly towel-dried his hair and raked his hand over it to restore some semblance of order. He looked wild, and dangerous, and she ached inside with the need to touch him.

He wrapped the towel around his waist and stood like a redwood, waiting for her to reach him. At least the towel hid part of those legs. How could he look so lean when he was clothed, when he had muscles like this?

Then she reached him, and a tiny smile curved his hard mouth, a mouth that looked as if it never smiled at all and yet he made the effort for her. This was Temple, she thought, not John. John smiled and laughed. When he was himself, he was an expressive man—unless he was playing another part, unless he had been someone else for so long that even John Medina was just a role for him now.

"For a minute there, I thought you were going to turn and run," he said in a low voice. "Don't be *that* reluctant."

"I know what to do." She sat down in the chair he held out for her, not caring if she sounded irritable. She *was* irritable. She hadn't had much sleep, and her nerves were raw.

He stood behind her, looking down, and she felt his stillness. Then he put his hand inside her open shirt and lightly smoothed his palm over her bare shoulder, the movement slow and absorbed, as if he couldn't go a moment longer without touching her. Only the thin straps of her camisole obstructed him, and they might as well not have been there. She shivered as that warm hand moved over her, pushing the shirt away just enough that he could stroke that one shoulder and upper arm. It was the most restrained, sensuous touch she had ever experienced, and her entire body reacted, nipples pebbling, stomach tightening.

Then he gently restored the shirt to her shoulder and moved around to take the chair across from her. When his back was turned she saw the thin, four-inch scar on his left shoulder blade. Even knowing it wasn't real, she couldn't tell how it was applied. It certainly looked genuine.

Then he sat down facing her, and she blinked in astonishment at the small diamond stud in his left ear. His ear wasn't pierced; she would have noticed before if it had been. And he hadn't been wearing an earring last night. Well, if the scar was fake, the pierced ear could be, too; he probably had the stud glued on. And the altered hairline looked real. All these small identifying characteristics were fake; with them removed, he would never be identified as Joseph Temple, despite having the same face. As long as there were no dental records tying them together, or DNA samples to compare, he was unidentifiable.

A waiter in black shorts and white shirt approached. "May I serve you anything from the bar?"

"We'd like to order lunch," John said, his French perfect.

"Of course, sir."

He ordered puff pastries filled with chicken in cream sauce for appetizers, potato soup, and a cheese and fruit tray afterward. Thankful she wouldn't be expected to choke down a full meal, including a meat course, Niema looked around at the beautifully landscaped courtyard. It was becoming more crowded now as others elected to have their lunch by the pool rather than inside. The murmur of conversation, punctuated by splashes, laughter, and the clink of silverware, made it reasonable that they would lean together over the small round table.

John adjusted the umbrella shading them to protect her from the sun, and also to partially block anyone's view of them from the house. Before he sat down he plucked his shirt from the chaise beside him and pulled it on over his head. She almost mourned as those pecs and abs disappeared from view, but admitted to herself that at least now she'd be able to concentrate better.

"I've been in Ronsard's office," he said, pitching his voice so that only she could hear. "I have the door code and got a good look at his security system. What's on the agenda for tonight?"

"It's fancy dress every night. Buffet dinner, dancing, just like last night."

"Good. People will be moving around, so it'll be difficult to keep track of us. We're going to dance every dance—"

"Not in high heels, I'm not. I'd be crippled."

"Then don't wear heels."

She gave him a dirty look, though of course he couldn't tell since she was still wearing the sunglasses. "You're the one who provided the wardrobe. Heels are the only suitable shoes I have with me."

"Okay, we'll dance a few dances." He looked in danger of smiling again. "I'm going to be making it pretty obvious we're together, putting some strong moves on you, so don't panic."

"Why the strong moves?" Her throat had gone dry. She wished the waiter would hurry up with the mineral water John had ordered.

"So, if anyone notices us going off together, they'll just think we're looking for someplace more private—such as your room."

And instead they would be going through files. "What about Ronsard? And Cara?"

"I'll take care of her. Ronsard's a bit trickier. We may have to take our chances and hope he'll be too occupied to come to his office." He paused. "Here comes the waiter." He leaned over and took her hand, thumb rubbing lightly across the backs of her fingers. "Walk with me after lunch," he was murmuring when the waiter set down the crystal goblets of mineral water.

She drew back and picked up a goblet, sending a shaky smile in the waiter's direction.

"How much time do you need to plant the bug?" he asked when they were alone again.

"I'd like to have half an hour." She could probably do it in less time than that, but she wanted to be very, very careful with this one, because she was going to have to get into the wiring in the walls and she didn't want to leave any telltale marks. "What about the computer files? How long will it take on those?"

"Depends," he said helpfully.

"Thank you so much, Mr. Information."

He fought another smile. "I don't know what system he uses, if it's password protected or encrypted—though I'd be very surprised if he doesn't at least have a password. I have to get the password—"

"How on earth can you do that?"

"People usually write it down somewhere handy. Or it's something obvious, like their mother's name, or their kids—"

"Ronsard has a daughter," Niema said. "Laure."

"A daughter? That wasn't in our information," John murmured.

"She's an invalid. He adores her, and is very protective of her privacy. For security reasons, very few people know she exists. She's so ill, she may not live long." A lump rose in her throat as she remembered Laure's skeletal face, with those dark blue eyes so like her father's, and her mischievous, practical spirit.

"Then he'd take very seriously any incident involving her," John mused.

Niema sat up straight, and snatched her sunglasses off so he could get a good look at how furious she was. "Don't you dare," she said between clenched teeth. "If you involve that child I'll—I'll . . ." She couldn't think of anything bad enough, but her eyes promised severe retribution.

"I'll do whatever's necessary," he softly replied. "You know that. I don't put limitations on what I'm willing to do to get a job done."

"Yes, I heard that about you," she said just as softly, rage boiling through her veins with a suddenness that took her off guard. "They say you even killed your own wife, so why would you worry about upsetting a little girl?"

Leaden silence fell between them. John's face was absolutely expressionless, his eyes so cold and empty they looked dead. "Her name was Venetia," he finally said, the words a mere rustle of sound. "Why don't you ask me if I did it? How do you think it happened? Did I shoot her, or break her neck, or cut her throat? Maybe I just tossed her out a thirty-story window. I've heard all those scenarios. Which do you think is most likely?"

She couldn't breathe. She had wanted to hit him, say something that would make an impression on him, and she had evidently succeeded beyond anything she could have expected. She hadn't believed those wild stories, hadn't really believed he had ever even been married. To know that he had, to know that his wife's name was Venetia and she had existed, was to suddenly think that those stories could be true.

"Did you?" she managed to say, barely able to force the words out through her constricted throat. "Did you kill her?"

"Yes," he said and leaned back as the waiter approached with their meal.

She strolled with him across the lush, manicured lawn. She hadn't had a chance to recover, to ask him any more questions, after he dropped that bombshell at lunch. First the waiter had been there, setting out their lunch, refilling their water glasses, asking if they needed anything else, and by the time he left, Ronsard "happened" to walk by and stayed to chat.

Niema had scarcely been able to talk; she had managed a few short answers to Ronsard's questions, but her lips were numb and she kept seeking refuge in her water glass. She remembered eating a few bites of lunch, but she had no idea how it had tasted.

After lunch, John put his trousers on over his dry swim trunks, then took her hand and led her out here. The hot sun beat down on her, bringing welcome warmth to her cold skin. She felt as if her heart were breaking. Innocence was an invisible fortress, keeping one safe, and oblivious to some things that were too horrible to contemplate. But now she no longer had that innocence, that obliviousness; she was aware of the pain, the horror, the cost. What must it be like for him, to have lived through it?

"John, I'm so sorry," she whispered.

She saw his surprise. Evidently he had expected her to be repelled by who he was, what he had done, maybe even frightened of him. She searched for the right words. "I didn't mean to hurt you. I hadn't believed the stories, or I never would have brought it up."

"Hurt me?" He sounded almost disinterested. She couldn't see his eyes behind the sunglasses, and she wanted to snatch them off his face. "The truth is the truth."

His hand was so warm and so strong, wrapped around hers, but the strength in his fingers was controlled so he wouldn't hurt her. He had never hurt her, she realized. Even when faced with her distrust and hostility in Iran, he had taken care of her, saved her life, held her in his arms while she grieved.

"Sometimes the truth is the truth, but sometimes it's something else. What really happened? Was she a double agent, the way I've heard?"

He made a noncommittal sound. Growing exasperated, she squeezed his hand. "Tell me."

He stopped and turned to face her. "Or what?"

"Or nothing. Just tell me."

For a minute, she didn't think he would. Then he shrugged. "Yes, she was a double agent. She did it for the money. There weren't any extenuating circumstances; she didn't have family in the Soviet Union, or in East Germany, that was being threatened. All her family was American, and they weren't involved at all. She simply wanted the money."

So there was no excuse he could give his wife; he'd had to face the truth that she was, simply, a traitor.

That would have been devastating for almost anyone; what had it been like for him, after he had dedicated his entire life to the service of his country?

"How did you find out?"

He began walking again. "There wasn't any one big moment of truth, just a lot of little things that began adding up and made me suspicious. I set a trap for her, and she walked right into it."

"She didn't know you suspected?"

"Of course she did. She was good. But I baited the trap with something she couldn't resist: the names of our two highest-placed moles in the Kremlin. Aldrich Ames never came close to this information, it was so restricted." His lips were a thin line. "I was almost too late springing the trap. This was during the height of the Cold War, and this information was so crucial, so valuable, that she decided not to route it by the usual method. She picked up the phone and called the Soviet embassy. She asked to be brought in, because she knew I'd be after her, and she started to give them the names right there over the phone."

He took a long, controlled breath. "I shot her," he finally said, staring off at the massive wall that surrounded the estate. "I could have wounded her, but I didn't. What she knew was too important for me to take the chance, the moles too important to be brought in. They had to be left in place. She had already told her handler that she had the names; they would have moved heaven and earth to get to her, no matter what prison we put her in, no matter what security we put around her. So I killed her."

They walked in silence for a while, going from flower bed to flower bed like bees, ostensibly admiring the landscaping. Niema still clung to his hand while she tried to come to grips with the internal strength of this man. He had been forced to do something almost unthinkable, and he didn't make excuses for himself, didn't try to whitewash it or blur the facts. He lived with the burden of that day, and still he went on doing what he had to do.

Some people would think he was a monster. They wouldn't be able to get beyond the surface fact that he had deliberately killed his wife, or they would say that no information, no matter how crucial, was that important. Those who lived on the front lines knew better. Dallas had given his own life for his country, in a different battle of the same war.

John had saved untold lives by his actions, not just of the two moles but of the ensuing events to which they had been critical. The Soviet Union had broken up, the Berlin Wall had come down, and for a while the world had been safer. He was still on the front lines, putting himself in the cannon's mouth, perhaps trying to balance his own internal scales of justice.

"Why didn't she sell you out?" Niema asked. "You're worth a pretty penny, you know."

"Thank you," he said dryly. "But I wasn't worth that much back then. I had high-level security clearance, so I was of some use to her, but she had her own clearance and access to a lot of classified documents."

"I can't imagine what it must have been like for you." Ineffable sadness was in her voice. She squeezed his hand again, trying to tell him without words how sorry she was for ever opening that particular can of worms.

He glanced down at her, then his head tilted up and he looked beyond her. He drew her closer to a huge flowering shrub, as if he were trying to shield them from view. "Brace yourself," he warned and bent his head.

His mouth settled on hers, his lips opening, molding, fusing. She put her hands on his shoulders and clung to him, her pulse pounding in her ears, her heart racing. Her entire body quickened with painful urgency, and she stifled a moan. His tongue was doing a slow, erotic dance in her mouth, advancing and retreating. He put his hands on her hips and drew her to him, lifting her, holding her so that they were groin to groin. She felt him getting erect, and she shivered with pleasure even while her inner alarm began clanging insistently. She fought to keep her legs under her and not sag against him like a limp noodle, which *he* definitely wasn't.

He lifted his mouth, holding it poised over hers. She stared up at him, dazed, and wished he wasn't wearing sunglasses so she could see his eyes. Still clinging to him she whispered, "Who's there?"

This time he did smile, his mouth curling upward. "Nobody. I just wanted to kiss you for being so damn sweet."

Violently she shoved away from him. "Sneak!" She stood

with her lungs heaving, glaring at him. She really, really wanted to punch him, but instead she had to bite her lip to keep from laughing.

"Guilty as charged." Taking her hand again, he resumed their walk across the lawn. "But what did you expect? I tell you something that proves I'm the ruthless bastard everyone says I am, and you apologize to me. Of course I had to kiss you."

"I thought it was for the job."

"Not always," he said, not looking at her. "Not everything."

CHAPTER
TWENTY-ONE

H igh heels would be a definite liability, Niema thought, going through her wardrobe in case she had overlooked a pair of shoes that was both dressy and flat-heeled, though she was certain she hadn't. High heels made too much noise, and it was impossible to run in them. A pair of ballet slippers would do nicely, but of all the different kinds of shoes John had had delivered to her, none of them were ballet slippers.

She stared at the gown she had planned to wear. It was a sleek black sheath with inch-wide straps that gradually widened to form the bodice, with the lowest point of the neckline squarely between her breasts. A sunburst of black cultured pearls was sewn at that strategic point, with strings of black pearls swinging from the sunburst. She had other gowns, but she wanted to wear the black so she would blend better into the shadows, if necessary.

Other than the sexy black heels, she had only one other pair of black shoes with her, and they were rather casual sandals, with stretchy straps. She pulled them out and stared at them, trying to think what she could do to dress them up. They would definitely be more comfortable to dance in than the high heels, but they looked like what they were: casual. Niema Jamieson wouldn't be that careless with her dress. She had classic taste in clothes and was never less than impeccably attired.

"Why couldn't you have been a slob?" she muttered to her alter ego.

She examined the gown again. It was sophisticated and understated, even with the dangling strings of black pearls, which glistened with a midnight iridescence that caught the eye. She reached up and flicked the strings with her finger, setting them to swaying. They would constantly call attention to her breasts.

She looked at the black sandals, then back up to the pearls. Curiously she examined the sunburst. The swaying strings weren't attached *to* the sunburst, but *under* it.

"Now we're cooking," she muttered and got up to get her tools. She knew why she was obsessing about her shoes, of course; so she wouldn't think about John and what he'd said about not everything being for the job. How was she supposed to take that? Was he referring to her or to something else entirely? There was so much in his past that he literally could have been talking about anything. Some guys led normal, open lives, with nothing more to hide than how many beers they had on the way home. John's past was so closed and convoluted no one would ever know all the bits and pieces of what made him who he was.

Obsessing about the shoes had obviously failed in its purpose, because she *couldn't* stop thinking about him. Losing Dallas had been difficult enough, almost too much to bear; what must it have been like for John, to not only lose his wife but for it to be by his own hand? She tried to dredge up some feeling, some sympathy, for his wife, but nothing was there. The woman had been selling out her country, costing other people their lives. To Niema's way of thinking, that didn't make her much different from the terrorists who used poison gas or random bombs to kill. Dallas had died stopping people like her.

Tonight might be the last time she ever saw John.

That thought hovered in the back of her mind all the while she worked with the sandals, using glue from her tool kit to attach the pearls to the straps. There had been other times she'd known could be the last time: When he left just before she came to France; when he was only a voice on the phone and she knew she might not be invited to the villa. But this was somehow more definite. Once he got the computer files, he would leave immediately.

She would stay until the end of the house party and leave as scheduled; by this time next week, she would be home and back at work, and this would be a fantastic story she could never tell anyone.

But for right now she felt vibrantly alive, more than she ever had before. Her very skin was more sensitive than she had ever before noticed. She took a long, relaxing bath in water scented with the bath crystals provided with her room, and washed her hair. She even took a nap, something she rarely did, but the events of the day had been taxing. She gave herself a manicure and pedicure, painting her nails a deep scarlet. If she never saw John again, by God, he'd remember how she looked.

She didn't want to have to come back to her room for her tools and equipment, but neither could she carry everything in the tiny excuse for a purse that was her evening bag. It had room for a credit card, a lipstick and compact, and a key. That was it. She tried to think of someplace to hide the tools and pistol, but she didn't know the estate well enough, plus it was crawling with people.

There was no way out of it; she had to come back to the room to retrieve the things. She wrapped everything, tools and pistol, in the black silk stole that matched the gown she was wearing and placed the parcel under her lingerie in the built-in drawers in the large closet. Then she took a deep breath, braced her shoulders, and prepared for a final act for the audience.

He was waiting for her at the foot of the stairs when she went down. He straightened, his blue gaze sweeping over her in a perfect imitation of an infatuated lover. Out of the corner of her eye Niema saw Ronsard watching them, his expression a mixture of ruefulness and concern. She waited until she caught his eye and gave him what she hoped was a reassuring smile. He spread his hands in an "I tried" gesture.

John followed her smile and his eyes narrowed, menace all but oozing from him. God, he was good. He should have gone to Hollywood; with his talent, he would already have a couple of Oscars to his credit and be making a lot more money than he was as a government employee.

She could do a little acting of her own, she thought. She slowed as she neared John, as if reluctant to take those last few steps. He frowned slightly and held out his hand to her in that arrogant gesture that demanded she come to him.

She did, silently putting her hand in his, and he led her into the ballroom where the same crowd as the night before was doing the same thing they had done the night before, only wearing different clothing. She went into his arms and he held her close, their feet barely moving, his head bent down to hers in the classic pose of a man who is totally absorbed in the woman in his arms.

"I had to leave the things in my room," she said in a low voice, the words muffled against his shoulder. "I couldn't carry them in this." She indicated the tiny evening bag.

"What? You couldn't put everything in your bodice with the SIG?" He glanced down at the fabric clinging to her breasts and the deep V of the neckline.

"Careful," she warned. "I've got a knife in there and I'll use it." She felt the movement of his lips against her temple as he smiled. "What kind of distraction did you arrange?"

"I didn't. I was afraid you'd scalp me. We'll take our chances."

"I'm good at taking chances." No sooner had the words left her mouth than she almost recoiled in shock. No, she *wasn't* good at all at taking chances. She used to be, but not now. Not any more.

He felt her stiffening in his arms and reacted by bringing her closer. "What's wrong?"

"Nothing," she said automatically.

"Nothing you're going to tell me," he corrected.

"Right."

Again there was that movement against her temple. After a moment he commented, "You're shorter than you were last night."

Trust him to notice something like that. "I'm not wearing heels. I doctored a pair of sandals so they match the gown." She stuck her foot out so he could see the pearls adorning the narrow straps.

ARD

He looked a little pained. "You butchered a Dior to decorate your shoes?"

"It's okay," she soothed. "Wearing sensible shoes was more important than the gown. Besides, black ops is off-budget; you don't have to account for what's spent, do you?"

"No, thank God."

"So, what time do we do it?"

"No set time. We keep an eye on Ronsard, and make our move when it looks as if he's occupied."

"What about Cara?"

"Taken care of."

"I hate to tell you this, but she's standing just over there."

"She won't be for long."

Cara was wearing a dazzling white tube gown, with her long blonde hair hanging straight down her back and rhinestones dangling from her ears. She knew she looked Hollywood flashy, but there was no way she could compete with these people in terms of jewelry and couture gowns, so she didn't try. California sexy was the style she tried for and achieved.

She flirted with several men, but the sexy Frenchman with whom she had played tennis that morning was safely anchored by his wife. Deciding to troll, she began moving around the room, stopping only to talk to likely prospects. She wasn't going to worry about Hossam's feelings one minute longer; he had no claim on her.

She didn't see it coming. Someone turned too abruptly, and a glass of red wine sloshed all over her white gown. She looked down at the awful stain in dismay, knowing she would probably have to throw the garment away. "I'm so sorry," the woman who had splashed her apologized, her face contorted

254

with dismay. "I don't know how this happened; someone jos-
tled me."

"It's perfectly all right," Cara soothed, even though it
wasn't. She didn't want to upset any of Louis's guests. "I'm
sure the stain will come right out. I'll just run to my room to
change." She brushed away the woman's offer to pay for the
dress and kept a smile on her face as she left the ballroom. She
seldom used the elevator, preferring the stairs in order to get in
some exercise, but tonight she chose the fastest route to her
room.

The smile was gone and irritation in its place when she got
off the elevator on the third floor. The long hallways were
deserted, with only indirect lighting from the sconces, but she
was glad no one was there to see what a mess she was. Taking
the key from her tiny evening bag, she jammed it into the lock
and pushed her door open, her hand unerringly finding the
light switch and flipping it on.

Light flooded the room at the same time a large hand
clamped over her mouth and an arm around her waist lifted
her off her feet. The door was kicked shut.

Panic screamed through her, making everything around her
go dim for a moment. She heard her own muffled screams and
knew the sound wouldn't carry beyond the room. She clawed
at the hand over her mouth, kicking and squirming in an
effort to escape.

"Hush, my love. There's no need to be frightened."

Hossam! Panic turned to rage in the space of a split second.
She slammed her head backward in an effort to smash his
mouth, but he only chuckled and tossed her onto the bed,
then landed on top of her before she could control herself
enough to scramble off the bed.

"You bastard," she hissed, no longer trying to scream.

He only laughed again, sitting astride her and capturing her fists. With no more effort than if he were handling a child, he looped a scarf around her wrists, then pulled her arms over her head and tied the scarf to the headboard.

"You bastard!" she said again, louder this time, shrieking it.

"Shhh, be quiet."

"I'll kill you for this! I'll tear your balls off—ummmph!"

"I told you to be quiet," he murmured, tying another scarf over her mouth. He sat back, eyeing his handiwork, and a smile spread over his dark face. "Now, my love, let's see if the magician knows any new tricks."

He took a knife from his pocket and pressed a switch. A gleaming blade shot out, the light catching the razor-sharp edges. Cara's eyes widened as she stared at the knife, then at him. She began bucking, trying to throw him off, but he squeezed her body between his thighs and ruthlessly held her still.

Muffled screams came from behind the scarf as he slipped the blade under the clingy material covering her breasts and slashed downward. The two halves of the gown parted as if it had been unzipped, baring her breasts.

Hossam paused to admire the view. Still holding the knife in one hand, he fondled her naked breasts, cupping them and stroking his thumb over her nipples, admiring the way they tightened. Then he levered himself off her. "Be still," he commanded. "I might accidentally cut you."

She forced herself to stillness as he slit the dress all the way to the hem and pulled the rags away from her. She wore nothing underneath. Modesty wasn't her strong suit, but now she squeezed her legs together in a useless effort to protect herself. Oh, God, was he going to kill her?

He stepped back and began removing his clothes. Wildly she shook her head, hot tears burning her eyes.

"Don't be frightened," he repeated, stepping out of his pants and standing naked over her. His penis jutted out from his body, telling her how ready he was. Desperately she kicked at him, trying to catch him in the balls, though she had no idea what good that would do since she was still tied and gagged.

Clicking his tongue in reproval, he grabbed her by one ankle and gave it the same treatment he had her wrists. Another ten seconds and her other leg was bound, and she was lying with her hands stretched upward and her legs spread obscenely wide.

"What a wild thing you are," he crooned, crawling on the bed between her legs. "Sweet and wild and . . . mine. Never forget that. You're mine."

She expected to be swiftly, brutally raped and had already braced herself for the violation. It didn't happen. Instead he bent down and pressed his mouth between her legs, and began loving her.

The contrast between what she had expected and what he actually did was so great that she couldn't stop the soft moan that vibrated in her throat. She arched, and he cupped her bottom in his big hands to hold her still.

The bright overhead light dazzled her eyes. She stared upward as pleasure zinged through her body, unable to raise her head to see. This was . . . this was so totally unexpected she couldn't quite grasp it was happening. He brought her to a hard, rapid climax that left her gasping, her eyes tearing from the force of it.

"That is just the first one," he murmured, leaning over her. "You know I would never, never hurt you. Tonight we will discover all the ways I can pleasure you, as no other man can." His dark eyes twinkled at her. "And afterward, perhaps I will let you tie *me* to the bed."

She moaned and arched as his long fingers slid into her, stimulating nerve endings that were still sensitive from her climax. Her fear had faded, because his hands on her were loving instead of brutal, and in place of fear a deep excitement was blooming. This was different, and kinky. She had never been helpless before during sex. Usually she dominated, because that was how she liked it.

But she liked this too, she found. She was totally at his mercy, naked and exposed in the bright light. He could do anything to her he wanted, and her mind reeled at the possibilities. Hossam was so big and powerful, and he tended to be slow at sex anyway. This was going to be a long night—wonderfully, deliciously long.

"It's time," John breathed into Niema's ear.

Her pulse leaped. She took a deep breath and felt herself steady. She tilted her head back and gave him such a vibrant smile that he physically checked, staring down at her.

Who was she kidding? The moment of clarity was almost blinding as they left the ballroom and climbed the curving staircase to the second floor. She *was* a risk-taker. She loved every minute of this. She didn't want to go home and resume her job; she wanted to stay in fieldwork, where she belonged. She had paid penance for five years, but John had wrenched her back into the life for which she was truly suited and she never wanted to leave it again.

She felt almost breathless with discovery, with an inner joy that spread through her as if she had finally returned to life, to being herself.

The long hallway was empty. With no one to watch them, they walked briskly down to her room. She retrieved the wrap from the closet and held it folded so the tools and pistol were in a pocket of fabric against her body, with the loose ends draped over her arm. "How about this?" she asked.

"Looks good. Come on."

They hurried back up the hall, but instead of going down the stairs they went straight across into the west wing. "I prowled around and found a back way," John explained.

"Ronsard's private quarters are in this direction, too."

"I know. The back way is through his rooms."

She rolled her eyes, but didn't bother asking how he'd gotten into Ronsard's rooms. Locks didn't mean anything to him.

This route wasn't without risk. There were fewer people to see them, but anyone who did would be staff who worked in the private section, and who would know immediately they didn't belong there. Guests or not, Ronsard wouldn't allow anyone to disturb his daughter.

John pulled her to a halt in front of a wooden door burnished to a high gloss. He turned the handle, and they slipped inside the room. It was a bedroom, she saw—a huge, lavish one. "Ronsard's," John whispered in unnecessary explanation. "There's a private elevator going down to the hallway where his office is located."

The elevator was small, but then it was meant to carry only one man. It was also surprisingly quiet and arrived without the customary "ding" of a commercial elevator.

The hallway they stepped into was also empty, which was good because there was no logical excuse for them to be there, especially stepping out of Ronsard's elevator. John strode to a door, pulled a small recorder out of his pocket and held it to the electronic lock. He pressed a button, and a series of tones sounded. A tiny green light on the lock lit up, there was a faint but audible click, and he opened the door.

They slipped inside and he silently closed the door behind them, then did something to the lock. "What are you doing?"

"Disabling the lock. If we're caught, the fact that the lock isn't working will at least cloud the issue in our favor a bit, but I'd still have to come up with some reason for our being here."

"Boy, you have this planned down to the last detail, don't you?"

"I don't intend to get caught. Come on, move your pretty butt and get to work."

CHAPTER
TWENTY-TWO

Niema looked around while John sat down at Ronsard's desk and turned on the computer. Another setup, far more elaborate, was hooked up on a desk on the other side of the room, but he ignored that one. She checked the jacks on what must be Cara Smith's desk; there were three separate lines coming into the office, but the phones themselves were only two-line phones. The computer was on a line by itself, then. She looked at the phone on Ronsard's desk; it was identical to the other, with two lines coming in. The first line would be the business line, she guessed; the second, his private number.

There was a closed-circuit television on Ronsard's desk, also, showing the hallway outside. She followed the line on it to the wall, making sure where it connected. She liked to have a room's wiring laid out in her mind, so she knew exactly what she was looking for and at.

Ronsard's phone jack wasn't behind his desk, probably because he didn't want it in the way. She followed the lines again; the jack was behind a long leather sofa that sat against the wall. Carefully she pulled the sofa out, lifting one end to make certain there were no telltale bangs and thumps.

Kneeling down on the floor, she unfolded her evening wrap and removed the black velvet pouch that contained her tools. Laying aside the SIG, she quickly unscrewed the jack, then disconnected the wires and stripped the plastic coating to separate the wires.

The usual wiretap had a receiver or recorder close by. In this instance, that wouldn't do any good because she had no way of retrieving a tape or listening to the calls. The CIA operative in place here didn't have access to Ronsard's office. John had slipped a digital burst receiver to him; he would trigger a signal to retrieve the audio data, which he would then send by his usual route to Langley. Even if he were discovered with the receiver, nothing could be made of it because the information was digitalized. It looked like an ordinary pocket radio; it even worked as a radio.

Quickly she attached the inductive probe tip to only one of the line terminals, which didn't make a complete circuit and hence couldn't be picked up by an electronic sweep. She interfaced the leads to the junction, keeping the leads less than three inches long. The short leads made the phone bridge impossible to pick up by electrical deviations. Next she hooked up two nine-volt batteries as a power source for the receiver/transmitter and began putting everything together in the receptacle.

"Almost finished," she said. She estimated she had been working about twenty minutes. "Are you in yet?"

"Still working," John murmured absently. "The files are password protected."

"Did you try 'Laure'?"

"It was my first shot."

"Nothing in the desk?" She had been aware of him opening and closing drawers, but thought he might be looking for paper files, too.

"No." He was swiftly examining everything on top of the desk, looking for anything that might contain the password.

She screwed the jack plate into place, then repositioned the sofa. "What if it isn't written down?"

"Unless he's a fool, he changes the password on a regular basis. If he changes it, then the current one is written down somewhere. If you're finished there, look for a wall or floor safe."

"Don't tell me you're a safecracker, too."

"Okay, I won't tell you."

Swiftly she checked behind all the paintings hanging on the wall, but there was only wallpaper there. A huge, thickly woven rug covered the floor and she threw back the edges, but again found nothing. She got out a screwdriver and, moving around the room, examined all the outlets, because sometimes dummy outlets concealed small hiding places. "Nothing," she reported. She gathered her tools and the pistol, slipping them back into the folds of her evening wrap.

John picked up a book and ruffled all the pages, holding it spine up to see if anything fell out. He paused, looking at the well-thumbed book. Niema walked over to look at the book, putting her tools down on top of the desk: *A Tale of Two Cities.*

John flipped to a page with a down-turned corner. "It's here. Nobody reads this more than once, unless they have to."

"It's a classic," she said, amused.

"I didn't say it wasn't good, but it isn't something you read over and over." He ran his finger down the page, looking for anything that jumped out at him. "Guillotine."

Turning back to the keyboard, he typed in the word. ACCESS DENIED flashed on the screen.

He shrugged and consulted the book again. "Dickens was damn wordy," he grumbled. "This could take all day." He tried "monarchs." ACCESS DENIED.

"Monsters" was rejected, then "enchanter."

The file list opened on "tumbrils."

"How about that," John said softly. "I was just shooting in the dark."

"Lucky shot." Except he wasn't just lucky, he was so highly trained that instinct and experience put him several jumps ahead of almost everyone else, allowing him to see the significance of a battered copy of a classic lying in the open on Ronsard's desk.

He slid a disk into the A drive and began calling up files and copying them onto the disk. He didn't take time to read any of them, he just copied them as fast as possible, one eye on the closed-circuit monitor the entire time.

Niema moved around behind the desk. "I'll watch the monitor," she said. "You copy."

He nodded, and the A drive began whirring almost continuously.

A moment later, watching the monitor, Niema saw the door at the end of the hallway open.

"Someone's coming," she whispered.

John glanced at the screen, but didn't pause in what he was doing. "That's one of the security team," he replied.

"Do they do door checks?"

"Maybe." The reply was terse. Since he had disabled the lock on the door, it would open if anyone tried it.

Niema put her hand in the folds of the evening wrap. The pistol grip felt cool and heavy under her fingers. The guard began walking down the hallway toward the office. Her heartbeat picked up and her mouth went dry.

The hallway was a long one; on the small screen, it seemed to stretch out endlessly, with the guard becoming bigger and bigger as he approached. Niema found herself counting his steps. Nineteen, twenty, twenty-one—

"Don't lose your cool," John cautioned softly but didn't look up from the list of files. "Almost finished here."

The guard strode past, never even pausing outside the door. Watching him on the screen, hearing his footsteps pass by the office, gave her an odd sense of unreality because the sound came from a different direction than the activity she watched on the screen.

"That's it." Quickly he punched the release, and the disk popped out. He slipped it into a protective sleeve and put it in his inside jacket pocket. Then he turned off the computer, restored everything on the desk to its original position, and touched her elbow. "Ready?"

"I'll say."

She turned to go to the door, but suddenly he grabbed her arm, pulling her to a standstill. "More company."

She looked back at the monitor. The hallway door was opening again. Someone had stopped in the doorway, half turned away as if he were speaking to someone on the other side of the door. The tiny figure on the screen had long dark hair.

"Ronsard," she whispered, a cold twist of panic tightening her stomach. He wouldn't be in this long hallway unless he were coming to his office.

John exploded into motion, literally lifting her off her feet. In two long strides he was beside the sofa. He set her down and began stripping out of his tuxedo jacket, carelessly dropping it on the floor. "Take off your underwear and lie down," he ordered, his tone low and urgent.

They had only seconds, seconds before Ronsard would be coming through that door. Her hands shook as she pulled up her skirt and reached under it for the waistband of her panties. Pretending to have sex was such a cliché, trotted out in hundreds of movies, that no one would believe it, especially not someone as sophisticated and savvy as Ronsard. That was precisely why it just might work, because he wouldn't believe Temple would be so hokey.

Of course John, being John, wouldn't depend on a torrid clinch to give the impression he wanted. No, he wanted underwear off, clothes disarrayed, as if they truly were just about to make love.

Her heart was pounding so hard she could feel her pulse throbbing under her skin. She skimmed her panties down her thighs and let them drop, then hurriedly kicked them away and lay down on the sofa.

Leaning forward, John tugged her skirt up to her waist and pulled her legs apart, kneeling between them with one knee on the sofa while he tore open his trousers. She went numb with shock. Only the cool air washing over her naked flesh told her this wasn't a weird dream, but it had to be. This was carrying pretense further than she was prepared to take it. She couldn't be lying here half-naked with him between her spread legs and witnesses likely to come through the door at any second.

He bent down and licked her, his hard hands pushing her thighs wider as his tongue probed inside her, depositing moisture. Niema's entire body jolted and he held her down, his mouth pressed between her legs. She swallowed a shriek, her breath strangling in her throat. Oh God, he was going down on her—Ronsard would . . . She couldn't let herself think of Ronsard walking in on them now but this must be what John had planned, to be caught in an act so intimate no one would dream it was pretense—

How could it be pretense when he was actually doing it?

She whimpered and reached down, her hands sliding through his hair. She wanted to push him away but couldn't, her hands simply wouldn't obey. Bolts of sensation shot through her body, arching her in his hands. How long would she have to endure this? How long? Five seconds? Ten?

Time had become elastic, stretching beyond recognition. She shook her head in wordless protest, helplessly speared under the dual lash of fear and pleasure. Something hot and wild spiraled in her. She couldn't do this, couldn't bear it, not with his mouth on her body making every muscle tighten past endurance.

She found the strength to push weakly at his shoulders. He slid upward, his tongue swirling around her clitoris in a quick caress that nearly shot her off the sofa, but he quickly controlled her and shifted into position between her legs.

"Easy," he whispered and pressed himself to her opening.

No. He couldn't actually be doing this. Not here, not like this. She didn't want their first time to be like this.

Everything was happening too fast; her body hadn't had time to prepare itself, even with the moisture he had given her with his tongue. How *could* she be prepared, when she couldn't believe what he was doing, not now, not like this?

He pushed slowly into her and she wasn't nearly wet enough, her inner tissues yielding reluctantly to his intrusion. "Scream," he said, the word almost soundless.

Scream? That would certainly bring Ronsard—but that was what John wanted. The realization seared through her dazed mind. Anyone up to no good wouldn't make that kind of noise, which was guaranteed to attract attention, or be doing what they were doing.

He put no limits on what he would do to get the job done.

He withdrew a little then thrust again, forcing himself deeper, inch by inch. "Scream," he repeated, demanding now.

She couldn't. She didn't have enough air, her lungs were paralyzed, her entire body arching under the almost brutal lash of sensation. Every nerve ending felt electrified, her loins clenching as she fought the relentless swell of pleasure. She fought him too, not with her fists but with every muscle inside her, clamping down, trying to hold him, prevent him from going deeper and pushing her beyond control.

She wasn't strong enough. He thrust slowly past her resistance, bracing his hands on either side of her rib cage and leaning over her. Quick, shallow breaths panted between his parted lips; his eyes were narrowed, brilliant, the blue more intense than she had ever seen it before. With one swift movement he pulled down the left strap of her gown, baring her breast. Her nipple was already tightly beaded, flushed with color. "Scream," he insisted, thrusting harder. "Scream!"

Her head thrashed back and forth on the cushion. She choked back a sob and desperately struck out at him, trying to squirm away. She couldn't, she didn't want to, dear God please don't let her be climaxing as Ronsard walked through that door, she couldn't bear it. John caught her wrists and pinned them to the sofa, relentlessly probing ever deeper.

She couldn't stop it, couldn't contain it. She convulsed, waves of sensation pulsing through her loins. She sank into the climax, head thrown back and eyes closed, breath halted, everything fading around her until her only focus of existence was the searing pleasure. She did scream then, silently, beyond despair, as she waited for the door to open.

The door didn't open. There was nothing but silence in the hallway.

The sensual paroxysm began to ebb, the tension fading from her trembling flesh until she lay limp and pliant beneath him, her legs still open and her body still penetrated. She couldn't think, couldn't move. She felt hollow, emptied out, as if he had taken everything.

Humiliation crawled through her like lava. She turned her head aside, unable to look at him. How could she have climaxed in such a situation? What kind of person was she? What kind of man was *he*, to do this? Tears burned her eyes, but she couldn't wipe them away because he still held her wrists pinned.

Time stopped.

Ronsard wasn't coming into his office. She didn't know where he had gone, but he wasn't here. She waited for John to withdraw, waited for a moment that stretched on and on until the tension was more than she could bear and she had to look at him again, had to face him.

His expression was set in almost savage lines, his eyes so bright they seemed to burn her. He seemed to have been waiting for her to look at him. "I'm sorry," he said, and began moving—not away from her but inside her, thrusting, forging a deep, fast rhythm, and pierced her to her very core.

He came hard, gripping her hips while he plunged and bucked, his head thrown back and his teeth grinding together to hold back the hoarse sounds in his throat. He sank against her, panting, his chest heaving as he gulped in air.

She didn't say anything, couldn't think of anything *to* say.

LINDA HOWARD

Her mind was emptied, dazed with shock. Nothing she'd ever read in Miss Manners covered this situation. The bizarreness of that thought almost made her laugh, but the laugh turned into a sob that she choked back.

Carefully he levered himself away from her; her breath caught at the drag of his flesh leaving hers. He pulled her to a sitting position. "Are you all right?"

She nodded silently, swinging her feet to the floor and pushing her skirt down to cover her thighs. He neatened himself with brisk movements, tucking in his shirt and fastening his trousers.

Her panties were lying on the floor in front of the desk. John picked them up and held them out to her. In silence she took them. Her legs felt too wobbly for her to trust them, so she sat on the sofa and worked the panties up her legs until she could lift her hips and tug the flimsy garment into place. She was very wet now, the moisture dampening her underwear and drying stickily on her inner thighs.

He walked around the desk until he could see the closed-circuit monitor. "The coast is clear," he said, as calmly as if nothing had happened. "I don't know where Ronsard went."

Shakily she got to her feet and gathered her evening wrap, fumbling with the folds to make certain they still held everything securely. John shrugged into his tuxedo jacket and straightened his tie, then raked his fingers through his hair. He looked cool and controlled.

"Are you ready?"

She nodded, and he checked the monitor again. "Here we go," he said, taking her arm and ushering her to the door.

Somehow she controlled her voice, and found the words. Somehow she sounded as casual as he did. "What about the lock? Are you going to fix it?"

270

"No, he'll just think it malfunctioned. This type does occasionally."

He opened the door and swiftly looked out, then ushered her into the empty hallway. He was pulling the office door shut, his hand still on the handle, when the hallway door abruptly swung open and a guard stepped through. He checked when he saw them, shouting something as he automatically reached for his weapon.

John was moving almost before the guard saw them. He pushed Niema against the wall as he went down on one knee, going for the weapon in his ankle rig. The guard panicked and fired too soon, the bullet plowing into the floor ten feet in front of him. John didn't panic. Niema saw his face, calm and expressionless, as his hand swept up. He fired twice, the first shot in the chest and the second, an insurance shot, in the head. The guard jerked like a puppet with broken strings as he crashed backward through the open door.

John gripped Niema's hand and with one motion pulled her to her feet. Screams rose beyond the open hallway door and running footsteps pounded toward them. "Come on," he said and shoved her toward the left exit, and people poured through the door behind them.

Upstairs, the three shots froze Hossam. He leaped off the bed and grabbed his pants from the floor, jerking them on as he ran for the door. He grabbed his shoulder holster as well, sliding the weapon free.

"Hossam! Don't leave me like this!" Cara's voice was sharp with panic—he had long since taken off the gag—but he ignored her and ran out the door. He did have presence of mind to slam the door closed as he went out, but that was all he took the time to do.

Barefoot, he raced down the hall to the stairway at the end and instead of using the steps he put his hand on the rail and vaulted down to the next tier, again and again until he reached the ground floor. The shots seemed to have come from directly below and to the right, which meant they were near Ronsard's office.

The long hallway was jammed with people, some of them Ronsard's guests who were exclaiming in horror. The security personnel were trying to clear them out of the hall, but the arrival of a huge, half-naked, armed man had the guests shrinking back.

"Where?" Hossam shouted.

"Out this entrance," a guard replied, pointing to the door. "It was Temple and one of the women." Hossam wheeled and plunged into the night.

Where would Temple go? Hossam briefly paused, thinking. He would try to get transportation, rather than get away on foot, but the guests vehicles were secured in a fenced area. The estate vehicles, however, were not. Hossam ran barefoot across the damp lawn, heading for the garage area.

Bright emergency lights flashed on all over the estate, lighting up the area like a football field. Armed men swarmed the lawn. Hossam yelled, "The guest vehicles! Check them!"

A large group formed, racing for the secure area. Hossam ran on toward the garage, his weapon held ready. Damn, this guy Temple had piss-poor timing! He'd had Cara ready to come for about the tenth time when he heard the shots, but he'd had to jerk out of her and leave her on the brink, still helplessly tied to the bed.

The long, shadowed garage was silent as he moved down the row of cars and Land Rovers and Jeeps. "Are you here?" he whispered.

"Here."

Hossam whirled as Temple stepped out of the shadows, towing a woman behind him. "Go, man," he hissed, pulling a set of keys out of his pocket and tossing them to Temple, who released the woman to catch them with his left hand. "The green Mercedes there."

"Thanks. Turn around."

Sighing, Eric Govert turned around. He just hoped he wouldn't be out too long, or Cara would be hysterical with rage. He never heard Temple move or felt the blow that left him stretched out on the cold concrete floor.

CHAPTER
TWENTY-THREE

J ohn bent down and scooped up the big man's
weapon and tossed it to Niema. "Here, hold
this."

She pushed that pistol, too, into the bundle of her evening
wrap. It would look suspicious if they didn't take the weapon.
He unlocked the car with the automatic lock release on the
key ring and they got in. "Get down on the floor," he said,
putting his hand on the back of her head and pushing to make
sure she obeyed.

She crouched in the well of the floor as he started the car
and hit the garage door opener. The door began to slide
upward and the automatic light came on overhead. He glanced
at her and smiled, and shifted into gear. The powerful car shot

forward, tires grabbing traction so smoothly there was no squeal or burning rubber.

The first shot shattered the window above her head, spraying glass over the interior of the car. She bit back a startled cry, covering her head with her arms as a second shot went through the passenger door and the back of the seat not three inches from John's arm, the bullet making a funny *whfftt* sound as it passed through the leather and fabric.

He floored the gas pedal, smoothly shifting through the gears. With each new gear the increased G-force pushed her hard against the seat. "Stay down," he said, and ducked a split second before the drivers' side window shattered.

The gates. He was heading for those massive, steel-barred gates. She barely had time to brace her hands before the impact. Metal screamed and glass shattered, and she heard more shots, the rapid coughing of automatic fire. She was thrown sideways, her head banging the gear shift. One of the heavy gates, torn off its hinges, landed half on the hood.

"Are you all right?" John shouted as he shifted into reverse. The gate spun and slid to the ground. He shifted gears again and the car shot forward, bumping over the gate, metal bars clanging.

"Yeah," she yelled, but she didn't know if he heard her over the gunfire. He wasn't returning the fire, using all his concentration to drive. She fumbled for the two weapons in the folds of her wrap; the first one she touched was the big one the Company man had been carrying. She got to her knees as she thumbed off the safety.

"God damn it, stay down!" John roared, reaching for her as if he would shove her back into the floor.

"Just drive!" She jerked away, wrapped both hands around the heavy weapon, and began firing out the window. Even if she didn't hit anyone, return fire would at least make them duck for cover. If she didn't do something, the car, with them in it, would be shot to pieces.

The heavy weapon bucked in her hand, the deep cough deafening her as hot casings ejected into the car. One bounced off her bare arm, leaving behind a sting.

The car wasn't running as smoothly as before; it jerked and hesitated, the engine cutting out. Some of the bullets had hit something critical but at least they were off the estate grounds. More shots zinged after them, but they sounded like hand-guns, which meant the shots didn't have their range. "We have to ditch the car," John said, turning his head to check behind them. The rearview mirror was nothing but a shattered metal frame, the mirror blasted into tiny pieces all over them.

"Where?"

"As soon as we're out of sight. With luck, they won't find the car until morning."

Niema peered over the shredded remains of the seat back. The estate was lit with so many lights it looked like a minia-ture city. Dozens of lights bloomed as she watched, neatly spaced apart in pairs—headlights. "They're coming," she said.

They went around a curve, and a thick stand of trees hid the estate from sight. He drove off the road, slowing so the tires wouldn't churn up the ground, easing the heavy vehicle into the trees. They bumped over limbs and rocks, and bushes scraped at the once-pristine paint job.

He didn't touch the brake pedal, just in case one of the tail-lights was still working. When they were far enough off the road that passing headlights wouldn't glint on metal, he stopped and killed the engine. They sat in silence broken only by the engine pinging and hissing, listening to the pursuing vehicles roar past their hiding spot.

They were less than a mile from the estate. "Now what?"

she asked, her voice sounding funny, but then her ears were still ringing from the gunfire. The car interior stank of burnt gunpowder and hot metal.

"Do you feel like a nice run?"

"It's my favorite thing to do in the middle of the night, wearing sandals and a two-thousand dollar dress, with a hundred guys chasing and shooting at us."

"Just be glad the sandals aren't high-heeled." He rapped his pistol barrel on the inside lights, shattering covers and bulbs so there wouldn't be any betraying light when they opened the doors.

Gingerly she climbed up from the floor. Shards of glass dusted the seats, her shoulders, her hair. It was very dark under the trees. The door on her side wouldn't open; a bullet had probably hit the lock mechanism. She crawled over the gear shift, glass tinkling and gritting with every movement she made.

John got out and reached in, bodily lifting her out of the car and standing her on her feet. "Shake," he directed.

They both bent over, shaking their heads and flopping their arms and clothes to dislodge any clinging bits of glass. Her arms and shoulders were stinging a little, but when she cautiously felt them her fingers came away dry, so at least she wasn't bleeding. It was a wonder they were even alive; not being cut by that hail of glass went beyond wonder into miraculous.

But when they straightened, her eyes had adjusted more to the darkness and she saw that half of John's face was darker than the other half. Her stomach plummeted. "You're hit," she said, fighting to keep her voice even. He couldn't be shot. He couldn't. Something vital in her depended on his being okay.

"By glass, not a bullet." He sounded more irritated than

anything else. He took the silk handkerchief from his breast pocket and held it to his forehead. "Do you have both pistols?"

"They're in the car." She leaned forward into the car and retrieved both weapons. "What about my tools? Leave them?" She definitely didn't want to lug them around.

"Hand them here."

She gave him the velvet pouch, heavy with tools. He took the tools out and threw them, one by one, as far as he could into the trees and underbrush. If the bag of tools was found, Ronsard would wonder what they had been used for, and since they had been spotted coming out of his office he would then no doubt have a complete physical search done of all the wiring, and he would find the bug. A physical search was the only way to find it, but then no bug could be hidden when the wires themselves were examined.

"Got your wrap?"

"Why do I need it?" ֊

"Because it's black and will hide some of that skin you're showing." She got the wrap and her evening bag out of the car, though she had to gingerly feel around until she found them. The evening bag was useless; there wasn't anything in there they could use, not even money. All her money, passport, everything, were back in her room. She wasn't worried about the passport; the name on it was false, and John would get them back into the country even without one, but money would have come in handy.

John took the bag from her, but instead of throwing it away he tucked it in his pocket. "Come on."

Running in the woods in the dark was too dangerous; they risked turned ankles at least, and possibly broken bones, so they picked their way through the trees and underbrush, pausing every so often to listen for pursuit. They could hear traffic on the road, growing more and more distant as they angled away from it. They couldn't hope that Ronsard's men would be stymied for much longer, though.

They came out of the woods onto a secondary road. "We'll follow this for a while," he said. "It's easier traveling, and while it's dark we can see them a lot sooner than they can see us."

"Are we going anywhere in particular, or just running?"

"Nice."

"Why Nice? Why not Lyon? It's closer."

"Ronsard will be watching the airport in Lyon, and all the car rentals. He'll expect us to go there."

"Then how about Marseilles?"

"Our yacht is in Nice."

"Really. I didn't know we had a yacht."

"The *Company* has a yacht, and the yacht has a computer with a satellite up-link. I'll be able to get this information to Langley and let them start work on it immediately."

"Nice it is, then."

He took a knife from his pocket and knelt at her feet. Grasping a fistful of fabric in his hand, he inserted the knife about level with her knee and slit her gown sideways, cutting off the bottom half of the skirt. "You have more things in the pockets of that tuxedo than Snoopy has in his dog house," she commented. "I don't see how it fits as well as it does."

"I have a very good tailor."

Now that they were out from under the trees, she could see that his head was still bleeding. He cut a narrow strip off the swath he had just removed from her gown and tied it over the cut. His tuxedo was torn and dirty, and when she looked down she saw that what remained of her gorgeous Dior gown was in the same condition. The remnant of the fabric he draped around his neck.

They began running in an easy jog, because they weren't wearing running shoes and the impact of the hard asphalt through the thin soles of their evening shoes jarred every bone and muscle as it was.

"Are we going to run all the way to Nice?" she asked after about a mile.

"No, we're going to steal a car."

"When?"

"As soon as we find one."

She tried to find a stride that was easier on her feet and legs, and tried to keep her mind focused on the present. While they were being shot at she hadn't had any trouble focusing, but now there was nothing but the rhythmic slap of their shoes on the asphalt, the easy sound of their breathing, and the night sounds surrounding them. With nothing posing an immediate threat, her thoughts zeroed in on what had happened in Ronsard's office.

She didn't want to think about it, but couldn't stop. Maybe it had been inevitable, given the tug of sexual attraction she felt for him, had felt from the moment she set eyes on him in Frank Vinay's office. He struck sparks off her, made her feel so alive she sometimes thought her skin couldn't contain her. Those kisses they had shared—maybe the setup had been pretense, but her response hadn't. With every touch, every dance, every kiss her anticipation had built until it was a wonder she hadn't climaxed as soon as he licked her.

If only it hadn't happened that way. If only he had been making love to her, instead of setting a scene for their cover story. For her, their coming together had been a cataclysmic event. For him, it had been a job.

Maybe that was what hurt so much. She wanted to mean something to him other than just another job, another means to an end. She was afraid . . . dear God, she was afraid she loved him.

She would have to be a Grade A fool to love John Medina.

Loving a man who traveled was one thing; thousands of women did. Loving a man who drew in danger with every breath was something else thousands of women did. Cops, firemen, high-iron men, oil-well riggers—they all had dangerous jobs and they were gone for long stretches of time. But at least they lived in the sunlight. At least their lives were real. John was always setting a scene, doing a job, working an angle. He was almost always someone else. She would never know if he was dead or alive, or if he was coming back even if he was alive.

She couldn't love like that. She couldn't *live* like that.

"Car," he said, breaking the agonized chain of her thoughts, gripping her arm and urging her off the road. "Get down." Headlights speared toward them through the darkness, the car moving fast.

She lay flat on her face in the weeds, with the evening wrap draped over her arms and shoulders and the remnants of her skirt covering her bare legs. John lay beside her, between her and the road. The car zoomed past.

Slowly they sat up. Until they stopped running, she hadn't been aware of how her feet and legs were aching. She rubbed her hands up and down her shins. "Maybe barefoot would be better than these shoes."

"On the ground, yes, but not on asphalt."

The thin straps were rubbing blisters on her feet. She eased the straps to a different position. "I'm developing a problem here."

He squatted beside her. "Blisters?"

"Not yet, but getting there."

"Okay, running is out. We need to get transportation tonight, though, because we'll be a lot easier to spot on foot during the day. I wanted to get farther away before I liberated a car, but that can't be helped."

"What difference does it make?"

"If a car is stolen practically in Ronsard's backyard, do you think he won't hear about it and figure we're the ones who stole it? Then he'll know what kind of car we're in and can have people watching for us."

She sighed. "Then we walk."

His hand closed gently over her foot. "I don't think that's an option, either. We'll come across a farm soon, or a village, and I'll get whatever's there, even if it's a tow truck."

"Until then," she said as she got to her feet, "we walk."

CHAPTER
TWENTY-FOUR

Ronsard was more coldly furious than he'd ever been in his life, but more at himself than anyone else. After all, in his business one could expect treachery. What he hadn't expected was that he would have been so completely fooled. Nor had he expected that as many security personnel as were on the estate wouldn't be able to stop one car from leaving. They were supposedly professionals, but they hadn't performed as such.

He had one man dead, and another, Hossam, suffering from a concussion. Hossam had been found lying on the garage floor, only half-dressed and unconscious. Having correctly guessed that Temple would try for one of the estate vehicles, he had evidently been taken from behind. Why Hossam had been wearing only his pants when he was supposed to have

LINDA HOWARD

been working was a puzzle, until he noticed that Cara was nowhere to be found and sent someone to investigate. She was found tied to her bed, naked and furious. He had been wondering if he would have to kill Hossam for assaulting her until her concern, when she found he had been injured, reassured him that whatever had been going on in her bedroom had been consensual.

Ronsard's guests were shocked and uneasy. The violence of the night's events had forcibly brought home to many of them exactly what sort of world their host lived in. It was all very well to flirt with danger, to boast to their friends that they had been guests at the notorious Louis Ronsard's luxurious estate, to give him information that made them feel wicked and notorious too, but the reality of it was more brutal than they could have guessed.

He imagined none of them had ever seen a man who had been shot in the head. Then all hell had broken loose outside as Temple made his escape, with a hail of automatic fire that sounded as if a small war was being waged on his front lawn, the car crashing through his front gates, his guards scattering as small-arms fire was returned at them. It wasn't just his security that had been breached, but theirs. They no longer had the illusion of safety. Most of them were leaving come the morning.

As a host, his night had been a fiasco. As a businessman, it was worse than that.

Temple and Niema had been in his office. What Niema was doing there, he couldn't imagine. Perhaps she was Temple's partner, perhaps not. Witnesses to the shooting in the hallway had agreed he was manhandling her, shoving her around, dragging her outside. On the other hand, Temple had been driving the car; who other than Niema had been shooting at his guards? It was possible Temple had been both driving and

286

shooting; difficult, but not impossible, and Temple was a trained assassin.

What had they been doing in his office?

The lock wasn't working. It had been, however, when he left the office the last time, because he automatically, from ingrained habit, tried the handle every time he left.

He stood in his office looking around, trying to see what Temple could have seen. What would he have been interested in? The computers, of course. But there was nothing on Cara's that would have been of interest to him, and the information in Ronsard's computer was password protected.

The password. He walked to his desk and surveyed the items on top of it. Nothing looked disturbed; his copy of *A Tale of Two Cities* was exactly where he had left it.

And yet—

And yet, the instinct for survival that had stood him in such good stead told him that Temple had somehow breached the security in his computer as surely as he had breached the estate's security. Ronsard couldn't afford to assume otherwise. Nor could he afford to underestimate his opponent, a man who evidently appeared and disappeared at will, and who had access to government documents before they were made public. Such a man was a man with power either behind him, or in his own hands.

They had to be found. With one phone call to the authorities in Lyon he had immediately thrown a net over the airport, then, when one of his more observant men saw where a car had been driven off the road and found the Mercedes abandoned, extended that net to the car rental services also.

They were on foot, unless Temple stole another car. Ronsard arranged that he be told immediately if any thefts were reported.

He sat down at his desk, drumming his fingers on the wood. Lyon was the most logical immediate destination—but perhaps Temple would go in the opposite direction, for that reason. Do the unexpected. Keep your opponent off balance, guessing.

This would be like a game of chess, with moves and countermoves. The key to victory was planning ahead, anticipating every move his opponent could make.

Marseilles was to the south—a larger city than Lyon, with a huge, busy port. It was farther away, but once there, the chances of escaping went up dramatically.

The port. That was the key. Temple would escape by water.

The village was a small one, no more than fifteen houses loosely grouped on each side of the road. John selected an older model Renault that was parked in front of a cottage, as the older cars were easier to hotwire. Niema stood watch while he eased the car door open and felt under the dash for the wiring harness. The interior light was burning, but he didn't have a flashlight and had to take the chance of someone seeing the light. With his knife, he stripped the wires of their plastic sheath.

Three cottages away, a dog roused from its doggy dreams and barked once, then fell silent. No light came on in any of the cottage's windows.

"Get in," John whispered, moving aside so she could crawl in from that side and not make more noise by having to open and close the passenger door, too. She wasn't a four-year-old, and the Renault was small; she banged her knee on the gear shift, her head on the interior light, and her elbow on the steering wheel. Swearing under her breath, she finally maneuvered herself into the passenger seat.

John wasn't laughing, but his mouth wore a curve that said he wanted to. The small interior light gave her the first clear look at him since they left the estate, and her heart skipped a beat. The right side of his face was streaked with dried blood, despite his efforts to wipe it off. His once-snowy shirt was rusty with dirt and blood, his hair was tousled, and beard stubble darkened his jaw. With the black strip of silk tied around his head, he looked like a disreputable, Armani-clad pirate.

If anyone saw them the way they looked now, they were busted.

He twisted the wires together, and the engine began trying to crank. It coughed, the fan turning, and he slid into the seat and gently pressed the gas pedal. With a high-pitched hum like a sewing machine, the car started. Without closing the door, he put in the clutch and shifted into low gear; the car began rolling as he let out the clutch. Fifty yards down the road, he closed the door.

"What time is it?" she asked, slumping in the seat. Her feet were throbbing. She eased them out of the sandals, knowing she might not be able to get her shoes back on and not caring. Sitting down was such a relief she almost groaned.

He glanced at his wristwatch. "A little after three. With luck, we have two or three hours before anyone notices the car is missing. Why don't you try to get some sleep?"

"I'm not sleepy." She wasn't. She was exhausted but not sleepy. She was both hungry and thirsty, and really, really needed to soak her aching feet in cold water.

"You will be. When your adrenaline drops, you'll crash."

"What about you? Don't you have adrenaline?" she snapped, though she didn't know why she was suddenly crabby.

"I'm used to it. I've learned how to work through the crash."

"I'm okay."

She wasn't, though. She glanced at him. His strong hands were steady on the wheel, his expression as calm as if he were out for a Sunday drive. Maybe she looked that calm, too, but inside she was shredded.

"Do you want to talk about it?"

"No," she said, appalled. There was no need to ask what "it" was. She didn't want him to be reasonable and logical and tell her to just look at what they'd done as part of the job. All she wanted was to get this over with and leave with some semblance of dignity still intact.

"We have to at some point."

"No, we don't. I just want to forget it."

He paused, and his jaw tightened. "Are you mad because you came, or because I did?"

She felt like screaming. God, why wouldn't he just leave it alone? "Neither. Both."

"That's certainly a definitive answer."

"If you want definitive answers, get a dictionary."

Another pause, as if he measured her resistance. "All right, I'll drop it for now, but we *will* talk."

She didn't reply. Didn't he understand? Talking about what happened was like touching a wound, keeping it fresh and bleeding. But, no, how could he understand, when it wasn't like that for him?

"How far is it to Nice?"

"A couple of hundred miles if we use the expressway, less if we go over the mountains. The direct route probably won't be the fastest, though, at least not in this car. It doesn't have the horses to climb the mountains at much more than a crawl."

"The expressway should get us there by six-thirty or seven, though."

"In the neighborhood. We have to stop and steal another car."

"Another one?"

"We're too close to Ronsard's estate. He'll hear about this as soon as it's reported. We need to ditch this one."

"Where?"

"Valence, I think. I'll look for something there."

They were serial car thieves, she mused. Well, she had wanted excitement. John Medina certainly filled the bill; there were no dull stretches while in his company. But home was looking better and better, as a refuge in which she could deal with the idiocy of having fallen in love with him. She thought of her peaceful house, with everything specifically arranged to her liking—except for the double hook-and-eye latches on every door and window.

"If I can get a flight out, I'll be home by this time tomorrow," she said, then remembered her passport. "No, scratch that. No passport. How am I going to get back into the States?"

"We'll probably take military transport home."

We? He intended to travel with her? That was news. "You're going back to Washington, too?"

"For the time being."

He didn't expand on that, and she didn't ask. Instead she leaned her head back and closed her eyes. Even if she couldn't sleep, she could rest.

"A baker reported his car was stolen early this morning . . . here." Ronsard put his finger on the map. The village was thirteen kilometers from the estate, on a small, narrow road that wound in a general southwest direction and eventually bisected the expressway. Several of his security people were gathered around the desk while he spoke on the telephone to a friend with the local authorities.

If Temple went south, he would have been in the same rough area as the village. "What make and color is the car? Do you have the license?" He wrote as he listened. "Yes, thank you. Keep me informed."

He hung up and tore the sheet of paper off the pad. "Find this car," he said, handing the sheet to his men. "On the expressway to Marseilles. Bring him back alive, if possible. If not—" He broke off and shrugged.

"And the woman?"

Ronsard hesitated. He didn't know the extent of Niema's involvement. He had personally searched her room and there was nothing suspicious there. Could Temple have kidnapped her? There was one thing of which he was absolutely sure: The man was obsessed with her. The intensity with which he had watched her couldn't be feigned. He could still feel that way if they were partners, but if they weren't, Temple was the type of man who wouldn't balk at kidnapping if she wouldn't go willingly.

The Niema he knew was funny, a little sharp-tongued, and kind-hearted. He remembered the way she had shown Laure how to apply the makeup she had acquired, the gentleness, the way she didn't talk down to Laure as if being ill had somehow stunted his daughter's ability to understand.

For Laure, he said, "Try not to hurt her. Bring her to me."

CHAPTER
TWENTY-FIVE

They reached Valence before dawn. John cruised down the streets, looking for a promising target. The city had a population of over sixty thousand, so he should be able to find another car without a lot of trouble.

He glanced over at Niema, sitting as erect as a soldier, and his lips compressed into a grim line. He'd almost gotten her killed tonight. He had been so certain this would be an in-and-out job, the sort he could do blindfolded, but instead they had barely escaped with their lives.

He was still taking risks with her life. He knew it, and yet he couldn't bring himself to make the call that would get them picked up, not now, not with what he'd done to her in Ron-

LINDA HOWARD

sard's office lying between them like a snake coiled ready to strike if he tried to move it.

One phone call. That was all it would take. They would be picked up within the hour and flown to Nice, where he would up-link the files and finish the job. But the way things were now, she would move heaven and earth to go home and get away from him. He couldn't let that happen, not with things the way they were between them.

He had gone to a lot of trouble to keep her from realizing how focused he was on her, and now that was working against him. She thought she was nothing more to him than a means to an end. What would she say if he told her the truth, that even though the love-making in Ronsard's office had started out as a cover, he had seen the opportunity to have her and ruthlessly used it. What was worse, he would do it again. He'd take her any way he could, whenever he could.

Everything he'd said at Ronsard's, everything he'd done, was the truth. That was why Ronsard had so easily believed the cover, because it was true. But Niema didn't seem to see it, even though he knew she wanted him, was so physically aware of him she had climaxed with startling speed. Maybe he was too damn good at his job, at playing a role. He was tired of role-playing; when he kissed her, damn it, he wanted her to know he was kissing her because he wanted to rather than because it was what was called for in some unwritten script.

A police car was coming toward them in the other lane. He was so preoccupied he almost missed how it slowed as it approached. Then instinct kicked in and reflexes took over. "We're made," he said, downshifting and taking the next right on two wheels. There was no point in being subtle; it didn't matter if they knew he'd seen them. What mattered was getting this car off the street before they were picked up. He jammed the gas pedal to the floor, needing to make the next turn before the police were able to turn around and fall in behind him.

Niema jerked to full attention. "That fast?" she asked incredulously.

"Ronsard has a lot of money. He can make a stolen vehicle a matter of prime importance." He pushed the little car as hard as he could, its motor whining. The next turn was a left, and that one too was made on two wheels. He killed the headlights and took the next left, which brought them back out on the street from which they had originally turned off.

Niema was trying to brace herself against the dash, the door, anything to keep from being slung all over the car.

He took a right. They were now, with luck, going away from the police car. The narrow street he was on was winding, and dark; unless he touched the brakes, they shouldn't be able to locate him.

He was good at driving without using the brakes. He down-shifted whenever he needed to slow to take a curve, letting the engine do the work.

"What now?" she asked. She had given up on trying to brace herself and was on her knees on the floor. In spite of everything, a hint of cheerfulness had returned to her voice. He remembered the way she had grabbed the heavy pistol and returned fire as they were crashing the gates; far from getting hysterical, she thrived on excitement.

"We stay with the original plan. Dump this car, get another one."

"Is there any chance of getting a little food while we're doing all this?"

"If we can find a stream where we can clean up. We're too noticeable the way we are."

She looked down at her bare feet and tattered gown, then at his bloodstained tuxedo, and shrugged. "So we're a little over-dressed. I don't think washing our faces and hands is going to help much."

She was right about that. They needed a change of clothes before they were seen in public; they were too noticeable. And he'd forgotten about the black strip tied around his head, but he couldn't remove it until they found some water, because the dried blood had stuck the material to the cut and if he pulled it off he'd start the damn thing bleeding again.

On the other hand, if the next car he stole had a full tank of gas, he could also steal some food and water and they wouldn't need to stop again until they reached Nice. They could shower on the yacht and have clothing delivered.

"We also need to find a secluded area for other reasons," she pointed out.

"Understood and obeyed."

He left the Renault parked behind a shop and removed its plates. The next car they came to, he removed those plates, replaced them with the Renault's, then they went back to the Renault and put the other car's plates on it. When the local police found the car and compared the plates to the ones on the car reported stolen, they would think it was a different car. They would eventually figure it out, but at least this would slow them down a little.

"Where to now?" Niema asked. She was tired, but at least John had found a bush behind which she had relieved herself, so she wasn't in any physical discomfort, other than her sore feet.

"We walk until we find another car."

"I was afraid you were going to say that. Why didn't we just take the car we put the Renault's plates on?"

"They were too close together. We would automatically be suspected. We need a car on the other side of town."

She sighed. The last thing she wanted to do right now was walk to the other side of town. No—the last thing she wanted to do was get caught. She bit her tongue to hold back any complaints that might slip out.

They walked for forty-five minutes before he spotted the car he wanted. It was a Fiat, parked at the top of a small slope, and it was unlocked. "Get in," he said, and she thankfully crawled in. Instead of hot-wiring it, he put it in neutral, braced his hands on the frame, and started it rolling. He hopped in and they rolled silently down the slope, away from the owner's house. He let it roll as far as it would and then did the hot-wiring thing. The engine was another sewing machine, but it ran smoothly, and that was all they required.

Ronsard paced quietly. He didn't like leaving everything to his men. He understood Temple, he thought, at least he didn't underestimate him. His guests were gone; there was no reason for him to remain here.

The phone rang with another update. The Renault had been found in Valence, but there was no report of Temple or Madame Jamieson. The plates on the Renault had been switched with those from a Volvo, but the Volvo hadn't been stolen.

"What other cars have been reported stolen within the past twenty-four hours?"

"A Peugeot was taken from behind a house a kilometer from the Renault. A Fiat was also stolen, but that was some distance away. And a Mercedes was reported stolen, but the owner has been out of town and does not know how long the car has been gone."

The Peugeot was the most likely, Ronsard thought. It was the closest. And yet . . . perhaps that was what Temple wished him to think. "Concentrate on the Mercedes and Fiat," he said. "I will be joining you by helicopter in two hours. Find those two cars."

"Yes, sir," came the brisk answer.

It was noon when they reached Nice. Niema was so tired she could barely think, but somehow her body kept moving. They were met at the dock by a man in a small outboard, to take them out to the yacht that was moored in the harbor. He had to be Company, Niema thought. He was American, and he didn't ask any questions, just competently steered the boat across the harbor and brought it alongside a gleaming white sixty-footer.

She wasn't too tired to be amazed. She stared up at the yacht, with an impressive array of antennas bristling from its top. When John had said "yacht," she had expected something about twenty-five or thirty feet, with a tiny galley, a tinier head, and bunk beds in a cramped cabin. This thing was in an entirely different category.

John spoke quietly with the other man, giving him instructions on the disposition of the stolen Fiat. It was to disappear, immediately. There were other instructions as well. "Keep us under surveillance. Don't let anyone approach us without warning."

"Got it."

He turned to look at Niema. "Can you make it up the ladder?"

"Do I get to take a shower and go to bed if I do?"

"Absolutely."

"Then I can make it up the ladder." She suited action to

words, setting her bare feet on the rungs and using the last of her energy to climb to the deck. John made it as easily as if he had just woke from a good night's sleep and started fresh. He looked terrible, but she couldn't see any sign of fatigue in him.

He opened the hatch door and led her inside. The interior was surprisingly spacious, with everything built in that could be built in, the design both sophisticated and luxurious. They were in the middle of the boat, in a large salon outfitted with pale golden wood and dark blue trim; a full galley lay beyond. John ushered her past the galley, into a narrow hallway, or whatever it was called on board a ship. If a kitchen was a galley, a bathroom was a head, and a bedroom was a cabin, then a hallway had to be something else too.

"Here's the head," he said, opening a door. "Everything you'll need is there. When you're finished, take either of these cabins." He indicated two doors in the hallway past the head.

"Where will you be?"

"In the office, up-linking to a satellite for a burst transmission. There are two other heads on board, so don't feel you have to hurry."

Hurry? He had to be joking.

The head was as luxuriously appointed as the rest of the boat. All of the cabinetry was built in, to save space. The glass-enclosed shower was spacious by anyone's standards, with gold-plated fixtures. A thick white terry cloth bathrobe hung on a hook behind the door, and a bath mat with a pile so thick her feet sank into it covered the glazed bronze tiles on the floor.

She investigated the contents of the vanity and found everything she could possibly need, as John had said: soap, shampoo, conditioner, toothpaste, a new toothbrush, moisturizer.

In another drawer was a blow dryer and an assortment of brushes and combs.

She was so tired all she wanted to do was fall in bed and sleep for the rest of the day. They were safe, the job completed. She had done what she signed on to do.

She should feel satisfied, or at least relieved. All she felt was a great hollow pain that had started in her chest and now seemed to fill her entire body. It was finished. Over. John. The job. Everything.

"I can't let him go," she whispered, leaning her head on her hands. She loved him too much. She had tried to fight it for weeks now; loving a man like him was a tough thing to do. She had already loved one damn hero, and losing Dallas had nearly destroyed her. What she was risking now was too devastating to even contemplate, but there was no turning back.

Nor could she see any future for them. John was, essentially, a lobo. They had worked as a team on this job, but that wasn't likely to happen again. By necessity he had to limit the number of people who knew his real identity, and carefully control any contact with them. She still didn't understand why she was one of those few people, despite what he said about being taken by surprise and blurting out his real name. John Medina didn't blurt out anything: Everything he said, everything he did, was toward some aim.

So why had he told her? She was nobody, a low-level tech with a talent for electronic surveillance. He could have kept quiet and let her go on believing his name was Tucker, or he could have come up with some other name; God knows he had a list of them tucked away somewhere in that convoluted brain of his. She had no way of knowing the difference.

She would drive herself crazy wondering about him, what he was doing and why he was doing it. No sane woman could possibly love him, but if this job had taught her one thing, it was that she wasn't sane. She was an adrenaline junkie, a risk-taker, and though she had spent the past five years fighting her own nature, punishing herself for Dallas's death and trying to shape her life, her personality, into a more conventional pattern, she could no longer maintain the illusion. All John had to do was walk through a door and beckon her, and she would go with him—anywhere, any time.

It angered her that she could be so defenseless against him. If he had shown any corresponding weakness, she wouldn't feel so hopeless. He liked her, she knew; physically he had responded when they kissed, and he had certainly risen to the occasion in Ronsard's office, but a physical response from a man was so automatic she couldn't let herself read any importance into it. Men were, as he himself had pointed out, simple creatures. All they required was a warm body. She had filled that requirement.

She could stand there all day running the details around and around in her mind, like a rat trying to escape from a maze, but she always came back to the same end: She couldn't see a future with John. He was what he was. He lived in the shadows and risked his life on a daily basis, and kept his personal life to a minimum. She even loved that part of him, because how many people in the world could do what he did, make the sacrifices he had made?

All she could do was hope she saw him now and again. Even every five years would be enough, if she could just know he was alive.

Shuddering, she pushed away that last thought and at last moved into action, stripping off her filthy clothes and stepping under the warm shower. She put her mind in neutral, soaping and scrubbing and shampooing, scrubbing away at a

LINDA HOWARD

stubborn dark stain on her thigh until she realized it was a bruise.

Getting clean made her feel marginally better, though the face she saw in the mirror was still pale and strained, her eyes shadowed with exhaustion. She took full advantage of the amenities provided, brushing her teeth, smoothing moisturizer into her skin, blow-drying her hair. There was even a tube of medicated cream, and she dabbed that on the raw places on her feet.

The grooming rituals had a sedative effect, easing the tightness of her nerves. She could sleep now, she thought, and even managed a smile to herself. As if sleeping had ever been in any doubt! She planned to spend at least ten hours horizontal, more if she could manage it.

She would deal with her dirty clothes later, she decided, and wrapped herself in the thick, soft robe. All she wanted to do now was sleep.

She opened the door and froze. John stood just outside the door, naked except for a damp towel wrapped around his waist. He had already showered; small beads of water still clung to the hair on his chest. Niema knotted her hands into fists, wrapping them with the robe sash to keep from touching him, flattening her palms against that warm, muscular wall and feeling his heart beat beneath her fingers.

"Are you finished?" she asked in surprise.

"It only took a couple of minutes. Load the disk in the computer, up-link to the satellite, and send a burst transmission. It's done."

"Good. You must be as tired as I am."

He blocked her exit from the head, looking down at her with an unreadable expression in his blue eyes. "Niema . . ."

"Yes?" she prompted, when he didn't say anything else.

He held out his hand to her, palm upturned, utterly steady. "Will you sleep with me?"

Her heart gave a powerful thud that made her feel weak. She stared up at him, wondering what was going on behind that impenetrable blue gaze, and then realized it didn't matter. For now, nothing mattered but being with him. She put her hand in his and whispered, "Yes."

He put his arms around her and lifted her off her feet almost before the word was out of her mouth. His mouth closed over hers, hungry, devouring, hot. He tasted of the same toothpaste she had used. His tongue stroked urgently in her mouth and she met it with her own. She wrapped her arms around his neck and lost herself, pleasure and joy exploding through her veins.

He dropped the towel where he stood. She lost the robe somewhere on the short route to the nearest cabin. She didn't know exactly how he got her out of it, but he did. They fell on the bed. Before she could catch her breath he levered himself on top of her and pushed his legs between hers.

His penetration was abrupt and forceful. She cried out, her back arching, her nails digging into his shoulders. His penis was so hot and hard it felt like a thick, heated pipe pushing into her unprepared body. His whole body was hot with urgency, his muscles shaking as he probed deeper, working his entire length into her. His mouth covered hers, swallowing her moans as excitement swirled through her. This wasn't part of a job. This wasn't pretense. He wanted her.

He was in her to the hilt, a heavy, stretching presence. He buried his head against her shoulder, shuddering with relief as if he couldn't have borne another moment unconnected to her.

This wasn't the John Medina she knew, this man with his

desperate need. He was always so controlled, but there was nothing controlled about him now.

She smoothed her hands down his back, feeling the powerful muscles rippling just under his skin. "There's a concept I want to introduce to you," she murmured. "It's called foreplay."

He lifted his head from her shoulder, smiling wryly. Propping himself on his elbows, settling more comfortably on her and in her, he framed her face in his hands and pressed a kiss to her mouth. "I'm a desperate man. Any time you let me touch you, I'm going to get inside you as fast as I can, before you have time to change your mind."

The words shocked her, hinting at a vulnerability, a need, she never would have suspected he felt.

He moved, a slow stroke that set off a small riot in her nerve endings. She gasped, her legs rising to clasp his hips. "Why would I change my mind?" she managed to ask.

"Things haven't always been . . . easy between us."

Things weren't easy between them now. There was tension and pain and uncertainty, an explosive sexual attraction, even a spark of hostility caused by the clash of two strong personalities. There was nothing serene about her relationship with him, never had been.

She slid her fingers into the damp strands of his hair, holding him as she lifted her hips and did her own stroking. "If I wanted an easy ride, I'd find a merry-go-round."

His entire body tightened, and his eyes burned laser blue. He seemed to lose his ability to breathe. She did it again, lifting to take him deep, then clamping all her internal muscles on him and holding him tight as she pulled back, milking him with her body. A harsh groan burst out of his throat. "Then hold on tight, honey, because it's gonna be long and hard."

"Actually," she purred, "it already is."

The smothered sound he made was almost a laugh. "That wasn't what I meant."

"Then show me what you did mean."

That look was back in his eyes again, that unreadable wall behind which something elusive moved. "A lot of different things," he murmured. "But for now, we'll concentrate on this one."

CHAPTER
TWENTY-SIX

Niema woke in his arms the next morning. She lay quietly, still drowsing, slipping back and forth between sleep and awareness. She was curled on her left side and he was a solid wall behind her, his legs tangled with hers and his arm a heavy weight over her hip. His breath was warm on her shoulder.

She hadn't slept with a man like this since Dallas, she thought sleepily, the name resonating gently in her mind. No—*John* was the last man she had slept with. The realization was a shock. She remembered that awful time in Iran, the way he had held her and gentled her to sleep, then held her the next morning while she wept, when she woke and realized he wasn't Dallas, that Dallas would never again hold her in the night.

She couldn't see the clock, but it was almost dawn; the sky was beginning to lighten. They had been in bed—what, sixteen, seventeen hours? Making love, sleeping, making love again. He had gotten up once and brought back a tray of bread and cheese and fruit, and that had been their supper. Other than that they hadn't left the cabin except to visit the head.

She felt lethargic, content to be right where she was. Her entire body was relaxed, sated, well-used.

His lips brushed the back of her neck and she realized he was awake. She made a slight nestling movement, sighing with pleasure. How she enjoyed this, waking in the early morning, held close by the man she loved; there were few things in life more satisfying.

His morning erection prodded her, rising insistently against her bottom. She started to turn over but he stayed her with a murmur, adjusting his position and guiding himself to her opening. She arched her back, giving him a better angle. He put his hand on her stomach, bracing her, and pushed. He went slowly inside her; she was morning soft, morning wet, but their positions made her body yield reluctantly to his intrusion. She breathed through her mouth, trying to stay relaxed. With her legs together there wasn't much room inside her; he felt huge, stretching her to the limit.

The sensation bordered on pain, but was also its own turn-on. She pressed her head back against his shoulder, struggling to contain the feeling and yet take more of him. Another inch pushed into her and she moaned.

He paused. "Are you all right?" His voice was low, smoky with sleep and desire.

She didn't know. Maybe. "Yes," she whispered.

He stroked his right hand up to her breasts, lightly rubbing his fingertips on the lower slope, the way he had learned she liked. The subtle caress lit a gentle glow of pleasure, prepared her nipples for more direct contact. That came from his thumb, slowly moving over them, circling them until they hardened and stabbed into his covering palm. It was scary how fast he had caught on to all the small subtleties of how she liked to be touched, scary that his attention had been so focused on her that he hadn't missed a single hitch in her breath. After just one night, he knew her body as well as she did.

He slipped his left arm under her, curving it around her waist and cupping his hand over her mound. His middle finger slid between her fold, pressing lightly on her clitoris. Not rubbing, just pressing, holding his finger there. Then he began to thrust, using long, slow strokes that moved her body back and forth against his finger.

She cried out, jerking under the lash of pleasure. He whispered something soothing and steadied her, then resumed the motion.

"I wanted you the first time I saw you," he murmured. "God, how I envied Dallas!" His right hand stroked up and down her torso, piling sensation on top of sensation. "I stayed away from you for five long, fucking years. I gave you every chance to settle down with Mr. Right, but you didn't take them and I'm through with waiting. You're mine now, Niema. *Mine.*"

Her thoughts reeled with shock. He wasn't given to a lot of swearing: For him to say what he just had was a measure of the strength of his feelings. "J-John?" she stuttered, reaching back for him. She hadn't had any idea any of that had been going on inside him. How could she? He was too damn good an actor.

His hips recoiled and plunged in a steady, unhurried motion

that was completely at odds with the way his heartbeat was hammering against her back. "I talked you into coming on this job because I couldn't let you go." His mouth moved on her neck, finding that exact spot between neck and shoulder where the lightest touch made her go limp with pleasure, and a bite would light her up like a Christmas tree. He licked and kissed, holding her quivering body as she strained against him. She tried to part her legs, to lift her thigh over his, but he anchored her leg and held it down.

Niema squirmed, almost frantic with need. As good as his finger felt between her legs, with her legs held together the contact wasn't quite enough; his strokes inside her weren't quite deep enough, or fast enough. He had brought her to the boiling point, with touch and words, but wouldn't let her go over it.

"You were right," he breathed, the words hot on her skin. "I could have found someone else to plant the bug. Hell, I could've planted it myself. But I wanted you with me. I wanted this chance to have you."

"Let me put my leg over yours," she pleaded, almost mad with frustration. "Move faster. Please. Just do *something!*"

"Not yet." He kissed her neck again. Her right hand, reaching behind to grab him, clenched hard on his butt. "In Ronsard's office—"

"For God's sake, confess afterward!"

He laughed and moved her hand, dislodging her nails from his ass. "I didn't mean to go that far. I've never lost control like that before." He nuzzled her ear. "I had to taste you, had to kiss you—and then I had to have you. I wanted our first time to be in a bed, with a lot of time to spend loving you, but I couldn't stop. I forgot about the job. All that mattered was having you."

He was saying things any woman in her right mind wanted to hear from the man she loved, Niema thought dimly. But, damn him, he was saying them when she was on the verge of dying. And maybe what he was saying was turning her on even more, because every word seemed to go straight to her very core.

"You seem to think the end of this job is the end of us. Not by a long shot, sweetheart. You're mine and you're going to stay mine."

"John," she gasped. "I love you. But if you don't start moving your ass this very minute—!"

He laughed, a deep-throated sound of pure pleasure, and obeyed her command. He lifted her thigh over his hip and moved hard and fast, going deep. She stiffened, her legs trembling, and erupted in a violent climax. He joined her before her tremors had ceased.

Afterward, she couldn't stop trembling. The pleasure had been too intense, too prolonged, and she still couldn't quite believe all the things he had said. She twisted around to face him. Immediately his expression became guarded.

She managed a smile, though her heart was pounding so violently she could barely speak. "Don't think you can get away with saying things like that only when my back is turned." She touched his face, cradling his cheek in her palm. "Did you mean them?"

A shudder wracked him. "Every word."

"So did I."

He caught her fingers and pressed them to his lips, then folded them in his hand. For a moment he seemed beyond words.

She kissed his chin. "I don't expect more from you than you can give. I know who you are, remember? You have a job to do, and I won't ask you to give it up. I'll probably go back into fieldwork myself—"

"Why am I not surprised?" he asked in a wry tone.

She couldn't seem to stop touching him. All those long hours in bed with him had only made the yearning worse, instead of sating it. She stroked her hand over his rock hard chest, pressed a kiss to his throat. "We'll work it out. We don't have to make decisions now, or even tomorrow."

His eyebrows rose and he rolled, tucking her neatly beneath him. Propped over her on his elbows, he said in amusement, "You're being very gentle with me."

"I don't want to frighten you off."

"After waiting five years to have you? Sweetheart, you couldn't frighten me off with an elephant gun. But you're right about one thing: We don't have to make any decisions other than what to eat for breakfast. We can steal a few days just for ourselves before we go back to D.C."

"Can we?" That sounded like heaven—nothing to do but sleep late, make love, lie in the sun. No roles to play, no disks to steal. They could just be themselves. She still couldn't quite take in everything he'd said: How could she not have known, not sensed his attraction to her? But maybe she had; maybe that was what she had picked up on when they were in Iran that made her so uneasy. She hadn't been able to tell what it was, because John was so good at hiding what he was thinking, but she had known there was some tension there. Would she have been ready earlier to hear what he was saying? She didn't know.

They were together now, and that was all that mattered.

CHAPTER
TWENTY-SEVEN

J ohn made a call on the radio, and a couple of hours later the man with the outboard brought some clothes to the boat: jeans, T-shirts, underwear, socks, and sneakers. "Have you heard anything on Ronsard?" John asked as he took the bundle of clothes.

The man shook his head. He was dressed much as he had been the day before, in cotton pants and a pullover shirt, with dark sunglasses that prevented anyone from seeing his eyes. "Nothing since last night. His men were all over Marseilles. Looks like you lost them there. We'll keep tight surveillance on the yacht, though, just in case."

Niema waited until the Company man left, then went out on the deck. "Clothes," she said with satisfaction, taking the bundle from John's arms. "Thank God. Being naked when you have clothes to put on is one thing, but being naked when you have no choice is nerve-wracking."

He reached out and fingered the thick bathrobe she had tightly belted around her after showering a few moments ago. "You look clothed to me—too damn clothed for my taste."

"That's the point. If you have to work for something, you appreciate it more." She stepped away from that encroaching finger and headed back below deck.

"Then you should consider yourself the most appreciated woman in the civilized world," he growled.

Maybe he hadn't meant for her to hear him, but she did. Her knees went a little weak. Every time she thought of the things he'd said that morning her heart started thumping hard and fast. She was so happy she was afraid she might fly apart.

They would face problems in the future, probably in the near future. She didn't know what form their relationship would take, whether there would be any formal commitment or just an unspoken arrangement as lovers whenever they happened to be together—which might not be very often. But all of that was in the future. For right now, for these couple of stolen days before they caught a military transport back to the States, all they had to do was love each other.

He hadn't said he loved her, but he didn't have to. She felt it every time he touched her, with a wrenching blend of tenderness and almost savage lust that made his hands tremble, or when he looked at her with his emotions naked in his eyes. John was so controlled that the very fact he let her see what he was feeling told her more than words ever could.

She didn't have to have any promises, any plans. Not today. Not tomorrow. Maybe losing Dallas had made her afraid to count on the future; all she knew was that she was happy just having John now.

He came below deck and leaned against the door frame, watching as she took all the articles of clothing out of the bag and placed them on the bed, dividing them into his and hers stacks.

"Are you going somewhere?"

"No, I just want to get dressed. I guess I can't believe Ronsard has given up, and if there's trouble I want to be wearing more than a robe."

John strolled forward and hooked a finger in the belt around her waist, pulling her against him. She went willingly, looping her arms around his neck. "We're safe enough here on the boat," he said. "The only way anyone can get to us without being seen is from underwater. We're under constant surveillance, and the boat has electronic countermeasures in place in case anyone tries to eavesdrop."

"So we have to stay on board until we're picked up?"

"I wouldn't mind a couple of days of downtime." A slight smile curved his lips. "On the other hand, I'm not Superman, either, so we might as well get dressed."

He stripped off his tuxedo pants, which was all he was wearing, and was in shorts and jeans by the time she stepped into a pair of underpants. He eyed her feet. "You need Band-Aids on those blisters before you put on socks and shoes. I'll get the first-aid kit."

Niema sat down on the bed and examined her feet. The blisters didn't look bad and weren't bothering her; the antibiotic cream she'd put on them the day before had helped a lot, plus she had been barefoot since coming on board the boat. Still, he was right: They needed protecting. Runners learned to take care of their feet.

He came back with a small white kit in his hand and sat down beside her. "Feet up," he said, patting his lap.

Smiling at the luxury, she turned around and lay back on the pillows, lifting her feet onto his lap and giving herself up entirely into his hands. These strong hands gently cradled her feet, dabbing cool ointment on the blisters and covering them with adhesive strips. He performed the task with the same fearsome concentration he applied to everything.

Still holding her feet in his hands, he looked up at her: "Did you know the feet are an erogenous zone?"

Alarmed, she said, "I know they're a ticklish zone." She tried to regain custody of her feet but with very little effort he controlled the motion.

"Trust me." His tone was both soothing and cajoling. "I won't do anything to tickle you."

She was trying to jackknife into a sitting position when he pressed his mouth to her right instep. She fell back on the pillows, her breath tangling in her throat, spikes of pleasure shooting all the way to her groin. She sucked in a deep breath. "Do that again."

"My pleasure," he murmured, caressing her instep with his tongue and eyeing with interest her hardening nipples.

Niema closed her eyes. What he was doing was incredible: She didn't have the least inclination to laugh. His touch was firm, almost massaging. His tongue unerringly found the most sensitive spot on her instep, stroking it until she had to choke back moans of pleasure. Then he turned his attention to her left foot, shifting so he was facing her and a foot was in each hand. He divided his attention between them, kissing and licking and sucking until she could no longer hold back those moans. Her body twisted and arched, and her breathing became ragged.

She was scarcely aware of when he deftly slipped her panties down her legs, only that he was cupping her bottom in his hands and lifting her up to his mouth. His hair was cool on the insides of her thighs, his mouth hot as he stabbed his tongue into her. She was so aroused that she began climaxing in moments, the sensation so intense that blood roared in her ears and reality contracted until it existed only in the sensation between her legs.

When she finally managed to open her eyes, he was smiling at her. "See?"

"Wow." She stretched languidly. "Do you have any more tricks?"

He laughed as he stood up. "A few, but we'll work up to those."

He had taken the edge off her interest in getting dressed, but she did it anyway, then joined him on deck. The sun was bright on the water. She looked across at the crowded beach and the city beyond. "I wish we could go into the city," she said as she slipped her sunglasses on her nose.

"Maybe later. Let's see if we pick up anything else on Ronsard before we go into the city." He picked up a pair of binoculars and scanned the beach.

"Looking at the topless women?" she asked, pinching his butt. "I thought you were too sophisticated for that."

"A man never gets too sophisticated for that," he murmured and laughed when she pinched him again.

Late that afternoon he got another report from the Company men on shore. Ronsard seemed to have pulled his men; though there was still surveillance in place at the airports, no one was actively beating the bushes for them.

"Looks like we can do a little sightseeing," he said.

She was aware he was indulging her. "You've been to Nice before, haven't you?"

He shrugged. "I've been to most places before."

"What do you do for relaxation?"

He thought about that for a moment. "Hide away on a boat on the Riviera and make love to you," he finally answered.

"You mean . . . you never just get in a car and drive? Rent a cabin somewhere in the mountains, go fishing, look at the scenery?" She was aghast, wondering how anyone could live under such unrelenting stress.

"Like a normal person? No."

Mr. Medina, that's going to change, she thought staring at him. When he had downtime, she would make certain he relaxed some place where he didn't have to constantly watch his back or keep up a cover. That would probably be the only way they could be together, somewhere so isolated they would have to make an effort to see another human being.

John radioed in that they were going ashore.

"Do you want surveillance?"

He thought about it. "How many men do you have?"

"We can keep the yacht covered, or we can cover you, but we'll be stretched thin if we try to do both."

It was a calculated risk, Niema knew. Just because Ronsard's men hadn't been spotted didn't mean they weren't there. But everything in John's life was a calculated risk—and lately, so was everything in hers. This was how it would be, she thought; this was the life she was choosing, the life she wanted.

"Put one man on us," John finally said.

"Will do."

He tucked his pistol into his waistband at the small of his back, then put on a lightweight jacket. Niema had found a straw tote in the cabin and she dropped her pistol into it.

The yacht had its own motorized dinghy, and they went ashore in it. The sun was low in the sky, the light mellowing, the shadows deepening. They walked for a while, strolling along with the other tourists. They stopped for a cup of coffee at a sidewalk café; she browsed through some lovely little shops and started to buy a six-foot long, sky blue scarf, only to realize she had no money. "I'm broke," she told John, laughing as she pulled him out of the shop.

He looked back. "I'll get the scarf for you."

"I don't want you to get the scarf. I want you to get some money for me."

"Independent hussy," he remarked, tugging free and going back into the shop.

She waited on the sidewalk, arms crossed and toe tapping, until he rejoined her with the scarf wrapped in tissue paper. He dropped the weightless package in her tote, and a kiss on her nose. "That's from me. As for operating money, I'll have more funds delivered to us tomorrow."

"Thank you." Over his shoulder she caught a glimpse of a man watching them. He quickly turned away and entered a shop. She said thoughtfully, "Do you know what our Company tail looks like?"

"I spotted him when we left the dinghy. Khaki pants, white shirt."

"A man wearing black pants, white shirt, and a tan jacket was watching us. He went in one of the shops when he saw me looking at him."

John moved immediately, though without haste, curving his arm around her waist and walking with her into the nearest shop. Once they were inside he walked quickly through the shop, with the owner sputtering after them, and out the rear entrance. They were in a narrow cobblestoned alley, dark with shadows, open at both ends. He turned to the right, so they were going toward the shop in which their unknown watcher had gone.

If the man followed them into the shop and out the back, he would instinctively turn left, in the opposite direction from which he had come. If they could get out of the alley before he decided he'd been made and came after them, they would shake him.

They almost made it. The man burst into the alley when they were two doors from the end. The shopkeeper was squawking in his wake, frustrated that people were using her shop as a shortcut. He ignored her as if she were no more than a mosquito, brushing her off as he drew a pistol from the shoulder rig beneath his jacket.

The shopkeeper screamed and rushed back into her shop. John shoved Niema into a recessed doorway and dove in the opposite direction, pulling out his pistol and rolling as he hit the ground. The first shot clanged into a metal trash can. The second shot was John's, but the man jerked back into the shop.

"Run!" John said, and fired another shot at the doorway of the shop. "I'll keep him pinned."

She was reaching in the tote for her pistol, but at his command she took off at a dead run, knowing any delay could hinder him. Ahead of her, people were scattering away from the mouth of the alley, screaming and rushing for cover.

She reached the end and whirled around the wall, flattening herself against it and peeking around. John was working his way back, firing carefully timed shots that chipped large chunks of brick off the building. When he was near he wheeled and grabbed her wrist and they ran down the street, dodging through confused and alarmed pedestrians.

"Do we head for the dinghy?" she gasped, setting into stride.

"Not until we shake them. I don't want that boat identified."

Meaning the boat wasn't just a place for them to crash. It had classified stuff on board; maybe the boat itself was classified.

As they ran she pulled the tote bag off her shoulder and dug in the bottom of it for her pistol.

"What are you doing?" he asked, taking a look behind them. "Right!"

She wheeled right. "Putting the pistol where I can get to it without having to dig," she growled, jamming the weapon under her waistband in back as he had done and pulling her T-shirt out to cover it.

A shout followed them. Unfortunately, the streets were still crowded with tourists, and heads turned to follow them as they ran and dodged. All anyone chasing had to do was follow the ripple of disturbance.

"Left," John said, and they turned left as smoothly as if they were joined at the hip. "Right." They took the next right. If they could get people looking in different directions it might create enough momentary confusion for them to gain some ground and slip away.

They dodged onto a small side street, bright with flowers growing in boxes and in pots set on narrow stoops; the doors were gaily painted, and children wrung the last moments of sunshine from the day. John increased his speed; they had to get off that street fast, before any kids got hurt.

They turned right, down an alley so narrow sunlight never penetrated it; they had to run single file. The street ahead of them was purple with shadows, alive with people. Lights were winking on.

Someone barreled into John as soon as he emerged from the alley and they went crashing to the ground. For a split second Niema thought it was an accident, then arms grabbed her from behind and she reacted automatically, driving her elbow back into a gut that wasn't as hard as it could have been. The guy whooshed out his breath in a violent explosion. She ducked out of his hold, whirled, and poked him in the little notch beside his eye. She didn't have the proper angle, back to front, but he went down anyway, writhing on the ground and vomiting.

John grabbed her wrist and yanked her into a run. She looked back and saw her assailant lying unmoving on the ground. The man who had tackled John was kind of half sitting, half lying against the wall. He wasn't moving either.

"Don't look," John still towed her by the wrist, so fast her feet barely touched ground. "Just run."

Her stomach turned over. "I didn't mean—"

"He did," he said briefly.

They dodged down yet another street and found themselves in a part of town where the streets seemed to branch off each other like tangled spaghetti. Ahead of them a trio of men cut across an intersection, weapons drawn. One of the men spotted them and pointed. John pulled her down the nearest bisecting street.

"How many of them are there?" she panted.

"A lot." He sounded grim. He angled back toward where they had seen the three men, hoping to come out behind them. They ran up a narrow, picturesque street, with flower boxes in the windows and old women selling a few wares on their doorsteps, from tatted lace shawls to homemade potpourri. One woman shrieked at the gun in John's hand as he and Niema ran by. A sharp angle took them to the left, and a dead end. Niema whirled and started back, but John caught her arm and pulled her toward him.

She heard what he heard. The street behind them slowly fell silent as the old women grabbed up their wares and vanished into their houses. The sounds of traffic came from a distance, but here there was nothing.

Louis Ronsard strolled into view, a slight smile on his sculpted lips and a Glock-17 in his hand. The big pistol was leveled at Niema's head.

John immediately moved at a right angle away from her. The gun didn't waver from her head. "Stop right there," Ronsard said, and John obeyed.

"My friends," he said lightly, "you left without saying good-bye."

"Good-bye," John said, without expression. He made no move with the weapon in his hand, not with that big 9mm locked dead center on Niema's forehead.

"Drop your weapon," Ronsard said to John. His dark blue eyes were arctic. John obeyed, letting the pistol drop to the street. "You abused my hospitality. If the guard hadn't surprised you, you would have gotten away with it. I never would have known you got into my computer. You did, didn't you? Otherwise you wouldn't have been leaving my office at that time, you would still have been in there working."

John shrugged. There was no point denying it. "I got what I went after. I copied everything; I know what you know."

"To what point, my friend? Blackmail? Or did you want exclusive access to the RDX-a?"

It was Temple who answered. As Niema watched, John's face altered ever so slightly, his eyes taking on a flat quality.

"Whoever has the compound will make a lot of money in a very short time. Plus . . . I have some uses for it."

"You could have bought whatever amount you needed."

"And *you* would make the money."

"So that's what this is all about? Just money?"

"It's always about money."

"And her?" Ronsard indicated Niema. "I assume she's your partner."

"I don't have partners."

"Then she is . . . ?"

"She isn't involved in this. Let her go," John said softly.

In a heartbeat Ronsard had the gun off Niema and on John, his finger already on the trigger. "Don't play me for a fool," he said, his voice low and deadly.

Niema slipped her right hand up behind her back and gripped the pistol tucked in her waistband. Ronsard caught the motion out of the corner of his eye and started to turn, but she already had the pistol out and leveled at his head.

"Perhaps," she murmured in her best Medina imitation, "you should be asking *me* the questions. Drop the pistol."

"I don't think so," Ronsard said, still holding his weapon on John. "Are you willing to risk your lover's life? He wasn't willing to risk yours."

She shrugged, as if it didn't matter. "Just move over there beside him."

Both men froze. John seemed to have stopped breathing, his face going white. Ronsard stared at her in astonishment, then began laughing mirthlessly. Niema didn't dare take her eyes off Ronsard, but she was almost paralyzed herself by the risk she was taking. With John's history, a wife he had killed rather than let her betray two men, for another lover to betray him would be devastating, so devastating that not even his superhuman control could hold. His reaction was crucial, because Ronsard had to believe it.

"My apologies, Monsieur Temple," Ronsard said to John. "It appears we were *both* used."

"Sorry, darling." She gave John an insincere smile. "I have the disk. While you were sleeping last night, I sort of confiscated it." He knew that was a lie. Not only had she not left the bed last night except to visit the head, getting the disk didn't mean anything now that the information had already been sent to Langley.

She looked back at Ronsard, to keep his attention on her instead of on John. "I would introduce myself, but it's better if I don't. I'd like to put a proposition to you, Louis—one that would benefit both of us."

"In what way?"

She smiled again. "The CIA is very interested in . . . reaching an agreement with you. We don't want to put you out of business. You could be very valuable to us, and vice versa. You have access to a lot of very interesting information—and we're willing to pay you well for it."

"So would other governments," he said, his eyes still cold.

Niema kept an eye on John as well as Ronsard, willing him not to spoil the setup. "Not as much as we can. And there's an added bonus."

"Such as?"

"A heart."

The softly spoken words fell into a silence that seemed complete. John started, then halted himself. Ronsard's face twisted with hatred. "You dare," he whispered. "You dare bargain with my daughter's life?"

"I'm offering the services of the United States government in finding a heart for her. Those are services you can't match, no matter how much money you have. Even a new heart might not save her, but at least she'll have a chance to hold on until other cures can be found."

He hung there, a father's anguish on his face. "Done," he said roughly, no haggling, no jockeying for position. His love for Laure was genuine and absolute. He would do anything, even sell his soul to the devil, to save her. Working with the CIA was nothing in comparison. He lowered his weapon and nodded toward John. "What about him?"

"Mr. Temple?" Niema shrugged as she lowered her own weapon. It was a risk, but one she felt she had to take to make this agreement work. "He's . . . a bonus, so to speak. I wasn't expecting to have his aid in the job, but since he was there, and so good at it, I let him do it." She had to keep John's cover, she thought. His identity as Joseph Temple couldn't be questioned.

John bent down and scooped up his pistol. Niema couldn't read his expression. His face was still pale, his eyes as dead as she had ever seen them. He started toward Ronsard.

"Temple!" she said sharply, just as a sound drew her attention to the right.

Two of Ronsard's men came around the corner. Their gazes locked immediately on John; he was the prime target of their hunt. They saw the pistol in his hand, saw him moving toward Ronsard. Niema knew, in a nanosecond of stark vision, what was going to happen. She saw their weapons train on him. He was momentarily too focused on Ronsard to react as quickly as he normally would have.

She didn't hear herself scream, a hoarse sound of rage and terror. She didn't know she was moving, didn't feel her hand holding the pistol as it began to rise. All she could hear was her heartbeat, slow and ponderous, as if it pumped molasses instead of blood. All she knew was—not again. She couldn't watch him die. She couldn't.

There was a distant roar. A blue haze of gun smoke. The stench of cordite burning her nostrils. The buck of the weapon in her hand as she fired, and kept firing. A crushing force hit her, knocked her down. She tried to stagger to her feet, but her legs wouldn't work. She fired again.

Someone else was shooting, she thought. There was a deeper roar . . . wasn't there? John. Yes, John was shooting. Good. He was still alive. . . .

The lights seemed to go out, though maybe not. She wasn't certain. There was a lot of formless noise that gradually reshaped itself into words. Something was tugging at her, and it hurt worse than anything she'd ever felt in her life, pain so sharp and all-consuming she almost couldn't breathe.

"—damn you, don't you die on me," John was raging as he tore at her clothes. "Do you hear? Don't you god damn die on me."

John rarely swore, she thought, fighting through the pain; he must be really upset. What on earth had happened?

She was hurt. She remembered now, remembered that crushing blow that knocked her down. Something had hit her.

Shot. She'd been shot. So this was what it felt like. It was worse than she had ever imagined.

"Don't die," John was snarling as he pressed down hard on her side.

She wet her lips, and managed to say, "I might not, if you'll hurry and get help."

His head jerked around and he stared at her. His pupils were pinpoints of shock, his face white and strained. "Just hold on," he said roughly. "I'll stop the bleeding." He looked beyond her, and his expression was savage. "You'd better use all the influence you have and get the best doctors in Europe, Ronsard," he said in a low, guttural tone, "because if she dies, I'll fillet you into fish bait."

Washington, D.C., three weeks later

Niema carefully got out of bed and made her way over to the lone chair in the hospital room. Her legs were steadier, she was walking more every day now, though "more" in this case meant a few minutes longer, not any great distance. She had come to hate that bed, though, and was spending as much time as she could in the chair. Sitting in a chair made her feel less like an invalid.

The last IV drip had come out that morning. She was scheduled to be dismissed from the hospital the next day. She would complete her recovery at home; Frank Vinay had visited and said it had been arranged for her to have help at home until she was strong enough to manage by herself again.

Being home again would be nice, she thought. Excitement was one thing, but a woman needed peace and quiet when she was recovering from a gunshot wound. Too much of the past three weeks was a blur, at best, or a huge blank forever lost from her memory. She vaguely remembered being in intensive care in some hospital in France. Louis Ronsard might have been there. He had held her hand once, she thought.

Then she had been flown from France to the States, back to D.C., and brought here. She didn't remember the flight at all, but the nurses told her that was what had happened. She had gone to sleep in France and woke up in D.C. That was enough to disorient anyone.

Every time she surfaced it had been to incredible pain, but she had stopped taking any painkiller a week ago, when she was moved out of intensive care into a regular room. The first couple of days had been rough, but after that every day had been easier.

The last time she'd seen John was when she'd been lying in that narrow, deadend street in Nice. He'd had to disappear, of course. He couldn't hang around, either as Joseph Temple or John Medina. She hadn't asked Mr. Vinay about him, either. John would either show up, or he wouldn't.

Only a small lamp was on in the room; after the bright lights of intensive care shining on her day and night, she wanted only dim lights now. She turned on the radio to an instrumental station and turned the volume low. Easing back in the chair, she closed her eyes and let her mind drift with the music.

She didn't hear any strange noise or feel a draft from the door opening, but slowly she became aware of John's presence. She opened her eyes and smiled at him, not at all surprised to find him standing in the shadows across the room.

"Finally," she said, holding out her hand to him.

He came to her so silently he might have been drifting on smoke, his gaze moving hungrily over her, darkening with pain as he catalogued each pound she had lost. He cupped her face, rubbing his thumb over her bloodless cheek as he bent down and lightly pressed his mouth to hers. She put her hand on the back of his neck, something in her easing as she felt him warm and vital under her touch.

"I couldn't stay away any longer," he said in a low, rough tone. "Frank kept me informed, but I—it wasn't the same as being here."

"I understood." She tried to stroke away the new lines that bracketed his mouth.

"When you go home tomorrow, I'll be there."

"Someone is staying with me—"

"I know. I'm the someone." He crouched down in front of her and folded her hand in his.

"Good. You can help me get back on my feet. The physical therapists here won't let me do as much as I need to be doing."

"If you think *I'm* going to do anything more than let you sleep and eat, you're way off base."

"Really? I thought you'd have incentive to get me up to my fighting weight again."

"Why's that?"

"So you can show me the rest of your tricks." She grinned at him. "I can't wait. I've been lying here for the past week wondering what they are."

The tension in his face relaxed as a smile touched his mouth. "It'll be a while before you're in shape for any of that."

"Depends on how fast you *get* me into shape, doesn't it?"

"We're going to take it nice and easy. A ruptured liver isn't something you get over in a day or two."

She was also missing part of her spleen, and the bullet had shattered two ribs. On the other hand, John was still alive, and that was the most important thing. He'd have been shot down in front of her if she hadn't drawn their attention.

"What were you *doing?*" she asked, drawing back and frowning at him as she was finally able to ask the question that had been nagging at her since she'd regained consciousness. "Why were you going for Ronsard like that?"

"The bastard held a gun to your head," he said simply. "And I lost control. I do that a lot where you're concerned."

"This can't keep happening."

"I'll try to do better." The tone was dry now—very dry.

"The deal I made with Ronsard—I haven't talked to Mr. Vinity about it. Will it hold?"

"Hold? They're ecstatic."

"The whole thing seemed like a good idea at the time. All he wants is money to take care of Laure; he doesn't care where it comes from or how he gets it." She paused. *"Can* you find her a heart?"

"We're trying. The odds are against it, but we're trying." He sighed. "And if we find her a heart, that means a healthier child somewhere won't have that chance."

"With the information Ronsard can provide, a lot of other lives will be saved, though."

They were both silent, the ethical considerations weighing heavy on each side of the argument. Where one stood, she suspected, depended on whether or not one's child was involved. She understood Ronsard's single-minded devotion to his daughter; someone else whose child was waiting on a heart wouldn't be at all understanding.

She put her hands on the arms of the chair and slowly pushed herself to a standing position. John stood also, his face anxious, his hands outstretched to catch her as if she were a toddler taking her first steps. She grinned up at him. "I'm not that fragile."

"You are to me," he said, and remembered terror swept over his face. "Damn you, no more heroics, do you hear me?"

"Leave them to you, is that it?"

He took a deep breath. "Yeah. Leave them to me."

"I can't." She put her arms around him, resting her head on his chest. "Heroes are few and far between. When you find one, you gotta take care of him." How fortunate she had been, she thought, to have loved and been loved by two such men as Dallas and John—extraordinary men by any standard.

Slowly his hands stroked up her back, his touch light so he wouldn't accidentally hurt her. "That's exactly what I was thinking."

Niema turned her lips against his chest, breathing in the hot male scent of his skin. She had lost the thread of conversation as soon as he touched her. "What's that?"

"When you find a hero, you gotta take care of her." He tilted her chin up with his hand. "Partners?"

A slow, delighted grin spread over her face, dispelling the aura of fragility. "Partners," she said, and they shook hands on the deal.